Philippa East grew up in Scotland and originally studied Psychology and Philosophy at the University of Oxford. After graduating, she moved to London to train as a Clinical Psychologist and worked in NHS mental health services for over ten years.

Philippa now lives in the Lincolnshire countryside with her husband and cat. Alongside her writing, she continues to work as a psychologist and therapist. Philippa's prize-winning short stories have been published in various literary journals. *Little White Lies* is her debut novel.

Little White Lies

Philippa East

ONE PLACE. MANY STORIES

HQ
An imprint of HarperCollins*Publishers* Ltd
1 London Bridge Street
London SE1 9GF

This edition 2020

1
First published in Great Britain by
HQ, an imprint of HarperCollins*Publishers* Ltd 2020

ISBN: 978-0-00-834401-6

Printed and bound in the United States of
America by LSC Communications

For Dan

For the longest time, the police could only find fragments of her, despite all our search posters, all our appeals; a few seconds of grainy, jerky CCTV footage, the tiny handful of frames they retrieved from the hundreds of thousands they trawled. An image of a little girl who stands on the up-bound escalator of a Tube station, her pointed chin raised towards the top of the staircase, her face tilted towards the bright lights.

For years I had hardly anything but those fragments. Those fragments, our memories and a bruising gap. As a family, we floundered in a stubborn, hopeless hoping, with jobs and school and birthdays and Christmases all waterlogged with her loss.

That's how it was before at least, for those seven years that she was missing. It was when that was over that all the rest began, all that led up to that night on the bridge.

When I had to account for everything I had done.

And, ultimately, everything I had not.

Chapter 1

Monday 27th May:
Day 1

ANNE

They discovered me in my daughter's bedroom, elbow-deep in boxes. It had been twenty-five minutes from that single, surreal phone call to the moment my husband and the twins arrived home: plenty enough time for me to go wrong. I heard the front door bang and them pound up the stairs, Robert's heavy boots kicking the carpet and the twins' feet scrambling behind.

'Anne?'

'Mummy?'

'I'm so sorry about the vase,' was the first thing I said, before they could even say anything about the miraculous news. 'It slipped, a complete accident.'

In the doorway the boys stood breathless and wreathed in chlorine. They had been swimming but now their swim had been cut short.

'The vase?' said Robert.

'Downstairs,' I managed, unable to tell him straight the awful thing I'd done. With the officer's voice still ringing in my ears, I'd picked up the roses – the crystal vase of glowing red flowers, my husband's nine-year anniversary present to me – lifting them to sit on the living-room mantelpiece. Perhaps I'd been in shock, still hardly thinking straight, but the one idea in my head was to place them there as a glowing symbol to welcome her home because this was everything I had ever wanted, everything I had dreamed of and hoped for, ever since she was eight, ever since she went missing, through seven long and painful years. Now my heart was bursting and all I wanted was a beautiful sight for her, all I'd wanted was for it to be perfect. Instead the vase had snagged on the lip, and one moment I'd had the precious flowers in my hands and the next there'd been a crash, an explosion of glass and rose stems strewn all over the hearth.

Now the pieces were in the bin and the bruised roses in the sink, but all that mattered was that Robert was coming forward to hug me, kneeling down on the floor and taking me in his arms, an outpouring of happiness and relief that she was found.

The twins pushed in beside us, all anxious, curious blue eyes. 'But what are you doing?' Laurie said. Gently Robert released me. Now he could take in the papers scattered at my knees. The phone call had come when I was alone, so out of the blue, so completely unexpected, a voice I didn't recognize, a local officer I didn't know telling me this information that was so impossible, unbelievable, that I'd had to ask him again and again to repeat it, with that single, impossible fact.

Dead? She isn't dead?

No, Mrs White. No...

Kneeling in her room I must have looked a mess – flushed and unravelled, my hands grimy with dust from the papers – but I was so sure of what I wanted. I scraped my hair behind my ears. We hadn't been in this room for months but all the evidence was in here, a paper trail leading all the way back. 'Can you help me?' I said. 'I can't have her room looking like this. Please, Robert, not this way.' I wanted a home, a sanctuary, not a display of everything that had gone wrong. I couldn't let it be like that now.

Sam and Laurie knelt on the floor beside me too. 'But are you sure she won't want these?' Sam was saying. I leaned forward to bring blood to my head; there was so much crammed into this small space. For so long we hadn't known what to do with her room. Change it, leave it, even my sister Lillian hadn't been able to say, my sister who always had the answers to everything. To begin with, we'd tried to leave everything untouched, ready for her to come back to, but it was so hard to see her room like that, the toys, books, clothes a constant reminder that she wasn't here. I think it started with the photos the police needed for the posters and news bulletins, the school portraits we'd laid out on her bed. Small changes at first, small additions. Over time though, year after year, we'd hoarded so much in here that by now it resembled an incident room: the cork board above her desk cluttered with the small, flat cards the officers had kept handing over at the end of every meeting saying, *If there's anything you need, anything else you think of, just call*; the walls covered with newspaper articles about her own and other abductions that might somehow shed light; then the computer composites of how she might have looked, at nine, ten, twelve, my beautiful daughter; the boxes and boxes of posters Robert used to print up every year, all symbols of our search for her.

But I didn't want her to be faced with all this, so much pain and desperation and loss. It was a home she needed, her family to welcome her: normality, happiness, the hurt over now.

I steadied myself with a palm against the floor and looked up at Robert, my husband, standing upright again now. 'Please can you bring her things down from the loft?' I asked him. All the things we'd put away up there. 'I want her to see, I want her to have them.' Without saying anything, without questioning me or hesitating, my husband went to unclip the loft ladder. The thought of his goodness almost closed up my throat and I had to swallow my mouth dry to make it pass. This was all we'd ever dreamed of and Robert had stood by me all the years in between, so why was I terrified that it might all change now?

Laurie bumped my arm with a stack of papers he'd collected up and I added them to the almost-full box beside me. Did they really understand what we were doing here? How much had Robert been able to explain? Their sister who they had barely known was coming home – had they really grasped that fact? To them she'd been little more than a name, photographs, memories, but now their missing sister would be here, in the flesh. I looked down at them, my sons, the children Robert and I had made together, creations that had cemented our relationship. How good our family had been like that, and now we'd be five again, our whole family rejoined. And her room, my daughter's room, would be filled with her presence.

My phone shrieked; my shoulders jerked. I dragged my mobile from my pocket, Lillian's name flashing on the screen. Lillian, my sister, whom I'd called even before I'd rung Robert. The person I always called in my life, six years older, my sister who knew me, who helped me, who always, always knew what to do. I had left her a message – a garbled, frantic, delirious message – and now she was calling me back. My hands slipped on the screen as I swiped to answer. Above me, I could hear the loft floorboards creaking.

'Lillian?'

'Annie.'

'The police, down in London. They've found her.'

'I know, I heard. I got your message. But Annie, are they sure?'

'It's her, Lillian. They said she'd been... that she'd been—' But I broke off. There was so much that it threatened to overwhelm me; I had to focus on what mattered, all that counted: she was coming home. Right now she was still with police in London but home – Lincolnshire – was no more than three hours' drive away.

'We're going to come over,' I told Lillian. 'In just a few hours, is that still all right? If we come over and leave the twins with you?'

'Of course, Annie. We can make whatever arrangements you'd like.'

There were so many fears that were crowding my brain, but she made it all sound so simple and it *should* be simple; why couldn't it be? We would make this perfect, we would make everything right. As I fumbled the phone to hang up, already Robert was coming back down from the loft.

'Do you want these?' he was saying as he appeared in the doorway. His arms were heaped with clothes – a pile of tiny skirts and dresses. We had kept them, but hidden them away: a missing child's clothes. But she wasn't missing any more.

7

'Yes, yes, put them in the drawers.' I stood to open the dresser for him, wrenching the tendon of my knee.

'All right, Anne. Steady.'

But I had to be ready. 'What do you know? What did he tell you?' I had asked the detective to call my husband too; I had needed Robert to know everything I did – I couldn't trust myself to relay the facts to him myself.

'As much as he could. Everything they know.'

'So did he say –' I couldn't seem to stop the shaking in my legs – 'about how she just walked into the London police station, and about the house, and the little girl Tonia, and that she didn't – that Abigail never…'

I caught myself, stemming my words, glancing down at the twins, busy on the floor picking Blu Tack off newspaper clippings, so small and innocent in the face of this news. Robert laid the pile of clothes in my arms and I pushed them into the empty drawer. There was no way she would fit them now, but I didn't know what else to do with them, and all I wanted was to get this right. And it *would* be all right. Robert was here, beside me, helping me. I made myself slow, I made myself breathe, taking in Robert's scent, the woody, musky deep smell of him, this man I loved and who loved me, who had brought such goodness into my life. We were a family, we had survived these seven years: me, my husband and our beautiful twins. But even as I held her clothes, knowing in a matter of hours she'd be here with us too – real, alive, home – I couldn't stop other words, other images coming. 'But the man, Robert—'

'I know.'

'Robert –' my breath snagged in my throat – 'they don't

know where he is, he's still out there, somewhere, he could be anywhere—'

The drawer stuck on its runner and gave a shriek as I tried to push it closed. Robert caught my hand, his strong grasp steadying mine.

'Anne.' He turned me towards him so that I was looking directly into those warm, straightforward, honest eyes. I forced myself to hold his gaze and for the millionth time I wanted to tell him. He believed in me, he always had.

'Anne,' he said. 'I understand, I'm overwhelmed too, but they've found her, she's safe. Whatever has happened to her, you and me, we're in this together, and all of us are going to be just fine.'

I wanted to fall, to sink into his words and let them embrace me, hold me, make everything okay.

But he could never have said that, if he knew about the lie.

Chapter 2

Monday 27th May:
Day 1

JESS

I heard their car outside, the growl of the engine turning over in our road. 'They're here!' I said. We'd been sitting, waiting, bolt upright for what felt like hours.

I didn't wait for my aunt to ring the doorbell. I couldn't wait indoors any more, I had to go out, never mind the gloom and the drizzle coming down. A grey, rainy May half term. I hopped in the hallway tugging on my trainers and got outside just as Uncle Robert was pulling up next to the kerb. Mum and Dad were right behind me.

My Auntie Anne and the twins got out first, Sam and Laurie, my seven-year-old cousins. Her half-brothers, only babies when she'd gone missing. It hit me right then – they were almost the age that Abigail was then. She had been eight and I had been eight, but that was seven years ago now. Now I and my cousin would both be fifteen.

The boys stood clutching their backpacks like parachutes, their hair getting wet in the rain. 'Thank you,' Auntie Anne said to Mum – her sister – pushing them towards her. 'They said we couldn't all go at once. Even family.'

Now Uncle Robert got out of the driver's side, levering his square frame up. He wasn't Abigail's real father, only her stepdad, but I knew he loved her the same as any of us.

'Of course,' said Mum, reaching out an arm to the twins. 'They can stay here as long as you need. Fraser and I will do everything we can.'

'They thought it would be too much,' my aunt went on. 'They said she was agitated and—' She broke off, glancing down at the pale faces of the twins. My uncle stood with the engine turning over and the rain falling on his wide shoulders. He gave a reassuring smile. 'She was just confused,' he said. 'They meant at first. When they had to explain everything to her.'

The car was lit up inside, shedding its glow onto the ring of our faces. Agitated, confused – I couldn't understand what my aunt and uncle meant. I wrapped my arms around myself and jigged on the pavement. I only had a T-shirt on and it was unseasonably cold. 'What about me?' I asked. 'Shouldn't I come with you?'

'I'll come back here to collect the boys,' Uncle Robert was saying. He hadn't heard me over the engine. 'Once Anne and I have driven back home with Abigail.'

My cousin. Back home.

'They're driving her up from London now and opening a victim suite specially. ETA is ten-thirty p.m.' It didn't answer my question though.

'What about me?' I said again. I hugged myself. I imagined

hugging her. 'She'll want to see me.' I was remembering when we were six and Abigail broke her arm. A slip on a wet climbing frame, wood chips hard as tarmac from that height. Uncle Robert scooping her up, zooming her to the A&E in Lincoln, and she came home with a bright pink cast on. Then for the whole two months it took for her arm to heal, *my* arm ached from elbow to wrist. It had always been like that between us. Thinking what each other thought. Feeling what the other felt.

My cousin Laurie was rummaging for something in his backpack. Mum stepped forward. 'You have to wait, Jess. One thing at a time.'

'When, then?' I looked again at my uncle, his stocky frame, his big, shaved head. In the shadows, his expression was all mixed up. I chafed my bare arms where they prickled with a damp chill.

Dad checked his watch. 'You're going straight there?' he said, keen as always to know every detail. 'To this place – this victim suite?' It was barely a quarter past nine.

'We have to, Fraser,' said Auntie Anne. 'If they brought her and we weren't there!' Another car came growling up the street. 'There was a man,' she continued. 'A man had her all this time.'

For a moment the approaching headlights blinded me. I had to cover my eyes from the glare. A man? But they'd got her away from him now. They were driving her home, she was perfectly safe now.

'What else do you know?' said Dad. 'What else did they tell you?' Even with the twins there, it was all coming out.

Auntie Anne turned back to the car, digging in the foot-well of the passenger seat. 'Only to bring something,' she said. 'Something she might know, that we could talk about. Something she would remember.'

She held out a slim packet, the kind you rarely saw these days. Inside, a handful of photographs.

'Daddy, my book!' Laurie was still rummaging in his bag, but nobody seemed to be paying attention.

As my aunt lifted the flap, the glossy prints almost slipped from her grasp. 'We chose the best ones,' she said. 'The happiest ones.'

'Daddy!' Laurie's small voice was shrill. He was getting upset that no one was listening. 'I haven't got it.'

My aunt held the pictures out to show us, but it was too dark to see properly and the streetlights made everything look orange.

'This too.' My aunt drew something else from the car, something small and soft and blue. My heart did a tuck jump. Of course. I recognized it at once – Abigail's flopsy. With it, another swarm of memories came: us running races neck and neck, every grazed knee she ever had. Running, playing, sleeping like reflections of each other. Dad was always amazed at how vivid my memories were and I'd tell him, *because there was nothing that came after, because for me there's been nothing between then and now.*

'We kept him,' my aunt said. But of course, I thought. What else would you have done?

'Daddy,' said Laurie, 'the one you were reading me—' We were all so preoccupied and he was so little, unable to understand the enormity of this.

The little blue stuffed rabbit looked so small in my aunt's hands, smaller than I remembered as I reached out to touch it. Auntie Anne wrapped her hands around mine, pressing the soft toy between us. 'Jess – do you have something, anything else we could take with us? I think the more we can take, the better.'

I stared at her. Better for what? We were all here, Abigail's family, ready and waiting. Why would she need any more than that?

'Daddy! I've forgotten our book!' Laurie's words seemed to get swallowed up in the rain.

Now Uncle Robert came round the bonnet of the car. Dad met him with a kind hand on his shoulder. 'Thanks, Fraser,' my uncle said. Auntie Anne was still looking at me, her question hanging and the thrum of the car engine was going on and on. 'Jess,' she said again, 'can't you think of anything?'

The fur of the rabbit suddenly made me feel shivery, like someone was running a finger up the back of my neck. Mum was standing, watching us all.

And then Laurie's hand slipped on the strap of his backpack and all the contents went tumbling to the pavement.

'Laurie,' moaned Sam, 'look what you've done!'

Mum reached out, too late to catch the clothes as they fell. The pavement was wet, everything was getting soaked. 'Don't worry,' said Dad, 'it's fine, it's fine.' Both my cousins looked so desperate. But Uncle Robert smiled, a hero's smile, and crouched to scoop up the pyjamas, the toothbrush, the little pair of socks. 'It's all right, Laurie, we can read it tomorrow.' Mum helped him slide it all back into the bag. He lifted Laurie off the ground, then Sam too in his strong arms. 'It's all right. Everything's all right. Be good, boys, and I promise we'll see you very soon.'

My aunt was still looking at me. I still had the flopsy in my hand.

'Anne, love,' said my uncle, 'we have to go.'

She nodded but she still didn't move. Mum reached out to the twins – 'Come on, come inside' – and now Uncle Robert was re-opening the car door. Dad touched my elbow. 'All right, Jess. Come inside.'

I pressed the flopsy back into my aunt's hands. 'You don't need any more things,' I told her. 'You'll be there. She'll have *you*.'

It should have been enough. She should have known it was enough. Instead my aunt looked past me, her eyes searching out Mum's face in the dark. 'But Lillian, what do I say to her? What on earth am I supposed to say?'

Chapter 3

Monday 27th May:
Day 1

ANNE

In a puffy chair with a heart-shaped tea stain on the arm, my hands shaking, I tried to study the printed pages the detective had given us, one for me, one for Robert: *Reunification. Remain calm and speak in a soothing voice.* Remain calm, remain calm, but I kept thinking we should never have come so early because now we'd spent nearly an hour in this claustrophobic suite with a detective who put my whole being on edge, and for every minute on the clock that we sat here, I felt the past crawl one step closer and my anxiety rise yet another inch.

'She's already been interviewed and had a medical assessment,' the detective was saying, 'so you'll be able to take her straight home.' He was young and neat, had a long, oval face: DS McCarthy, Lincolnshire Police, brand new to the case and assigned at the request of the team down in London. It was completely irrational of me not to like him; there was nothing wrong with the way he looked, with how he spoke or anything he said, and all the officers before had been so kind and understanding, going to the ends of the earth to help us, so why should it be any different with him? And yet every time his grey eyes gazed at me without flickering, all I could think was, *you don't trust what anyone before might have said.*

'Will that be all right?' The grey eyes came to rest on me. 'We've assumed you're ready for that?'

I forced myself to hold my gaze steady and not lose my courage. I'd done my best to make the house look perfect, prepared her room and put framed pictures of her everywhere, but now I thought, what does it matter how neat the couch cushions are or how her room looks and whether or not I've hoovered the stairs? If a bomb is about to go off, what good will any of that do?

'Yes,' said Robert. The clock on the wall read twenty past ten. 'But the medical assessment – do you know if she's all right?'

The detective reordered the notes in his lap, as though all the answers about Abigail were in there. I pressed my wrists against the rough chair arms. I didn't want him to talk about my daughter. I wanted to tell him myself: she's mine and she's perfect, and I've loved her from even before she was born and I've loved her exactly like that ever since.

'Yes,' he said. 'Overall, physically, she's okay.'

Physically. But what about all the other ways to be hurt? The typed words on my sheet ran on: *Follow the child's lead. Don't assume s/he wishes to be touched straight away.* The page detailed nothing about what a child might say, what accusations they might blurt out.

I made myself look back at the detective. 'But what about the man? Where is he?' It sounded as though I was accusing *him*, but it was only because his grey eyes kept fixing on me, or on Robert, as though he was peering into every corner of our lives. I thought again, *you don't know how I feel about my daughter and you can't judge the mistakes I've made.* I didn't say it though, I just squeezed the flopsy in my lap.

Robert echoed me. 'Do you know where he is?'

The clock on the wall ticked: twenty-five past ten. DS McCarthy shook his head. 'We're looking but – we haven't found him yet.' A car crunched on the wet gravel outside. 'Now,' said the detective, 'they're here.'

When the door of the suite opened, we all stood up. The photographs went sliding from my lap and I didn't even try to pick them up. I was still holding her flopsy though – I had that at least. I drew on all my strength to stand there and just keep holding it out to her so she would know it was us and that we loved her – to stand there and not to burst into tears. There were so many phrases Robert and I had rehearsed, but overrunning all of these was the avalanche of words I was suddenly desperate to say, words I'd been living with all these years, wondering if I'd ever have the opportunity to say them. Finally, here and now, was my chance – before she could possibly say anything herself, what if I could put right what had happened, make it okay, and if I could do that, then nothing else would matter but that she was home now, rescued and safe and everything else would be forgiven.

They came together down the long aisle of the room. The police officer escorting her was pretty and graceful and had such a kindly face, and then next to her: my daughter. Robert reached for my hand, and I knew he was also shocked at the sight of her because, my God, she looked so different. All these years I'd pictured her the way I'd remembered: light and lithe as a ballerina, her golden skin, her rosy mouth, her plaited hair the loveliest blonde. Happy, shining, brimming with love – *that* was the version of her I remembered. Instead now her hair was dull and ragged and there was a pudgy thickness to her shoulders and thighs. Her face was so pale that all her freckles had gone – our family trademark completely disappeared. Now it was such a different Abigail I saw, like a side of her that I had pushed away or forgotten, or like a different person entirely.

Yet all of those physical changes I could have accepted, overlooked and not minded; it was what happened next that threw everything off, tearing up my script and all my good, brave intentions. The escorting officer didn't even touch her – she would have known better than that – the kind hand was only there to usher her forwards, but Abigail wrenched her arm from that kindness with a movement so brutal that even Robert flinched.

And with it, every word in my throat dried up.

They stopped in front of us. 'It's all right,' the female officer said, but then she seemed to fade into the background, along with all the others in the room – DS McCarthy and the blurred figure of some appropriate adult – and we were there alone, the three of us, a triangle of the most complicated love.

Abigail hitched the trousers she was wearing – dark purple jeans I had never imagined for her. I was so aware of Robert beside me and the fact that he wasn't holding my hand any more.

When she opened her pale, chapped lips it felt as though my whole world stood still and I thought to myself: here is where it all falls apart. Here is where the tidal wave comes, the force I never knew how to deal with and that I never managed to outrun.

With her free hand, she reached out and took the flopsy, almost idly, from my hand.

'So I'm going home with you now?'

The words were so innocuous, so devoid of emotion, so exactly the opposite of what I'd been expecting. It was as though a vacuum opened up in the room, sucking out everything I'd been bracing myself against and it left me frozen, ears ringing, completely lost as to what came next. It was only when DS McCarthy stepped forwards that I saw the aching mistake I had made:

That was the moment – the exact moment – when I should have hugged her.

She sat in the front seat of the car and we made sure the heater was on so she wouldn't get cold. All the way home, my heart scrabbled like a rabbit trying to escape its hutch.

'Are we going to the same house?' Abigail strained against the seatbelt, craning to see every road and turn-off we passed. In the wing mirror I glimpsed fragments of her face: her mouth, the discolouration around all of her teeth, and I thought, what on earth has done that? Later I discovered it was the cigarettes he'd given her, the ones she'd grown addicted to.

Robert nodded. 'The very same.'

She continued to crane, as though she couldn't believe him, and I thought, does she still not understand she's come home? At our front door, in the rain, I fumbled the lock and inside it felt as though we all tangled in the hallway, not enough space for us all. She put a white hand on the wall to steady herself, and stared up the stairs and through the doorways as though she feared something would leap out at her. I was so glad when we finally brought her into the clean living room, with the familiar coffee table and TV and a couch that we might sit her down on.

She stood in the middle of the room, her hands at her sides in tight little fists. 'Where are Sam and Laurie?' she asked. 'The twins?' So she remembered her brothers, even though they'd been so tiny when she last saw them, no more than babies. But she asked as though we were playing a trick on her, bringing her into this house without them.

'Don't worry,' Robert said. 'They're with Auntie Lillian and Uncle Fraser.' He smiled. 'They're seven now, did you know?'

She didn't answer and I jumped to fill the silence, silting up the room with words: 'Are you hungry? Do you want something to drink? Tea or juice or a biscuit?' Anything to make this more normal, because that's all I ever wanted for us, to have her home, to start again, to be the happy family we always should have been.

She sat down with a jerk on the couch and ran her hands over the soft leather as though it confirmed something to her: perhaps that this was really her home. 'This furniture is the same.' Her feet jutted out onto the rug and I could take in her shoes as well now: plain white trainers, like old-fashioned plimsolls. She was pushing her heels into the carpet. A few inches from her foot was a crushed rose petal I'd missed and the water stain still shadowed the hearth. Anything could still happen, hadn't I seen that? My heart was beating so quickly it hurt.

Robert sat down carefully in the armchair nearby, as though trying not to startle a wild, skittish creature. His gentleness had always steadied her, but who knew if it would still be like that now? 'Abigail? Is there anything at all we can get you?'

She sat there, her eyes seeking mine and her very presence demanded so much of me, her mother, a million words I should have been able to say; the little flopsy was slipping from her grasp but I felt freeze-framed, unable to move, unable to reach out and do anything to correct it. Then in a strange slow motion, Abigail slumped backwards into the cushions, her rough hair rubbing up against the leather. Her eyes were closing like a baby's, her head tilting, her voice already muffled with sleep.

'I don't need anything,' she said. 'Thank you. I'm just very, very tired.'

We found her one of Robert's old T-shirts and a clean pair of my leggings; we didn't have anything else for her yet. She got changed in her bedroom, behind the closed door, then crawled straight into bed without even pausing to brush her teeth. When we knocked gently, only minutes later, she was already asleep. She was gone.

Shortly before midnight, Robert left to fetch the twins and I went into our chilly bathroom and counted long breaths to slow my skipping heartbeats. When I had a hold of myself, I wiped my eyes, blew my nose and went back into her room.

I had promised Robert I wouldn't wake her and he needn't have worried; she was in a deep sleep, her breathing slow and steady. The cave of her bedroom was musty from all the books and toys we'd brought down from the loft; the dust we'd disturbed was scratchy in my throat. I questioned suddenly if we'd done the right thing, putting her room back like this. I had always been like that, so different from Lillian: making choices and then never being sure; and if there was ever a time I trusted my own judgement, since Abigail went missing, I hadn't seemed to be able to at all. In the soft light that followed me in from the landing, I moved aside the tangle of clothes she'd left on the low chair at the foot of the bed. I could make out the purple jeans, underwear, the plain blue acrylic jumper. Careful not to make a sound, I sat down.

In the quiet and dark, it felt so much easier. Asleep, she looked so gentle, so peaceful: the sweet, lovable Abigail I remembered. I'd been so afraid of what she might blurt out, but in the end there'd been nothing. Could I tell myself then that she'd simply forgotten? Should I make myself try and forget then too? I laid a hand on the bottom of the duvet, my fingertips finding the smooth buttons a hand-span from her feet. My daughter had found her way back to us, to a happy home, a happy family, and Lillian's advice years ago made more sense now than ever: if she had forgotten, why confront her with it now, and if the three of us made sure to say nothing, couldn't it be like it never even happened? Abigail stirred beneath the freshly washed sheets and on the pillow the little flopsy slipped sideways again, its long ears tilting over the edge of the bed. Abigail needed us, her family, to be strong for her – no doubts, no questions. Speaking about it could only risk ruining everything. Better to leave it then, bury it, unmentioned; better for everybody that way.

On the night-stand, Abigail's little clock glowed as the minute hand stepped gently over the hour: one day over and a new one begun. Still without waking her, I settled the little toy back in beside her, smoothed the blankets and stood up.

Chapter 4

JESS

I had to wait two whole days before I was allowed to see her. *Two whole days.* I badgered Mum all round the house, but all she could say was, *it's complicated*, like a bad status update. It maddened me the way Mum's rules were so rigid, the way her opinions were always right. Because what could be simpler than Abigail and me? Ever since we were tiny it had been that way.

I roamed upstairs, downstairs, hardly knowing what to do with myself. I couldn't even get hold of Lena – out of reach on a last-minute half-term holiday with her mum, a family package with her mum's new partner too, some Mediterranean island where mobiles barely worked. Without her, without Abigail, I had to hold all my excitement like a fat balloon in my chest.

Then finally, that Wednesday, we were on our way, Mum and Dad in the front seats of the car, me folded into the back. Driving all the way through town, seeing places and shops I passed all the time: Costa, Oxfam, WH Smith, estate agent, hairdresser, a new bridal boutique. They were the same but everything was different.

On her lap, Mum was holding the card we'd bought. So formal. Like we'd been invited to a birthday party. Mum's idea, but all three of us had had to go to choose it. I'd watched Dad thumb through all the ready-made messages: 'Congratulations.' 'With Sympathy.' 'New Home.' No one makes cards for an occasion like this. In the end Mum chose one labelled, *Blank inside for your personal message*. What were we supposed to write? I'd told Mum to just put: *With love from us all – cousin Jess, Auntie Lillian and Uncle Fraser*. Now Mum was running her fingers round the edges, giving the envelope a turn each time she reached a corner. The seams were sharp enough for paper cuts.

I closed my eyes. Behind my eyelids, my cousin rose up, the bright flick of her hair. So real, so close I could practically feel her. The memories came sweeping like a tide. Scraped knees, bug bites, skipping ropes, cartwheels. Her face, close up, like a copy of mine: same nose, same freckly forehead, same mouth, only the frame of her hair different between us, hers butter yellow and mine dark brown. Hand in hand and breath for breath, the pair of us at three, five, eight years old—

I opened my eyes. In the front seats, my parents were skirting an argument.

'We should have left earlier. You knew there'd be traffic.' That was Mum.

And Dad: 'I know. But we'll be there by five-thirty at the latest.' We were past the church now and heading round the one-way system.

'Yes, Fraser. But they said five. I saw you write it down.'

Dad's hands tightened on the wheel. 'Lillian,' he said. 'Not now.'

'You know it might upset her. Arriving late.'

'Listen –' Dad switched on the windscreen wipers, smearing wet across the glass – 'I don't know anything except that we're her family and they've asked us to come. I for one will be so damn happy to see her and there are bigger things to worry about than being a few minutes late.'

He pulled the handbrake as we stopped at the south-side traffic lights. *Thank you, Dad*, I wanted to say.

But even he had told me to prepare myself, his face all kindly and solemn when he'd knocked on my bedroom door last night. Dad was like that, always wanting to *talk* about things, always wanting stuff out in the *open*. I had to understand, he'd said, Abigail would look different, would be different now. Was I prepared for that? I couldn't just go running up to her, jumping on her, hugging her. She would need time.

I'd nodded, pretending to agree. But he had never known Abigail like I did.

The lights were green now and we were moving again. But in the front, my parents had both gone quiet. Mum was looking away out of the passenger window. I couldn't see her expression, only the angle of her head, the stiffness in her neck.

We took the turn-off onto Springfield Road and I craned forwards to look out of the front windscreen. Up ahead, my aunt and uncle's little patch of front garden was surrounded by a huddle of men and women. I recognized the set-up at once. Journalists, their collars raised against the untimely spring rain. For weeks, months, they'd reported her missing. Now they would write the best headline of all, the perfect ending to our story. I wondered what Lena would make of all this. She'd refused to believe it would end this way. That argument we'd had when we were thirteen, when I'd yelled that her parents' divorce was stupid and she'd flung back, *Jess, don't you get it? Real life isn't happily ever after. In real life, my parents are getting divorced and your cousin is never coming back!* It took me weeks to forgive her for that but what did it matter now? I'd been right.

The seatbelt was tight around my shoulder. The journalists looked as keen as bloodhounds. 'Go round the back,' I said to Dad. He nodded silently and heaved the wheel. As the car jounced over a speed bump, Mum put a hand to the dashboard to steady herself. She didn't have to say anything – the gesture was enough. 'Sorry,' said Dad.

We parked on the narrow, pot-holed road behind. Here the street was empty, just a dog barking somewhere with a steady, grinding bark. We got out of the car. Through the misty air, I could see up to where the road became a dead-end, to where a scrubby path led off through lopsided railings. Off to the sleek tracks of the railway line, where the fast trains didn't stop, just thundered through. I remembered how Abigail had always wanted to go up there. We weren't allowed though, Auntie Anne had been adamant – a girl had once fallen from the bridge down there. Still, Abigail used to stand and stare until I'd grab her arm and yank her back, off up the road to the corner shop or playground.

The envelope in Mum's hand was crumpled, creases running across the creamy paper. She handed the card to me and looked up at the house, the brown brick walls and white-framed windows gazing back down at us. She dug in her pockets like checking for loose change or bus tickets. 'What are you looking for?' said Dad.

'I'm not – nothing.' Mum took the card back.

Dad drew a hand down the bristles of his cheek, as if to smooth things out between them.

'Let's just go in,' I said.

I pulled down the sleeves of my jumper and tucked my thumbs in the cuffs, a move that always annoyed Mum. But for once she said nothing, just hitched up the zipper on her coat and headed through the little wooden gate at the bottom of the Whites' back garden. I followed behind and Dad brought up the rear, careful to drop down the latch of the gate after him as if there was something inside that might want to escape. On the slippery decking, Mum rapped on the whorled glass of the back door. We could hear sounds from inside and I could see wavering shapes. We waited.

'Knock again,' said Dad. 'Maybe they didn't hear us.'

'Annie knows we're coming to the back. I texted her from the car.'

'Well, just knock again.' He was reaching past her to bang once more when the door swung open and there was Auntie Anne.

I'd expected her to look filled up with happiness. Instead there were muddy circles under her eyes and a restless flush on her cheeks, like someone with a brand new baby – hair a bit rumpled, skin a bit pale. I tried to look past her, to catch a glimpse of Abigail.

My aunt ushered us in through the doorway and into the fug of the kitchen. Dad stepped on the back of my heel and mumbled another apology, and I was pressed up against the scratchy wool of Mum's coat. We stood crammed in with them between the blue kitchen units and shiny wall tiles. Mum held out the card to no one in particular until Uncle Robert reached out and took it. The twins stared at me, wide-eyed. In the background a kettle came to the boil, thrummed and thrashed then clicked itself off. There were fresh mugs laid out and a full jug of milk, but no one got up to pour the hot water.

I undid the Velcro fastening on my jacket, the sound a huge big scrape in the room. It was hot in here, way too hot. I pushed my fringe up off my face. Next to Auntie Anne, framed by the doorway to the hall, was a figure.

I couldn't take my eyes off her. But still nobody moved.

They'd said she'd look different, but she didn't to me. All right, so her skin was pale and she was heavier than me now but shorter. Her hair was an odd colour and she was wearing a weird combination of clothes. In bunched leggings and one of my uncle's huge T-shirts, she was wrong-shaped, wrong-sized, coloured in all wrong, but all that was like a costume I could see right through. I pushed forwards past Mum, past the chairs and the table and the waiting kettle.

I came to a halt in front of her. I could hear the sighing of her breath as it drew in and out – in time, it seemed, with mine. I held her gaze and she held mine.

'Welcome home, Abigail,' I said.

Across the great chasm of time, it was like the years were winding up, rethreading themselves. There was the tiniest pause, then, 'Hello, Jess,' she replied.

I smiled and summoned the magic words from long ago, when we were best playmates. Words that worked just the same for our fifteen-year-old selves.

'Come on then,' I said. 'Let's go up to your room.'

The house smelled the same as it always had – a scent of pine from some cleaning product, and the smell of oil and sawdust from Uncle Robert's overalls. Behind me, as we climbed the stairs, words floated, my aunt's hushed voice: '… the house was empty and the police haven't traced him…' I let the words fall away behind us.

On the landing, we came to a halt. Sam and Laurie's bunk beds showed through the open door to the left and next was my aunt and uncle's bedroom. Opposite that, the bathroom, and at the end of the hallway a spare room, for guests. Abigail gestured to the door nearest on the right. 'Here's my room.'

She was right. It had always been hers. But I hadn't expected the transformation.

She pushed the door wide and led me through. Pictures, teddies, board games, books. Skipping ropes, rosettes, the blue flopsy at the head of her bed. The articles, paperwork, search posters all gone, and all the belongings of eight-year-old Abigail laid out once again.

I stood in the doorway, on the threshold, as if by entering I'd break some spell. Then softly as I could, I stepped into the room and stood beside Abigail at her childhood dresser. On the polished wood a little glass frog squatted on a lily pad, its bulging eyes crossed and goofy.

'Albert McCroak,' she said. I made him take a few hops across the dresser and landed him gently beside her. As she slid a finger down the smooth curve of his back I noticed the tip was stained nicotine yellow, like our granddad's used to be. 'Ribbit,' she said. I grinned.

She looked up at me, as if waiting for what I might do next. Above her bed was the volume we used to always read. *Grimm's Fairy Tales*. I pulled it down and sat on the bed, opening the book across my lap. She sat down next to me. I could smell the tang of her teenage sweat and I listed towards her as the mattress dipped. I knew she didn't want to be hugged, not just yet, but I let our shoulders touch, let the clumped mess of her hair tickle my cheek. As we turned the pages in a hypnotic rhythm, whole worlds passed before us, stories we'd lived within, once upon a time. I'd never let myself forget them. I could feel the heat of her against my arm. 'We used to read these to each other,' I said.

She ran her hand over the pictures – beautiful watercolours I knew so well. 'The Frog Prince,' she said. 'Hansel and Gretel.'

So she *did* remember. The relief was like little bubbles in my chest. I leaned across and helped her flip forward. 'You always liked this one – with the donkey and the cat. The Bremen Town Musicians.'

'Yes. With the robbers.'

I turned more pages, searching for other stories she'd know, other ones to make her smile. 'Some of them were scary,' I said, 'but you were never scared.'

Abigail let the book slide from her lap and suddenly uncurled herself from the bed. I had to steady myself as the mattress shifted. What was it? It was like some word of mine had pinched her somewhere, snagged on something. She went to the window and folded back the curtains, peering out into the street, that narrow street we'd parked on. It was like she was still wondering when we'd arrive. Or waiting for someone else entirely.

The bedroom door creaked, and I jumped.

'Girls?'

Mum, come to check up on us. On the nightstand, the clock read ten to six. We'd have to be leaving before long, I knew. Mum had said we shouldn't stay too long. We didn't want to stress Abigail or tire her out. Or ourselves. I could read in Mum's eyes how she wanted to reassure me: *Don't worry, it will get easier, she's still adjusting, try not to mind…*

Don't you get it? I wanted to say back. Nothing is different between us. I haven't changed and neither has she. But Abigail wasn't saying anything, just standing with her forehead pressed against the window. In that moment, I saw my cousin as Mum did – like a stranger, awkward, not knowing where to put herself, even though she was right here, home, in her own room.

Silently, I got up and put the book of fairy tales back on the shelf. I felt hollow. I couldn't even find my voice to say goodbye, just swallowing empty mouthfuls as my cousin turned around, pressing the heels of her hands on the sill behind her. There's no way Mum expected what Abigail said next, and she even caught me giddily off-guard. It was just the kind of announcement she used to make when she was eight:

'Auntie Lillian, please, can Jess stay the night?'

We sat up in her room like little mice while downstairs the adults argued, trying to decide what to do. They hadn't planned for this, there was no protocol. What if it was too much too soon – but then if Abigail herself had asked? Upstairs I rolled my eyes and my cousin giggled, with that funny hiccupping laugh I remembered so well.

Finally, Uncle Robert put up a camp bed in Abigail's room and Auntie Anne made up the guest bed for Mum and Dad. She found us spare toothbrushes, and I could sleep in my T-shirt. As so we did, we stayed the night. All of us under one roof.

Sitting crossed-legged on the squeaking camp bed with her Mickey Mouse lamp on the floor between us, I didn't need to think of where she'd been, or who with, or what had been done to her there. I only needed to see her here. When my aunt brought the twins up to say goodnight, they hovered in the doorway, twining themselves round the frame. They'd been so little when she disappeared, only nine months old, too little, I imagined, to remember anything. Me though, I remembered everything. We listened to the thumps and bumps of the adults making their ways to bed. When at last the house fell quiet, it was just the two of us alone.

'All your stuff is here,' I said, looking round. It was like I was only taking it in properly now. I knelt on the camp bed and ran my fingers over a row of frilly rosettes pinned to the wall. Now, close up, I could see the Blu Tack marks from where Anne and Robert had had their notes, their pictures.

This rosette was for second place in a dancing competition, aged seven. I laughed. 'You hated ballet.'

She rubbed her cheek. 'I know. But Mum liked me to go.'

I sat back down. 'You loved reading, stories, that was your thing. And you were good at drawing. But mostly we made up our own games.'

She nodded, sliding down into the cocoon of her duvet. 'I remember. Tell me again, Jess, how it was between us.'

So I did. I told her about the games we'd played, the ones

we'd disappear into whenever she was upset. Dress-up, make-believe, once-upon-a-time. The thousand imaginary worlds we created, the nights we wouldn't let each other fall asleep because we didn't want to say goodbye. As I talked, other scraps of memory flickered: arguments, tantrums, Auntie Anne losing patience. Our games, though, had made everything all right.

'It can be the same now,' I told her. 'Just like before.' I'd been waiting to say that to her all this time. Now we were together and nothing could hurt us. Just like catching each other in the game of *Do-you-trust-me?* I didn't say the rest, but I think she knew. *I've only been waiting for you.*

I snuggled down in the warmth of my sleeping bag. My eyes grew heavy, I was so warm, so happy. I could hear her breathing, steady and deep. After a while, I switched off the lamp, and we went on lying there in the soft dark. Maybe I dozed off in that darkness, just for a moment, because when I next looked over she was sitting up in bed, staring at the far wall like it was a TV screen or a stage. I could see her – just – in the light from the landing, filtering under the bedroom door. She didn't look like Abigail in that moment. I didn't quite feel like myself. Something had shifted in the space between us, something had entered the bubble I'd made.

Maybe that was what made me ask, made me shape the question. A sudden need to fill a blank, a hole. My skin tingling like when we'd tell ghost stories, torches under our chins, my words came out slow, dreamy, as I whispered:

'*Abigail – what was it like?*'

At first she went on staring at the wall, not moving. I wondered if she hadn't heard me or whether she was pretending.

I suddenly wondered if she was even awake. But I could see her eyes glistening in the dark. She leaned towards me, turning her head.

'It isn't like anything,' she said.

Chapter 5

Friday 31st May:
Day 5

ANNE

Abigail slept so much more soundly that night. I knew because I stayed up, haunting the landing, listening, checking long after Robert said, come to bed. I pictured them in there, our family's two daughters, sleeping together as they used to as children. It had always been like that between them; calming each other like no one else could. There had been something unbreakable between them, something that hadn't broken, even now. Listening to Jess's whispers, finally my heartbeats slowed and I could slip away to my own room across the hall, leaving the door open, knowing she was only calling distance away.

By the morning, I had made a decision; I had woken with one bright thought in my head. Beside me, Robert was still asleep, his hefty, lion-like shape a mound under the covers. I thought of Jess, asleep in Abigail's room, of Lillian and Fraser next door, all of us gathered together. Why not take the opportunity? What better chance to show what she meant to us? Careful not to wake my husband, I eased back the blanket and slipped out from the warmth, and at first I pulled a jumper on over my nightdress, then took both off and got properly dressed. No one else up, the house fizzing with cold, I went downstairs.

In the kitchen, I opened every cupboard and took out bowls, plates, side plates, knives and spoons. All the boxes of cereal we had I pulled out: Shreddies, Weetabix, Coco Pops, Frosties. We had five flavours of jam in the cupboard: strawberry, apricot, blackcurrant, raspberry and the one that had always been Abigail's favourite: cherry. I set them all out so she could choose anything she wanted. I dug out a butter dish from the back of the cupboard – an old wedding present we never used – and unpeeled a hard block of butter from its wrapper. In the fridge I found orange juice, apple juice, milk; I laid out yoghurts with individual spoons. When the kettle boiled, I made a heavy pot of tea, and even folded eight napkins from a roll of kitchen towel.

I heard the footsteps on the stairs; soft light footsteps and I straightened up, a rush of love thrumming through me. 'Mummy?' I was so ready to welcome her, my beautiful daughter. When the kitchen door pushed open, I saw blond hair, thin shoulders, bare feet.

'Mummy?' The shape wavered and blurred. 'What's going on?' Not Abigail. Sam.

All right then. I made myself smile. 'Come on, sit here.' I pulled out a chair. 'Doesn't it look lovely?'

Sam rubbed at his eyes, a tiny frown-crease lining his fore-head. 'Is this for Auntie Lillian?'

I shook my head. Why say that? Just because I'd made it all look so perfect? 'No. It's for Abigail. A welcome home breakfast.'

I pushed him forwards and settled him into the chair. The clock on the microwave clicked over. Sam leaned his elbows on the table, his feet scuffing at the bare kitchen floor. 'I was sleeping, Mummy. You woke me up.'

Outside it was only just growing light – too early for any reporters to have gathered – but already I could hear birds singing: blackbirds and the croak of jackdaws. The kitchen felt chilly though; I couldn't understand why the boiler hadn't come on. Sam fiddled with the knife at the side of his plate, his thumb making a smudgy print on the blade.

'Sam,' I said. 'Leave that.' He set the knife back down. The clock on the microwave blinked again: 5:41, ridiculously early, I know. Sam shivered, his fingers sliding from the knife, from the table. 'Mummy,' he mumbled. 'I'm going back to bed.'

It was three hours later when the whole family finally appeared – Lillian and Fraser, Robert and the boys, Abigail yawning in the dressing gown I'd lent her, and a sleepy Jess by her side, pulling her jumper sleeves down over her arms.

Abigail sat down to eat with the rest of us and heaped up her share of cereal and toast. From where I sat at the other end of the table, she seemed happy enough – busy with milk and butter and jam – and I set to my own breakfast with a grateful sense of relief. It was only when I came to clear the plates that I realized, my heart twisting. She had hardly eaten a thing.

She spent the rest of the day wrapped in my thick pink dressing gown, watching TV, dozing. She was tired after the Bradys' visit. From the couch, she received all my yes-or-no questions: *Do you want a drink, have you had enough sleep, do you remember your flopsy, can you work the remote?* – with a steady expression. I

38

knew I was hovering, crowding her, but it was as though seven years of everyday mothering was now desperate to come out. She replied, *yes, yes, yes* to each one of my questions, but always with a pause beforehand, a tense little pause.

It was the same when she replied *yes* to Robert's suggestion. He had been set on the idea all week, ever since the first headlines got out. I knew what it meant to him. He wanted the chance to say: here we are, the family who never gave up, the family who never stopped trying and thank you for bringing her back to us at last. It wasn't as though I didn't understand. Hadn't my breakfast been about the same thing? When he came into our lives, he'd made a promise to protect her. Hadn't that been a condition of our love? And hadn't he spent these last seven years wracked with guilt at how this promise was broken? Now she was found and safe and at home. He had every right to be overjoyed at that.

The twins crowded round him as he broached the subject with Abigail, clambering next to him on the armchair in the living room, and I watched them all from the doorway.

Under the dressing gown, she was still wearing the T-shirt and leggings she'd slept in last night. They needed a wash but we hadn't got anything else for her yet. My daughter, home, and we didn't even have clothes.

Robert looped an arm around Laurie's shoulders and he spoke so gently and calmly to Abigail, explaining, reassuring – we'd only need to be out a few minutes, let them take a few photos, and she wouldn't even need to say anything, he would prepare a statement for us all, one even DS McCarthy would approve of. He could arrange it all with one quick call.

'What about it, Abigail? What do you think?'

Hugging a cushion, she looked at him. The little tense hesitation, a breath through her nose, a glance up at me and then: *yes.* Surely it was better this way, said Robert. It would stop them hounding us, get them off our front step, and yet I woke up the next morning with a pain in my stomach.

That afternoon, I sat on our rumpled mattress turning up a pair of my smart black trousers while Robert shaved at the corner sink. His electric razor was humming and the sound of it usually comforted me, but right now it felt like a needle against my teeth.

The trousers had been so long on her when she tried them on, whole inches pooling at her feet no matter how high up she hitched the waist. I'd measured the amount they'd need taking up but now the needle in my hand kept slipping, the thread twisting and tangling, making a knot that refused to pull through.

'Some of the reporters will be the ones from before,' Robert was saying over the buzz of his shaver. 'I'll never forget how they tried to help.'

I remembered too: how he had gone on and on calling up the news stations – at home and in London – begging them to provide fresh coverage, fresh appeals, even when the soundbites of information shrank to crumbs and every single lead dried up. He had done everything. He had never given up.

'I'm not sure.' When he didn't hear, I had to repeat myself. '*I'm not sure.*'

Now Robert paused his shaving, looking at me through the mirror, the razor hanging in the air. 'But I thought you were all right with it. All we're doing is sharing good news.'

I wiped the damp pads of my fingers on my knee, rethreaded

the needle. Lillian had tried when we were younger to get me to copy her own perfect efforts: stitches in rows like soldiers, each one alike, but mine had never come out like that.

'I am – I was, but don't you think we should wait? Why do we need to go out there right now, when we've barely even just got her back?'

'Anne, this is a *good* thing. All we're telling them is how happy we are. All they want is to write their happy ending. That's the only reason they've been standing out there. The sooner they've got that, the sooner I think they'll let us alone.'

I tugged at the trousers, pushing the needle through again, shaking my head. Robert set the shaver down on the shelf. The buzzing vibrations whined worse than ever. 'What is this, Anne? What is it you're so worried about?'

But how could I explain when I hardly knew myself, just had this feeling, a cold stone in the pit of my stomach, making sweat bead on my palms. How could I explain that it all felt so fragile, as though the slightest misstep would break everything apart?

In my panic, I found myself saying, 'Why do we have to be all on show? Why does it have to be shared with everyone? Just what is it that you're trying to *prove*?'

Straight away as the words came out, like catching my fingers in the slam of a door, I knew it was absolutely the wrong thing to say. In the mirror, it was written all over Robert's face.

'Robert,' I said. 'I'm sorry.' I pinched at the hems of the trousers, trying to press the stitches flat. 'I didn't mean that at all.'

He reached out and carefully turned off the shaver. The silence flowed in like a cool sluice of water. He came and sat along from me on the bed, in a patch of May sunlight. I reached out my hand, a gesture we'd done a hundred times over the years: our olive branch that had got us through the very worst of times. As always, he took my hand in his but this time, in his fingers, I felt the tension.

'Anne, it's not like that. I'm not trying to prove anything. By why are you acting like we've something to hide?'

When I held up the trousers, miraculously the hems stayed in place. I gathered them up and went to give them to Abigail. Robert was right, we had nothing to be afraid of. I had read his statement, it made everything clear; it would give the journalists exactly what they wanted and if Abigail hadn't said anything before, why should she now? All right then – as soon as she was ready, we would go.

'Abigail?' Her door was ajar, her bedroom empty, and her bed was made with uncanny precision. It was as though she had vanished into thin air or climbed out of her window or run straight out the front door. 'Robert,' I called out, 'where is she?'

'I heard her go into the bathroom,' he said from our doorway. By now he had his shirt on and was doing up the bottom button. 'Just knock for her while I sort out the boys.'

Of course. After all, hadn't we told her to get ready? At the bathroom door, I listened for her with the trousers bunched in my hands. She'd closed the door tightly and I couldn't hear anything – no sound of taps running or a brushing of teeth. How long had she been in there? Five minutes, ten? A sickly thought rose up, like something with claws climbing up my throat. Wild thoughts, paranoid thoughts, but I couldn't stop them stretching and thickening as I thought of the razor blades beside the bath, a dressing gown cord to loop from the shower rail and a whole box of painkillers in the cabinet over the sink.

I knew the lock on the door was loose and I lifted the handle up with a twist and shoved the door open – and there she was.

At first I couldn't make out at all what she was doing. She jerked back from the mirror and out of some instinct thrust her hand behind her back. Still, I glimpsed what she was holding: something small, black, circular.

'Abigail? I'm sorry. I shouldn't have barged in.' I told myself to keep my voice steady.

'No, I'm sorry,' she said. 'I should have asked first.'

'But what are you doing?' Her forehead was pale where she hadn't swept the colour yet and the front of my dressing gown was scuffed with powder. I told myself, you remember this from before, the way it can go, if she's challenged, if you get angry.

She looked at her nose, her cheeks in the glass. 'I'm just so white.'

The trousers slipped from my hand and I fumbled to catch them before they fell. I couldn't escape it as my mind fitted the pieces together, showing me suddenly what this meant: so pale, so white because of how she had lived, in conditions no child should ever have to live in. The thought was sickening.

I shook my head. 'Don't apologize. You don't need to apologize. Of course you can use my make-up if you want, I can even show you if you like, how to do it, how to get it right.' It was the kind of thing a mother would do for a daughter, another of the thousands of things we'd missed out on. But somehow this time an edge had crept into my voice; I'd glimpsed that look I knew so well, the bottom lip pushing out, the stubborn flare of her nostrils and I'd felt the old, old feeling: that raw, painful

43

discord between us. She set the compact down on the lip of the basin. It wobbled for a moment and then fell in, scraping down the enamel. I was ready for it; I knew what came next. I remembered her this way, this other Abigail; I remembered it and I braced myself.

Instead she turned away, a quarter turn back to the mirror, as though all the fight had gone out of her, or as though she'd had no fight at all to begin with. Seeing it drained my heart. Whatever I had expected, this was worse: this disconnect, this hollow gap. This closed-off, silent turning away.

I held up the trousers, right-sized now, filling up the space with my words. 'I've taken these up now so they should fit, and come through to the bedroom when you're done and I can quickly measure you for the rest.'

After a beat, she looked at me. 'You don't need to do that. I know my size.'

She must have seen the red climb my cheeks. She did. Of course she did. 'Okay,' I said when I could get my voice even. 'Just give me a minute.'

She stooped to wash the make-up off.

Downstairs, Robert was pulling out shoes for the twins. He didn't ask any questions as I went out of the back door and yanked open the bag by the wheelie bin. That's what I'd done with them, on her very first night; she must have wondered. The clothes were inside, safely nestled in the clean plastic – the clothes he had bought for her. Of course the size was on the labels. I carried the whole bundle back upstairs with me, including the neat white bra. Up in her room, she took them from me and placed them carefully on the bed, right next to the trousers I'd laid out. I took hold of myself. *They're only clothes,*

I told myself, *and she had to wear something. You needed the measurements and now you have them: size 14 and 36C.*

Once she was dressed – in the black trousers and white bra and the blue acrylic jumper – we finally made our way up the road. As we walked, Abigail in between me and Robert, and the twins on either side, I thought to myself, *we're all right, we're fine. We're a family reunited, and it's wonderful, a miracle that all five of us are here, walking down a sun-filled street together. Why should anyone think any different?* Laurie slipped his small, hot hand into mine and I tugged him a little, to make him keep up.

We heard them before we even reached the hall, and when we rounded the corner, the grass was beetling with reporters, more of them than I think even Robert had expected. Beside me, Abigail fell back a step. The journalists had seen us now and were jostling for position. 'On the steps? If you stand on the steps?' The press officer, a petite woman with blonde hair in a bun, was coming towards us, all smiles. She reached for Abigail, curling one hand about her elbow, and this time Abigail let the woman handle her just fine.

She positioned Abigail on the top step and Robert climbed up to stand beside her. He was clearly waiting for me to get up there too.

'And your boys?' Against the sun, I could make out the faces of our neighbours and friends, this tight-knit community that had accepted me and Robert, a community that had supported us through the ordeal of all these years.

'Mrs White? Anne?' The press officer was gesturing to me: come along, stand here, your sons will be fine. I looked up at them: my husband and my daughter. They looked nothing alike, never had, but he'd been more of a father than her real dad ever was. From the start, their bond had been so loving, so strong, and there'd been a naturalness, such an ease in his relationship with her; I'd envied it and I'd loved him for it, the joy that he'd brought to both of our lives. Then all through this ordeal, we'd been a team together. He'd never allowed himself to be pushed to one side. Now he reached into the pocket of his shirt and pulled out his crisp sheet of paper. He smiled down at me and I felt myself smile back as I climbed up beside them. We were still a team here today and suddenly I wanted everyone to see it.

With a deep breath, Robert read out the statement and it was perfect. I put my arms around both twins and I managed to say my bit too. Abigail stood there all the while, bravely, and didn't speak or add anything. The May sun was glinting in my eyes; I could hardly make out the reporters in front of us. It was only when the sun disappeared for a moment that I made out the cameras with their local and national and international logos, nothing at all between us and them, nothing hiding us at all. And I suddenly I realized why I'd balked at bringing her here. Suddenly all the knotted ropes in my stomach made sense. All the eyes of the world were on us and like a bloated cloud passing over the sun, the thought bloomed across my mind:

He will see this.

Chapter 6

Friday 31st May:
Day 5

JESS

They aired the story on the evening news. They started with the other girl: Tonia Dillon, six years old, taken by a man with chin-length blond hair. The same man, they said. Then about the teenager who'd brought her to Southwark Police Station, who said the child had been brought to her house.

I gestured Dad to move up on the couch, make room for me between him and Mum. I'd already seen coverage all over Twitter, but Dad had wanted us to watch this together. *For Abigail White's family, just being together again is a joy*, said the news anchor, and there they were – Auntie Anne, Uncle Robert and Abigail, up on the steps in front of some building, the twins cuddled in at my uncle's side. Five days in and it still sometimes felt like a dream. I squeezed my arm, checking the tender, sharp spots. Making sure I wouldn't wake up and find her gone again, like all those other times I'd dreamed she'd come back. But this news broadcast was true, the real deal.

You could catch the flash of cameras, sense the dozens of reporters. It was like in the beginning, when Uncle Robert had to keep calling the papers, making sure they covered her story. I knew the guilt he felt for not being there. Because he'd stayed at the hospital instead. He'd gone over that story with us a million times in the months after Abigail went missing, like he couldn't stop punishing himself. But even despite that, it didn't make sense to him – why there weren't witnesses with all those hundreds of people *right there*? He wouldn't let the media give up. They'd even staged a reconstruction. A Tube platform, overflowing with rain-soaked commuters, all these people pushing, pressing to get home. The train carriages bursting, a crush for anyone to get on or off. They showed us a woman with infant twins in a buggy, trying to keep her eight-year-old in tow. And then a tide of passengers pushing to get out of the carriages, and how, in a split second, Auntie Anne and Abigail got separated – bodies buffeted, hands wrenched apart. And they said how in her confusion, my cousin left the platform, made her way up and out of the station. And then there was that shot. The one where it wasn't an actress, it wasn't the reconstruction, it was the CCTV footage of my cousin herself, holding the hand-rail and standing on the right, just like you're supposed to, people packed in all around her. On the footage, they used a bright spotlight to pick her out. You know, in case you missed her. In another two shots, she drifts through the barriers and up the steps to the exit, and then that was it.

Dad turned the volume up on the TV. 'Where are they?' I said. 'What building is that?'

Mum lifted a hand to say, *shush*.

The camera pulled back and now I saw the lettering above them: the village hall. Uncle Robert read from a sheet of paper, his voice fuzzy on the TV speakers. *Our daughter has been returned to us after an eternity. We are overjoyed. It is a miracle to have her back with us, safe and sound.*

Mum rubbed at the skin between her forefinger and thumb, making Dad shift awkwardly.

'What?' I said. But Mum just shook her head.

To a clatter of camera shutters, Uncle Robert passed the paper across to Auntie Anne. *We ask for privacy at this time. Abigail has been through a great ordeal. But she's safe now and we will do everything to help her.*

A last shot, zooming in on Abigail. And that was that.

'Is that it?' I said. 'That's all they have to say?'

Dad scraped a hand down the stubble of his chin. Mum's lips were tight.

'They really didn't think it through, did they?' she said, ignoring me.

'I don't see how it can do any harm.'

'Really, Fraser? Drawing all that attention? Parading her like that, like a provocation? Putting the whole of themselves on show?'

Dad closed his mouth. Without another word, he switched the TV off.

I wished I could crawl under the cushions of the couch, into the warm, soft, silent space below. I knew, I always knew. I could read it, the atmosphere between them, clear as a weather forecast. But why, *why* did it have to be now when everything was supposed to be finally all right? Very carefully I stood up, the air as heavy as before a thunderstorm, and when I left the room, I made sure to close the door tight shut behind.

Upstairs in my room I pushed my ear buds hard into my ears. I didn't want to hear them, I didn't want to know. I felt like a kid again, fingers jammed in my ears, tears jamming up my eyes. They could go months, half a year and I'd think they were done, over it now, until the air would go tight again and just like that, I'd know. The pressure that would build to one of their rows. On my phone, I pressed the volume as high as it would go.

I almost missed it, I had my music on so loud – my phone screen flashing with Lena's pixie face. My phone pinged, and pinged again. I paused my track and swiped for her texts.

Oh My God! I saw on the news!

Tom texted me too, the message right after said, and I felt the familiar ache in my chest, the distance between us nothing to do with miles. I went to lean against the cool of my bedroom window.

Another text: Jess, can you believe she's back?

Outside, down the end of the garden, the wind caught the blue ropes of my old childhood swing, setting the plastic seat swaying. Nearby the grass was ragged from where Dad had been digging at something. Lena and I had been best friends since we were ten, but these last couple of years, ever since her parents divorced, we'd grown further and further apart. The two of us used to do everything together, but now there was Tom and other girls she hung out with, now there were parties she got invited to, without me. She'd got so busy with growing up, while all I'd done was try to keep things the same. Sometimes, like now, I felt the stab of it. The aching sense of how I'd fallen behind.

My fingers slow, I texted back.

Always knew she'd come home.

Because why else had I been waiting, stalling all this time, putting the whole of my life on hold?

Need all the deets! A pause. Then: Can't call, Mum barely letting me text. Home Sunday but really late, but see you at school??? Then a row of smiley-face emojis.

She was reaching out, so happy for me, so friendly. There was so much I wanted to tell her. I typed a reply, deleted it, tried again. But nothing I wrote explained how I felt. I just didn't know how to share Abigail with her.

Eventually, from the icons on my phone, I found a smiley face to send back.

School. I hadn't even thought about it, but half term was almost over, May was almost over, and school would start on Monday, in three days' time. In the morning, Saturday, when I came down to breakfast, Mum and Dad were both standing at the sink with their backs to me.

'I *know* anyone can read a newspaper,' Mum was saying, 'I *know* anyone can follow the news. But *seeing* her, Fraser.' Her tone was made even more bristly by the scourer she was rubbing over the draining board. 'He never gave her up.'

They still were picking at the edges of their argument, like fanning a flame instead of blowing it out.

'What are you saying? That he'll try to... when the police are—'

'The police have no idea where he is!'

'Seen who?' I interrupted. 'Try what?'

They both turned around. I sat down heavily at the kitchen table.

'Hey, Munchkin,' said Dad. 'Are you wanting some break-fast?'

I didn't say anything, just waited for one of them to finally explain. Instead, Mum pressed the button to jump the bread out of the toaster, and handed it to me. Like everything in our world was so normal.

I set the plate down on the table: two pale slices. 'When are we going to see her again?'

Dad sat down opposite and handed me the butter. Mum had already gone back to her scouring. 'Jess,' he said, 'you have to be patient.'

I looked at him silently. *But you saw how happy she was to see me*, I wanted to say, *and I've been patient for seven whole years.*

'You went to bed early last night,' Mum cut in. She did that, had a way of hauling up a question, putting me on the back foot. I was used to it, but it still worked.

'Yes,' I said. The toast on my plate wasn't properly done and the bread split when I tried to spread the butter. 'Anyway –' I pressed the knife down hard – 'you two were busy.'

Dad frowned, a sad frown, and opened his mouth to say something, but before he could, the doorbell rang. Mum turned from the sink and my parents looked at each other, not moving, just letting whoever it was stand out there on the step. What was wrong with them?

'I'll get it,' Mum said eventually.

She went down the hallway and I heard her open the door. I picked up my toast, dropping crumbs, and followed her out. A lady stood on our front step, an older neighbour I recognized from a couple of doors down. Mum ran errands for her sometimes, but I could never remember her name. She was beaming at Mum. '...like a miracle!' she was saying.

'Yes,' Mum said. 'On Monday night.'

The neighbour shook her white head like she still couldn't believe it. 'And you've seen her? How is she?'

'We saw them on Wednesday.' Mum glanced behind at me. She didn't say anything about my crumbs.

'Oh! How did that go?'

'She asked for Jess to stay over. In fact, we all stayed.'

'Well, isn't that lovely!'

The neighbour's beam reached me over Mum's shoulder. She looked like she wanted to hug me. I swallowed a dry piece of bread and smiled back. But we haven't made a single plan to visit again, I wanted to tell her. Don't you think that's unfair, don't you think that's stupid?

'So – will she be coming here at all?' the neighbour went on. 'Will we be able to meet her too?'

Mum's hand tightened on the edge of the door. I couldn't tell if she realized she was doing it, but bit by bit she was edging it closed.

'No. Not until—'

The neighbour's face was so shiny, so expectant. I listened for Mum's next words very carefully. Waiting for her to answer all my own questions too.

'Not until we know it's safe.'

Chapter 7

Saturday 1st June:
Day 6

ANNE

My sister was right – DS McCarthy too for that matter – it had been a bad idea to do the TV appearance. He might be desperate, wrote Lillian in her barrage of texts. *Reckless* and *unpredictable*. Who knew what he was capable of, this man who had abducted my daughter, what lengths he'd go to to get her back? The police were looking for him but he'd vanished and they couldn't say where, so don't go parading her around, my sister said. Until he's found, we all need to be very, very careful.

Because the thing about it, the thing that was so hard to understand, was that Abigail's discovery didn't happen the way you see in films. She wasn't 'rescued' and she didn't escape. She'd simply walked into a South London police station. Holding six-year-old Tonia Dillon by the hand.

We'd seen the news about Tonia, of course we had; we followed every missing child case. It was two days before that Mrs Dillon had reported her child missing. 'Kidnapped in plain daylight!' she'd cried to the 999 operator. The girl had been playing in their back garden, even though it was drizzling. Mrs Dillon had needed her out of the way; she was dealing with Tonia's father who'd come to demand his visiting rights. It was a neighbour who'd spotted the man from her window – early thirties, with longish, light-coloured hair. He'd chatted to Tonia and offered her something – sweets, probably, the police had said. Then he held out his hand and off they went. The neighbour watched them walk down to the end of the road and turn the corner. She waited, but they didn't come back.

Over five minutes had slipped past by the time the neighbour went running next door. Did Mrs Dillon have a friend, a relative with pale blond hair? She'd just seen Tonia going off with a man. The three of them roamed the wet streets for an hour but by then there was no trace of her.

So we'd heard Tonia's story. And that was where it all began for us.

Officers questioned the teenager who'd returned the lost child. She gave her name – said she was Abi – and her age, and an address a twenty-minute walk from the station. *And how and where did you find Tonia?* they asked.

The teenager said: the little girl was brought to the house where she lived. The officer read out the address she'd been given. *Who else lives there? Presumably some adults?* The teenager described a man: blue eyes, blond hair. When the officer asked, *and... is this your father?* Abigail, we were told, stayed quiet a long time. Then: *No. I don't think so.*

Then she said she needed to get back. *He won't cope without me*, she said. *He won't cope.* Instead, the officer asked her to repeat her name, her full name please, this time. She did, eventually, reluctantly. It was only then that anyone realized who she was. That she was my daughter. That's when they began to ask a lot more questions. But during that whole interview, they admitted, not once did Abigail ask to come home to us.

So now our house was like a bunker, as though we were waiting out a siege with Abigail at the centre of it all. Every move she made was like a pinch to my heart – if she yawned, if she coughed, if she changed TV channels – and at the same time within these stifling walls, I couldn't seem to stay still. I was as afraid as anyone about the man they were hunting, and yet there was something else that so unnerved and troubled me, something happening within these four walls. I kept remembering the look on Abigail's face when I'd stumbled across her in the bathroom, an avalanche of history I'd tried to keep at bay. Aged six, aged seven, I'd been so proud of her, seeing her behave herself so well, and it was so much of what Lillian approved of – the decent family Robert allowed me to create, but it hadn't always been that way and now more than ever, I couldn't stop thinking about the contrast: how Abigail had been and how I was, all that time in the years before.

The missed call I'd received last night and the voicemail sat like a lead weight on my phone, a few short phrases, threatening to unravel everything. *Annie, you know I have a right. Annie, please, I just need to know how she is.*

In the end, I had to get out. I tried not to think what it said about me that I needed to get away, that I had to leave her, my long-lost daughter, not even a week after she had come home. I was going out, and it was Robert who would stay, my husband who had always been so good with her. From the start, he'd brought out the best side of her: a child quick to laugh who came running for hugs, who let herself be kissed. And I became so much more patient with her, so much more competent, able finally to shower her with love.

When I told Robert what I needed, making up my reasons, he didn't question me or chide; he just nodded his big head as though to say, *I completely understand if you need to get some air.*

'An hour,' I told him. 'An hour and a half at most.' I just needed time to decide what to do, time to decide how best to protect her.

I dug my anorak out from the forest of coats by the front door and pulled out my walking boots from the wardrobe upstairs. Downstairs, Abigail sat cross-legged in my dressing gown on the floor of the living room where the twins had set up a board game. I'd expected them to be shy, cautious around her, but it was quite the opposite: they were so keen to be with her, to sit next to her, to play with her, it became overwhelming for her at times. I had to remind them to give her space. By now we had settled into some semblance of a routine: she slept late, ate a little breakfast, and spent most of the afternoon hours with TV. Yet it all felt so temporary, as though we were all on hold. All still pretending, acting, or waiting for the real show to start. Her physical presence seemed to be everywhere in the house, but I could look at her, my daughter, my child, and feel that she hadn't returned to us at all.

I crouched down beside them as though they were all tiny children, the fuzz of the rug bristling through my socks. On the floor, there were clue cards they weren't supposed to peek at, but Abigail had spread them all out, not following the rules.

'I have to go out for a little while,' I said to her. I picked up the cards and set them correctly. 'There's a project I volunteer at and I can't let them down. I can get you anything you need though, while I'm out?' I would have fetched her anything in the world.

She looked up at me with a face brighter than I'd seen these last six days, her gaze this time steady and direct. Wide awake, no traces of the way she had been last night, when I'd heard her from the landing, and then again when I'd stood at the foot of her bed, mumbled sounds because she was fast asleep and sleep-talking, a stream of words I couldn't decipher at all.

'Any food you'd like? I could pick up pretty much anything at Asda.' On the summit of her cheeks her teenage skin was dry and I wanted to place a cool hand on it, soothe away every tiny thing that hurt. I had touched her so little since she'd come home. 'Abigail?'

'Maybe I can come with you?'

My knees were numbed from crouching down and I couldn't seem to move. *Yes, yes, yes,* I thought, *you can come with me anywhere and it means so much to me that you asked,* but really, how could I take her with me, the whole point was not to involve her in this, to keep everything simple, everything separate – happy home, happy family – and so all I could mumble was, 'Not today, Abigail. Not to this.'

She nudged a blue disc from one empty square to another, the ragged curtain of her hair slipping down across her face.

I got to my feet with my legs burning, and left the house thinking, shit, shit, shit.

I'd never expected it to be like this. For years I'd imagined how it would be if she returned; that I would do nothing but cling to her, talk to her, sit with her for hours. I had pictured my daughter, her eyes, her smile, I had longed for the shining Abigail I remembered. I'd never thought it would feel like this: like being dragged back to the worst parts of myself.

All the way along the busy road to the canal, I fingered the phone tucked in my pocket. I'd never deleted his number though I told Lillian I had, and now it turned out he'd never deleted mine. I needed him to stay away, I had to find a way to keep the past in the past. If I opened a door I had worked so hard to jam shut, how much would I be risking then? From the road bridge I pushed my way through the scrubby grass down to the towpath; it was the first of June, officially the beginning of summer, but it had been a raw, cold spring and the banks were still a muddy tangle. As I headed downstream, ducks came scattering out of the reeds, setting up a wild quacking as they skittered away, a fan of ripples spreading out behind them. The slow water helped me to draw my breath. It felt as though I hadn't breathed since Abigail came home.

Just keep walking, I told myself, until you know what to do. Call him, don't call him, but you have to decide. The towpath was long enough; it ran all the way to Nottingham. I knew where I'd get to though, long before that. Soon enough I could make out the figures in bright yellow jackets, the work team dotting the canal banks in this project I'd signed up for last year: the renovation of the old lock. I'd thought it would help, and in some ways it had. We'd never spoken about Abigail here; the pain, the grief. This was a world apart from everything – from past, from present, from family, from loss. Here I was Annie, plain old Annie, and not *the mother of the girl who…* Sometimes, I'd just needed to escape. I'd never thought I would still need to escape now. Voices carried downwind on the breeze and I could hear the ring and chock of tools. I longed to be among them and get my hands dirty with a simple task, repetitive and focused. What had started out as an excuse – a lie to Robert about needing some air – perhaps would turn out to be true.

One of the volunteers straightened up as I got near them, a boyish figure, seventeen, eighteen, looking up at me from the uneven bottom of the lock. I undid my anorak; I hadn't needed it – no rain. 'How is it going?' I called. The volunteer – Cory was his name – smiled up with his face so friendly and open, looking like the kind of person who only wanted to help, the sort who would never do harm to anyone. I pulled my hands out from my pockets and zipped my phone away.

'We're good,' he called back and stooped to pull another staff of rotted wood from the sides of the lock. 'Have you come to help?'

They would have heard, all of them here, they must have, but even now they were good as their word, not mentioning anything. I nodded, blinking wind-blown strands of hair from my eyes. 'Can I? I just need to feel useful,' I said. Half an hour, I told myself, and then I'll decide and go home.

'Sure.' His smile was doing me the world of good. 'All right, wait here.'

He climbed up nimbly and headed to an older man across the little stone bridge. I could smell the canal water, deep and earthy, and I took in big lungfuls. 'Martin says you can help to take down the hut bricks.' Cory pointed to a structure that must have once been a little house. For the lock keeper? I headed across to them.

'We're preserving the bricks,' said Martin, handing me a hi-vis jacket. 'They can be recycled. It's an easy enough job though to pull them down and stack them.' His smile made sun rays in the corners of his eyes. Here I could pretend there was nothing but sunshine.

The bricks of the little hut were loose, the mortar around them crumbling, and Martin was right, I could pull them off with a quick sharp tug. Under my anorak, I could soon feel the sweat building and when the sun came out from behind the scudding clouds, it heated me from the outside too. With each brick I pulled, I seemed to gain courage, a belief that maybe I was stronger than I'd thought. Perhaps after all I could do this – return his call with no harm done. My thoughts, always so fast and so scrambled, fell into a slow order and I hid my face behind my hair, wiping my cheeks and nose on my sleeves, hiding my tears in the currents of the wind as I lowered the walls brick by brick.

I could only imagine how he, her father, would be feeling, knowing she was found, knowing she'd come home. He would have so many questions, ones the police could hardly answer: what exactly she looked like, how exactly she was, those myriad details that meant so much. Didn't he have a right to that at least? Surely it need be only one short conversation, telling him what he'd want to know but no more. And what if I didn't call and he simply turned up – emotional, demanding, volatile, high – wouldn't that be so much worse for Abigail? Wouldn't that reignite the worst in us all?

The volunteers were breaking for lunch; I straightened up and brushed the mortar dust from my hands. 'I can't stay,' I said, handing the yellow jacket back to Cory. 'Abigail's waiting for me at home.'

'See you soon?' Martin said and I nodded, and they both hugged me to say goodbye.

Even so, I'd stayed longer than I meant to and I walked back quickly, already feeling a thin chill as my sweat dried. A few minutes from home, in a place where the muddied path narrowed and was hidden from the main road by a copse of trees, I pulled my phone from my anorak pocket. My sister's voice was buzzing in my ears: *don't call him, Annie, don't let him back in,* but I ignored it. I *wanted* to call him, I realized now, it felt like a chance to set everything right. I could ring him, just once, and never tell anyone. I clicked the phone open.

Three missed calls from Robert, one text:

Come back.

Sick with guilt, I made myself run the rest of the way home.

When I got there, Robert met me at the front door, a finger to his lips.

'What is it? Is she all right?'

'DS McCarthy called. They're showing it.'

'What?'

'On the news, now. They've released his photograph to the press.'

My legs were like lead as I kicked off my boots and the sleeves of my anorak tangled as I twisted my arms free. In the living room, the BBC news was on the TV, but Robert had muted the sound. He pointed a finger to the ceiling: to the twins' and Abigail's bedrooms. 'I think it's best right now if she doesn't see.'

On the screen, there were shots of a house, a street, a car, nothing I recognized.

Wanted in connection...

Police are tracing...

Appeal for information...

The inevitable picture of her flashed up, our eight-year-old daughter frozen in time, but now the reporter was sounding another name out, and now came the shot of a man with blond hair and pale eyes.

'That's him,' said Robert. 'John Henry Cassingham.'

Six syllables that sounded so painful in my husband's mouth and I took each one, turning it over and over in my mind, trying to find any answer, any clue. But it was a stranger's name, a complete and utter stranger, and when I looked at Robert he shook his head too.

Gently, he took my hand in his. 'DS McCarthy is on his way.'

It had come to this: DS McCarthy in our house with his shiny shoes making divots in the living-room carpet.

Abigail sat opposite him, her big frame half sunken into the cushions of the couch; Robert sat beside her, a foot of space between them, and I stood in front of the mantelpiece, filling the gap where Robert's roses should have been.

'Do you remember the address,' the detective was saying to her, pushing his fingertips into the leather of our chair, 'that you gave us at the start?'

Abigail gazed across at the detective without blinking. 'Fifteen Martin's Road, in Southwark, in London.'

I swallowed. She reeled it off like a schoolchild reciting by rote, as though it was her home. This address, this place in

South London, so little distance, I realized now, from where she'd gone missing; just a walk through the rain from London Bridge.

'All right, well. On Monday afternoon we sent officers to the address.' His voice was soft, like suede, designed for gentle handling. 'The trouble is, there was no one at home.'

Abigail continued to gaze at him, childlike, open-faced. It had come to this: the detective here, struggling for leads, looking to my daughter to give him the answers and I thought, what on earth is this like for her? What sense is she making of any of this? Here we are, all gathered round her, piling her with questions as though she has the answers when she still hardly seems to understand that she's home.

'We know from a neighbour,' DS McCarthy went on, 'that Mr Cassingham came home mid-morning. And left again, with a duffel bag, about fifteen minutes later.'

'What are you saying?' I said. 'What are you trying to ask my daughter?'

His grey eyes came to rest on me and I made myself hold my own gaze steady. He said his next words to Abigail very quietly. I thought I had misheard him.

'Do you know anything about this, Abigail?'

I stayed right where I was. I was afraid if I moved, I'd slap him. The insinuation, the accusation in his tone as though somehow we were the ones under suspicion, as though my daughter were somehow responsible for this. 'Why should she?'

My daughter's fingers were picking at each other as if she couldn't keep them still, and I wanted to reach over and make her stop.

'Abigail?' The detective's voice was a soft murmur.

She slowly slid her gaze up to me, then away again to the window, to outside. She shook her head. 'Uh-uh.'

'There was a dark blue car,' DS McCarthy pressed on, his fingers pushing right into the arm of our chair. 'Like the one seen near Tonia Dillon's house. We got his details from the registration plate. We contacted the school where you said he worked. He hasn't been there since Monday morning.'

Abigail's shoulders hunched up to her ears, a shrug. I knew the detective was only doing his job: gathering information, piecing together clues. It was the way Abigail seemed so uncaring, so complacent, as though she couldn't see what the fuss was about, why the police were so desperate to find him; as if she didn't think her abductor had done a single thing wrong. For a blind moment, something slipped in me again and I had the sudden urge to grab her and drag her up from the couch, march her upstairs, and shake the answers out of her. *Explain yourself! Explain yourself!*

The detective looked as though he was bracing himself for what he'd say next and automatically I braced myself too. He leaned forwards.

'Abigail. Do you know where he is?'

Then the detective was gone and we were alone again. Robert put an arm around our daughter. I stood up. 'I'm going to check on the twins.'

As I climbed the stairs, I could hear Abigail's voice below me in the living room. 'I told them all this. They went over and over it in London.' Then Robert: 'It's all right. If you don't know, you don't know.' Even now, his simplicity allowed him to steady her: no sharp corners, no edges to get in the way. I knew it was something I should be grateful for, something that could only be good for my daughter; it was just that it brought an ache to my heart because I only wished I could be the same way.

The boys were sitting in their bedroom propped against Laurie's bunk; they'd been so good, keeping out of the way. On the carpet beside them, an abandoned iPad game blipped, a message flashing, *Restart game?* 'What's happening?' said Sam. 'What's going on?'

But I was looking at the mess on their desk: a whole pile of papers with her face on each, dozens of pictures of her: *Abigail White, missing, missing, missing.* All those posters that Robert had kept printing, more than he could use, the extras that had sat in boxes in her room. 'Why have you got these? What are you doing?'

Laurie jumped to his feet. I felt the sharpness of his elbows as he pushed up beside me, his voice shrill as he pressed his hands to the pages. 'We rescued them! When we were clearing her bedroom. We wanted to keep them.'

The computer game suddenly stopped pinging. I breathed in hard. I mustn't shout, I mustn't be angry. 'She's home now,' I said. 'We don't need any of this. You were there when we put all this away.' I scooped the accusing posters up, catching the ones that fell to the floor. I crumpled them, the paper unyielding, and crammed them into the bin by the door. When I was done I let out my breath. 'You can come downstairs,' I said. 'We're finished.'

Slowly, Sam uncurled himself from the floor. As he headed past me, I caught at him and Laurie too, hugging them to me. 'I love you,' I said, but their faces were sullen and as soon as I let them, they wriggled away.

I listened to their feet bang down the stairs, with something cold and hollow in my chest. I sat down on Laurie's bunk, the rockets and spaceships so innocent and familiar, symbols of everything I should be fighting to protect. I took out my phone, scrolling through my contacts to the old profile, stored simply as 'P'. The choice was gone; I knew I couldn't call him now. My hands heavy, I deleted his voicemail.

After a moment I deleted his phone number too.

Chapter 8

Sunday 2nd June:
Day 7

JESS

On Sunday I made Mum let me call them. When the phone rang it was Auntie Anne who picked up. 'And Abigail?' I asked. 'Can I speak to Abigail? Can she come to the phone?'

But Abigail was sleeping, Auntie Anne said, even though it was the middle of the day. 'The detective was here yesterday and it tired her out. I'm sorry, Jess.'

'Well, and how is she?' said Mum. 'Any dissociation, any nightmares?' She had been reading up on 'trauma symptoms'.

'No,' said Auntie Anne. 'Nothing like – that.' She paused. Something hung there, unsaid. 'But I'll get her to call you, shall I, Jess – when she wakes up?'

But Abigail must have slept right through because come eleven that evening she still hadn't called, and then it was Monday and I had to go to school.

I woke with a thick head, a shivery fever, like coming down with 'flu. Mum held the back of her hand against my forehead, not even checking with the thermometer, and said I'd be fine. I got her to drive me to school at least. I couldn't face the bus.

She wrote me a note too, for my teachers. Explaining everything that had happened.

When she dropped me off at the top of the road, it felt like I'd been away for years, not a week. Maybe that's what was making me feel so ill, the flip from one world straight into another. Lena was there though, waiting for me by the high green school gates. Standing by herself, and I was properly grateful for that. Around me, pupils off the bus shoved past, eyes on me, knowing about me, knowing what had happened. I didn't listen. I didn't look at any of them, only Lena. Her fair hair – that used to remind me so much of Abigail's – looked peroxided, so sun-bleached from her holiday. I stopped in front of her.

'It's really happened then?' she said.

She had a new piercing high up on her ear, the skin inflamed and red. Had she got that done abroad? I didn't know. She did all kinds of stuff on her own now, without telling me. Things she knew I wouldn't want to do. 'Yes,' I said. *So you see I was right* – said the voice in my head – *to hope, to wait, to refuse to move on.*

'Wow. Okay. And, you know – how is she?'

Her words seemed unreal, like her disbelief was rubbing off on me. I tugged at the strap on my bag, tightening it. 'She's fine. She's good.'

A shadow weighted Lena's expression. 'Really?' She had this thing about her these days, a skepticism I kept pulling away from. 'But all that stuff they said on the news...' She reached out to take my arm and I flinched back.

She stared at me. 'What?'

I looked back at my best friend, the heavy liner round her

eyes. We used to be two kids together. So what if Lena's parents had blazing rows, so what if my aunt and uncle still cried? Forget it, I'd say, let's play hide-and-seek. Then at thirteen, her parents separated, got divorced. And since then, she was always seeing the cracks in things, like she couldn't just let anything be pretty any more.

But I wouldn't let her be like that about Abigail.

'It's nothing.' I slid my arm behind my back. 'And everything is great with Abigail. You'll see.'

In the form room, I gave Mum's note to Mr Chalmers. He read it, then asked if I wanted him to let the class know. I said yes. Probably most of them had seen on the news, and better someone told them than they whispered behind my back. I sat down next to Lena and let him announce it. And then everybody knew for sure. Mr Chalmers told them not to trouble me with questions, but then he got called away to another classroom and then there was no one to stop them talking. I sat there with Lena, so glad she was next to me, choosing me over the other girls she got along with so easily these days. Somehow I'd never known how to fit in in groups – without Lena, I didn't have other friends.

Their questions came in a hungry swarm.

Seven whole years?

What's she like? Does she talk?

Bet she's got PTSD. Does she? Does she have that?

They wanted horror stories and gory details. I had nothing like that to give them, and what did I care if they were disappointed? I rubbed my arm absently where little patches still ached under the skin. She wasn't their cousin, Abigail was mine, and I knew her better than anyone. I answered their questions with a shrug of my shoulder, repeating, *she's fine, she's happy, she's glad to be home.* Like a record on repeat. The man, I said, they had dozens of police looking for him, and they'd find him, arrest him and it would be done. Their questions buzzed like wasps and I flicked them away.

But behind the buzz, something else was going on, a scuffle in the background, stifled giggles, a phone passed from hand to hand. Lena slipping out from our desk, sliding her way to the knot of girls in the corner. Snatching the mobile from them, glancing at the screen, her face drawing fierce. But just as our eyes met, the bell rang – time up – and she went to her class and I went to mine.

Just before the end of school, Lena texted me: Meet me after in the usual place?

For a while, I stared at my phone, the handset hidden under the desk, a glow filling up my chest. *The usual place.* Not far from the school and halfway between mine and Lena's houses, there was a play park, a sorry affair with a dented slide, peeling climbing frame and creaky swings. Little kids didn't go there much, but for years Lena and I had met there whenever we had something important to talk about, too big to bring up at home or at school. These last couple of years, we'd hardly gone there – so much felt different and only because *she* had changed. But the park, our park, was still there.

When the last bell rang, I headed straight out, ahead of the swarming crowds. I got there first. I swept the grit from a swing and sat down, the ridges of the rubber pressing through my skirt. The rest of the playground was empty, except for two small children playing in the concrete tunnels bored into the slope at the top of the park. A boy and a girl, about seven and four. Brother and sister, I guessed, but I couldn't see their parents anywhere. It put me on edge a bit, them being out alone like that.

I rocked the swing, its rhythm a comfort. While I rocked, I thought about another play park. Until she was five, Abigail's dad still had contact and she'd gone to see him every other Saturday. At his house, she'd sit in a room with drab brown curtains and watch repeats of some car programme, his favourite. Then he'd take her out to the park so he could have a cigarette, leave her to push herself on the swings. I'd asked her once: don't you mind? She just shrugged, like she didn't know any better. But after each visit there was always an argument, a tantrum, something. If not with her mum, then between Auntie Anne and him. It was my mum who'd put her foot down in the end. He lived abroad now, Spain or somewhere, and hadn't had contact with our family for years.

The park gate clanged. Lena was coming through the railings with her pearly hair catching the sharp sunlight, the same sunlight that was making me squint. I dug my toes into the wood chip as she came up. 'Hey.'

'Hey.'

She sat down with a bump beside me. 'Weird day, huh?'

I leaned back on my swing, hanging off the chains. 'A bit.'

We didn't say anything for a while. I was just glad she was here. I cocked the swing and lifted my feet, air rushing against my face as I swooped forwards. Times like this, we felt back to normal. Same as when we were ten, same as when we were twelve. Then Lena got hardened and it all started to change. Now, instead of swinging, she was fiddling with her bag, digging something from a zippered pocket. She pulled out a crumpled sheet of paper. 'I wanted to show you this.' She unfolded it and held it out to me, making me bring my swing to a halt. 'They were making stupid jokes about it, but I thought you'd want to see.'

I took the page from her and smoothed it on my lap. A printout of an old news article with a picture of a teenager, a boy, grainy and blurred, a woman next to him.

'I printed it out in the library,' she said. 'Tom said the page might get taken down.'

'Why? What is it?'

Lena twisted her swing, leaning over to point at the tight-printed text below. I scanned the lines. Something about a school football star, scoring three goals to win a local championship. Pictured here with his foster mother and soon to sit his GCSEs.

Football. Foster mum. 'I don't get it. Who is it?'

'Don't you recognize it?'

I looked again at the grainy photo, printed out in black-and-white. The boy looked fifteen, maybe sixteen. Handsome, I could tell – shiny fair hair, a wide mouth. He was looking right into the camera. His eyes, they sort of drew you in.

Lena stopped twisting, made her swing completely still. 'You really don't recognize him?'

'No.' And the shameful thing was, I didn't.

She pointed at the caption. The print was tiny, blurred. 'Look at the name.'

I did. And froze.

'And look at the date,' Lena carried on. 'I worked it out. If he's fifteen in that photo, say, he was only twenty-five when

73

he kidnapped your cousin. Twenty-five. I mean, that's *young*, right?'

I stared at the photo, his face clicking with that other image, shown daily, shown multiple times a day on the news. She was right. It was him, the name matched. Cassingham.

'Right?' Lena repeated. She pushed her swing back up against mine and I could almost feel her breath on my neck.

'Why are you showing me this?' My thumbs had turned white where I was pressing the page. 'I don't want to look.'

'This is the man who took her. Don't you care?'

'Of course I care!'

Lena's mouth went tight. 'But you act like nothing happened! You were just the same at school. "She's happy", "she's fine". Have you any idea how weird you sounded?'

'She *is* happy! She *is* fine!' I crumpled the page and stuffed it in my bag. 'I don't have to look. This isn't my job.' I stood up. I just wanted to go.

She caught me by the sleeve of my blazer. Her nails, black-varnished, were cold against my wrist. 'So, what is your job? Pretending nothing's wrong?'

My swing clipped my knee. I hated it – the way Lena was talking like Abigail was some *freak*, some *victim*. She was my cousin and I needed her to be fine. I tried to pull away, sick of my friend's words. As I did so, Lena's grip dragged my sleeve up.

She stared. Everything in my chest went tight.

'Jess. What is that?'

'It's nothing.' I wrenched away, trying to pull my sleeve back down. 'She was asleep. Having a bad dream.' I pushed away the images that came flashing – Abigail's eyes glistening in the dark, Abigail reaching for me from her bed.

Lena stared at the bruises. Five yellow fingerprints.

Then she said everything I didn't want to hear, words that summed up the chasm between us. 'Stop acting like nothing has happened to her. Stop pretending that nothing has changed. The stuff she's been through – you can't just ignore it. For your own sake, Jess, you need to grow up.'

I got home late and exhausted to find Mum and Dad in the study. There were papers, folders, ring binders everywhere. When she saw me, Mum got up off her knees, dusting invisible lint from her jeans. 'Where have you been?' she said. 'We're having a clear-out. You'll need to sort through your stuff too, so get changed and come and help.'

A clear-out? It was like Mum was trying to change everything too, when all I wanted was for it all to stay the same. Familiar, safe. I didn't want anything else. I wanted everything to be how it once was. I wished I could have said that to Mum, I wished I could tell her what had happened with Lena. But I knew how she got when she was on a mission, and the ragged edges of my parents' last argument still filled the house, just waiting for one of us to snag on.

In my room, I stripped off my rumpled uniform and hauled on a clean pair of jeans. In the study, I knelt on the floor as Mum pushed a tall cardboard box over to me. 'Here. This is mostly your old primary school stuff. Have a look through and give me everything you want to throw away.' The box was heavy, hard to pull towards me.

Dad was sitting at the desk, turning over pages in a tattered folder. Mum craned over his shoulder. 'Those are just old water bills. We don't need to keep them.'

'Wait. There are other documents in here too.' He went on turning the pages.

Mum stretched up to pull more stuff down from the shelves. She held out a fan of old dental journals. 'Throw or keep?'

Dad barely glanced up. 'Keep.'

'Really?'

'Keep.'

Mum dropped them into a pile beside him on the desk, the space already nearly full. I reached into the cardboard box and lifted out a few jotters.

'I don't think it's a good idea to keep her indoors the whole time,' Mum said, like it was a natural follow-on.

I knew at once she was talking about Abigail. She and Dad had probably been talking about her all afternoon. I kept my eyes on the rough jotters. Between the scuffed covers, my old childish handwriting clambered across the pages, sliding up and down the ruled lines. Every other story was about my cousin. Ever since I could remember, I'd been frightened of things: starting school, new people, the smallest changes in routine. But in my worlds with Abigail, it was never like that.

Dad put his ring binder down on the desk. 'It's hard to know, Lillian. There's still a lot for her to adjust to. Maybe it's good to let her get used to just being in the house –'

'*Her* house.'

'– first. And they still need to find him.'

I kept my head down, kept turning over the smudgy pages. On the top half of the space, left blank for pictures, I'd crayoned in drawings of flowers, starry landscapes, rainbows. Magical worlds I could never quite capture in pencil and crayon.

Mum shook her head. 'That could take weeks – months.'

'Not that long, surely,' said Dad.

But Mum had already changed her mind about Abigail. Her rules could shift and morph in a moment, keeping the rest of us running to catch up.

She lifted a stack of papers – they looked like old study notes, lines of her neat handwriting and streaks of highlighter pen. 'I'm throwing these out. Pass me the bin bag.'

Dad held up a black plastic sack. Mum tipped them in, then held the sides open towards me. 'Have you got stuff to put in here too?'

I looked at the spread of jotters on my lap. All my old stories. Worlds I'd never wanted to leave. 'I don't know yet. I haven't really looked.' I turned another page in the jotter. Me and Abigail in bright-coloured crayon. How old were we meant to be here – six, seven?

Mum lifted another armful of papers into the sack, tipping them away with hardly a glance. 'She was cooped up, Fraser, for years and years. Not just *cooped up*. Trapped. Held hostage. Don't you think she needs to know that it won't be like that now? And another thing... I really think they need to redecorate her room. How is she supposed to move on in a time warp like that?'

Dad stood up from the desk. 'Look, I don't know what's best. Maybe you need to let Anne and Robert decide. Maybe, for a change, we should leave it up to them.'

It felt like a whole set of windows had been suddenly slammed shut.

I stared down at the pile of jotters in my lap. Abigail stared back at me, her hair swirled in bright yellow, crayoned fingers entwined in mine. I needed her, I always had done. Ever since I could remember, I'd been frightened of this too. The intangible tensions I'd always felt in our house. But our happiness together had made everything safe.

Mum held the bin bag out to me, its mouth a gaping hole. 'Well?'

'No,' I said. 'I'm keeping them all.'

Chapter 9

Thursday 6th June:
Day 11

ANNE

When I went into her room, Abigail was sitting up in bed, her face puffy from sleep. Even though it was warm, she kept the duvet pulled up to her chin as though needing to hide herself underneath it.

'What's all that?' she said.

I sat down in the chair at the end of her bed and fanned the packages out on top of the duvet. With Abigail's sizings, I'd ordered a whole wardrobe of clothes online and by now the first few packages had arrived. I wanted her to put them on and to take her outside properly; I was glad Lillian had changed her mind and arranged this simple excursion, a trip to the hairdresser's. Yet now that it had come to it, my chest fluttered with nerves.

'I know it was hard for you to choose so I went ahead and ordered some things. I hope you don't mind, and listen, if you don't like any of them we can easily send them back, so just say.'

By now her – *his* – purple jeans and blue acrylic sweater

were stuffed deep at the bottom of the laundry basket and who knew when they would ever get washed?

She pulled one of the packages towards her and picked at the seal of tape with a blunt fingernail, peeling it off in a long slow movement, like a magician with a grand reveal.

Inside the layers of slippery plastic was a bright yellow blouse, the colour of sunshine. My face felt hot. 'Do you like it?'

She pushed her hands up inside the soft cotton and held it out in front of her, then looked inside the bag again as though expecting to find something else. 'It's pretty.'

'Here.' I pushed the other parcels towards her. 'There's lots more.'

She was frowning. 'These are supposed to be mine? To keep?'

'Of course,' I said. 'What else would they be for?'

Ten minutes later she came out of the bathroom, dressed. The new jeans just about fitted her and eventually she'd decided on a green jumper.

Now I could say it without it being a lie. 'You look lovely.'

She pulled at the inside seam of the jeans where it ran up the V of her legs, as though it was hurting her. It was true though – she really did look nice.

I stood up. 'Ready?'

It was warmer now but the day was still overcast, so I gave her my light coat to wear, the one with the hood she could pull up if she needed. The jacket I'd ordered for her online hadn't arrived yet. She looked so small inside it I wanted to take her hand, the way I used to, hold her tighter than tight. The words from Lillian's last call still rang in my ears. *Cooped up,* as though Robert and I were her jailers, not parents trying to keep her safe. That's all I was trying to do, I'd wanted to say to my sister.

This whole outing was Lillian's idea; she was allowed to change tack like that and still be right, and yet as soon as she'd suggested it, I'd felt ashamed for not thinking of it myself. We'd both seen how her hair looked, but it was Lillian not me, who'd thought to do anything about it.

As we put on our shoes, Robert came out from the kitchen in his overalls, ready for work. 'All set?'

Abigail pulled the zipper of my coat right up to her chin. 'Yep.'

'Call me if you need me. I'll be right at the end of the phone,' and he hugged Abigail and pressed a hot kiss to my cheek.

Outside, my car – a second-hand runaround we'd bought last year – was parked a little way up the road. We didn't need to drive, it was hardly far, but I wasn't ready to have her wandering the streets. When I blipped the car unlocked, Abigail pulled open the back door and I had to reach out and stop her. 'No,' I said. 'Here. In the passenger seat.' She wasn't a kid any more.

We found room to park one street away from the salon, squeezing into the one empty space. She stepped onto the pavement and I got out too, locking the doors behind us. I pointed over the road to the little walkway that we would cut through. 'Just across there. That's where we're going,' and I'd hardly finished speaking when she stepped right out from the line of parked cars, straight into the road.

A car horn shrieked. 'Abigail!' I grabbed for her, catching her by the hood of my coat. She stumbled as I pulled her backwards. 'What are you doing?'

She wrenched herself round, angry with me, confused. The anger in my own voice was the kind that whip-rides on panic. 'You can't walk out like that! You could have been killed!'

The look on her face, it was as though I had slapped her, and then it hit me – how on earth was she supposed to know? She hadn't grasped any of this, shut away with him, imprisoned from the world. Here she was, fifteen years old, and still naive as a child of eight. I took a deep breath; I let go of her coat. I had been holding onto her so tight.

'It's all right, Abigail, but please just listen. You have to look both ways when you're crossing a street. You have to listen for cars, you must always look. You have to wait for a gap in the traffic and never cross until it is safe.'

She gazed at me, still only half comprehending. 'Okay,' she said. 'I'll try to remember.'

My sister was waiting outside the salon; no doubt she'd got there ten minutes early. She was wearing a pair of tailored trousers, a smart scarf tucked into the collar of her blouse; I was wearing a jacket with a button missing. I remembered how I'd had such a go at her once, saying: *you think you're leading by example, Lillian, showing us how to be perfect like you. But the way you do it, you don't realize the effect. You don't know how you shame people into just giving up.* I wondered if she still remembered that now.

She'd taken an afternoon off work for this and I knew how big a sacrifice that was. I was grateful to her, really, and my sister was right, of course she was – how could I not have thought about it? Someone had tried to cut Abigail's hair, to give her a bob. Him, or Abigail herself? Whoever it was had made a mess of it, anyone could see. Did we expect her just to go about with it like that?

'Isn't Jess coming?' Abigail asked as soon as we came up.

Lillian smiled down at her. 'She couldn't. She's at school.'

Abigail's face fell, and I thought, how stupid of me – why hadn't we arranged this so Jess could come too? This was exactly the sort of thing they should do together, not Abigail with two grown-ups, hovering round her like flies.

It was a tiny salon that Lillian had found, tucked away from the market square and high street, and we were the only ones in there. Inside, two stylists were waiting for us, one with blue highlights and the other with a high, straight ponytail. They surely knew who Abigail was. Please be kind, I thought, and don't make this any more awkward than it already is.

There was a chair at the mirror for Abigail to sit in. The stylist with the high ponytail held a rustling robe out to her and swaddled her in the ink-blue folds. Lillian sat down on the soft couch nearby, her fingers reaching for a magazine. At the mirrors, the girl with blue highlights leant gently down to Abigail. 'What would you like? Just a trim or more of a change?' Their eyes met in the mirror.

Abigail lifted the robe to rub at her arm through the pink jumper and I knew she was scratching at the nicotine patch there. She still had cravings, hungry cravings, driving her fingers mad, setting them picking at themselves. She wore the patches that Robert had bought for her, two every day. We'd had to explain that cigarettes were bad for her, that there was no way we'd let her have those. We had to show her facts online to convince her; she couldn't seem to believe that they were harmful.

Now she stared at herself in the mirror. 'Just to keep it the same.'

I tried to hold my voice steady. 'It needs cutting, Abigail.' She must see it, her hair tousled and misshapen, hanging in clumps about her ears.

Up in the corner, a speaker spilled tinny music into the salon. 'We could do a fringe, for example,' said the blue-haired girl quickly. 'Here – I'll show you.' With the gentlest touch, she lifted a sweep of hair and laid it across Abigail's forehead. 'There, do you see?'

I did – Jess's features, Jess's image. The two cousins, how alike they had always been. From the start, their bond had been almost uncanny, and had only grown stronger when they had ended up living together. Me and Lillian. Jess and Abigail. What would have happened if the girls hadn't come along? To Lillian, getting together with Abigail's father was the biggest mistake I ever could have made. At nineteen, I thought my sister would never speak to me again: I'd fallen pregnant, the worst mess-up of all. We might have broken from each other then, it really might have gone that way, if Lillian hadn't discovered just two weeks later that she and Fraser were expecting too.

The blue-haired girl smiled at Abigail and me in the mirror. 'It'll look lovely, you'll see.' When the girl with the ponytail led her to the basin I finally sat down, at an angle so I could still see my daughter. Beside me, my sister turned the pages of the magazine, image after image of perfect people.

At the basin, Abigail lay back, her white throat exposed to the ceiling. 'Is that water okay?' the hairdresser murmured. I leaned in but couldn't hear what Abigail answered. 'Close your eyes then. Mind the shampoo.' The tendons in my daughter's neck stood out.

'How is Robert?' Lillian asked.

'Robert's fine.'

She waited. 'You know, you should just tell me if there's anything you need.'

Now the girl with the ponytail sat Abigail up and I watched as she neatly bandaged her head with a towel. By the mirrors, the blue-haired stylist was waiting with her scissors.

'We're fine,' I said to Lillian. Why did she always make me feel I couldn't manage by myself?

I could still feel my sister looking at me and I knew what she was thinking: *has she said anything? Has she ended up telling Robert?* If she'd come straight out and asked me I would have said, no, Lillian, of course I haven't. Even though I've wanted to, I've done what you told me, just like when we were children: keeping mouths closed and stained hands hidden, all because you couldn't stand being in the wrong, would rather tell a hundred little lies than ever be to blame.

Six years apart and we were so different. Growing up, Lillian always wanted control over everything, which meant controlling me, her little sister, too. Who knew why she was the way she was? As far as I could ever tell, she was born that way. Who could tell why I was how I was? Always getting things wrong, always clumsy.

Wet and combed out, Abigail's hair looked softer and smoother, all the frizz and tangles wetted down. I wanted to gather that smooth hair in my hands. Expertly, the blue-haired girl trimmed the lengths, getting rid of the jagged, messy strands.

'I can come over if you need. Help with the twins.'

85

'I know.'

Lillian turned another page. 'Work will understand.'

'I *know*. It isn't that.'

'What then?' Her fingers were pinching the magazine and I knew I would have to tell her what had happened. It was impossible for me to hide things from her and I still needed her advice; the only person who knew absolutely everything, who even as a child didn't ever make mistakes but who always, always fixed mine. Fixed them, or hid them; to her, either would do.

The hairdresser placed the blade of her scissors to Abigail's forehead. My daughter flinched, her head jerking. I half rose from my seat but the hairdresser laid a child-like hand on her shoulder. 'It's all right,' she said. 'Just keep your head still and your eyes closed.' The scissors inched their way across Abigail's forehead. I sat back down.

When the stylist turned on the hairdryer, a sudden shrill noise above the music, under its roar and behind the flicker of Abigail's hair, I said: 'Lillian, he called me.'

My sister's hands went still on the glossy page she wasn't reading. She knew exactly who I was talking about. My chest went tight as I remembered the fight: the biggest fight Preston and I ever had, me in our back garden, Preston high, raving, so angry he tipped over the garden bench. Our mum was already so sick by then; our dad barely managing to cope. It was Lillian who'd had yet again to help.

Lillian hated that I ever saw Preston after that and still let him share custody of Abigail. She hated that I kept trying to make things work, that I kept on believing we could find a way through the anger, arguments, tantrums and mess. In the end, it only stopped because Lillian put her foot down. After Mum died, she just wouldn't have it any more. In the end, it all stopped because she kept us apart.

'Annie.'

I felt myself flush deep red. *You know better than that*, her tone said. I'd known she would be angry and now, as always, I felt irresponsible and stupid, wreaking havoc on myself yet again. And yet she would never really understand about Preston. We'd met at school, he was two years above me, and Lillian had left home by the time we got together; twenty-four years old while I was still eighteen. By then she was in the middle of her nursing training, had met Fraser and was ready to settle down.

'He *is* her father,' I tried to explain. 'Whatever happened, that hasn't changed.'

But Lillian would never understand the way that it felt: as though she'd set too perfect an example to follow. Preston was someone who made more of a mess of things than I did. When I got together with Preston, it felt like a relief.

I couldn't catch her next words through the roar of the hairdryer. 'What?' I said.

She said it louder. 'You keep on picking at him, like a scab. You never drew that line, Annie, you never let go.'

'We haven't spoken in over ten years!'

'Why can't you leave it to the police then? They kept everything separate before. You know they'll already have contacted him.'

I saw DS McCarthy's clean shoes digging themselves into the carpets of our home. I hated the thought of him involving himself in this. And I could feel some stubborn part of me saying, so what if he called me? It was just like when we were children and I'd feel the temptation to blurt everything out, whatever childish misdemeanour I'd done, an urge to confess that burned like vinegar, so tired of trying to be perfect all the time.

'He was part of my life. He was so much of Abigail's.' But even as I said it, I found myself thinking, *but wasn't that exactly the problem that caused it all?*

When my sister looked up from her magazine, her eyes were as cool and determined as they'd been in our childhoods. No matter how my guilt would burn, nothing would hurt as much as Lillian's sharp fingers, pinching the skin on the back of my arm.

'It doesn't matter,' I said, my voice gone small. 'It was only a voicemail and I didn't reply.'

The roar of the hairdryer fell silent. In front of the mirror, Abigail opened her eyes and gazed at her reflection, touching her fingertips to her new fringe. The girl with blue highlights said, 'There. Do you like it?'

Abigail touched her forehead and nodded: *Yes.*

Lillian carefully folded her magazine closed. Only now did I see that her hands were trembling. 'Please don't contact him, Annie, all right? For Abigail's sake and your own. We shut the door on all that, we agreed. She has a wonderful family now: you and Robert and Laurie and Sam. Please stop trying to unravel it all.'

Lillian was right, of course she was. Don't contact him – how hard could that be? As Lillian took Abigail up to the counter to pay, I made myself a promise. Even if he rang again, I wouldn't answer, I would delete his voicemails without even listening. I would put the whole thing out of my mind.

I think I wanted something to cement my decision. Afterwards, once Lillian had left us, instead of taking Abigail straight back to the car, I made her follow me into the store I'd spotted next door. I had a desperate urge to buy her something here and now, something I would pay for and something I would know for sure she would want. It was as though I needed to bind her to me, as though drawing that line required me to bring her this close.

'Where are we going?' she said as she followed me in through the stiff glass doors, the handles greasy with all the hands that had grasped them before.

'Just come with me.'

Inside, the clothes shop was bigger than I'd expected, stretching back with row upon row of outfits. They had a sale on: bright red markers were sticking up from the racks and coat hangers hung askew with their items tangled. She followed me down a narrow aisle, her hands hidden in the pockets of my coat, her shoulders bumping against the rails. 'You've already bought a load of clothes for me. I won't need any more.'

I gestured to the racks and shelves full of fashion. 'I just want you to pick one thing and let me buy it for you. I want to do this for you, please. It's my way of saying ... of saying ...'

Well, what was I trying to say? You're mine, I'm a good mother to you, I promise from now on I'll do this right?

She ran a hand down a rail of outfits, the skin around her nails raw. 'But the rest of what you ordered will be arriving soon, the coat and everything. And there isn't anything else I need.'

'I know that, Abigail, but can't you just pick something that you want?'

I didn't shout, I didn't, but when she reached out, I knew how impossible I'd made it for her. She didn't want anything, she had made that clear, so now she was doing it only to please me and only for my sake would she pick anything at all. Her hand closed on whatever was nearest her: it wasn't a choice, only a stubborn, rebellious submission. She pulled it sharply from the display, sending a pile of necklaces clattering to the floor and held it out to me.

Without another word, I carried it to the cash desk and fumbled in my bag, my wallet thick with all the notes I'd wanted to spend on her.

I set her choice down. 'Just this, please.'

A pink plastic bangle, price: £2.49.

Chapter 10

JESS

Mum declared the whole outing a success.

On Friday when I got home from school, they were all there – Dad in the kitchen boiling pasta and Auntie Anne helping Mum set out serviettes and plates in the dining room. Mum had put out flowers, a centrepiece for the table. A huge beautiful bunch.

'What is this?' I asked. 'What's going on?'

'Well,' said Mum, admiring her handiwork. 'I just thought we should celebrate.'

I found Abigail across the hall, watching TV in the living room with Uncle Robert and the twins. I stopped in the doorway. Her new hair. It was sleek and glossy now, one side tucked neatly behind her ear. It was when she turned to see me that I noticed the fringe. Just like mine. Mum was right, I decided. A total success.

She was sitting on the floor, Sam and Laurie watching her from the sofa. I got the sense Uncle Robert was holding them back, like they might otherwise go clambering all over her. Or like they'd already climbed on her and she'd elbowed them off.

I took a cushion from the couch and slipped down beside her. Like slipping into a waiting space, familiar and warm, feeling the perfect connection between us. I remembered our games of *Do-you-trust-me?* Hovering together, our breaths in time. Falling backwards into each other's arms. Leaning out into space from the climbing frame, arms clasped, suspended in time, half flying. In that game, it would feel like I became her. Like through some brilliant magic I was in her body and she was in mine. It was how I knew she'd always catch me. Six, seven, eight – every few months we'd play that game. Like checking we still could.

'I've been waiting for you to get home,' she said to me now.

I pushed away thoughts of what Lena had said, the fact that my best friend and I had barely spoken since. Sitting here, with Abigail, how could anything else matter? Here with Abigail, I didn't need anyone else.

Now I noticed the bracelet she was wearing: an odd, cheap-looking thing. I pointed. 'Is that new?'

Abigail looked down at the plastic band on her wrist as if she'd only just remembered it was there. Her face seemed thinner than the first time I'd seen her, not so puffy. It felt so strange that this was only our second meeting since she'd come home. My whole week had been so full of her.

She nodded. 'We got it yesterday.'

'You and your mum?'

'Yes. She wanted to buy me something special.'

She rotated it, the light catching on its glossy surface. There was no clasp or catch. An unbroken circle.

'Like a present?'

Abigail frowned. 'I don't know. I don't think so.'

'Well,' I lied, 'it's nice.'

It was a Disney film they were watching, a really old one, *Beauty and the Beast*. Where they'd found it, I had no idea. I'd thought Mum had thrown out those old DVDs years ago. The animation was cruder than I'd remembered, but the colours hadn't faded and the songs were as familiar as ever. I stretched one leg out and bent the other to fold my arms on my knee. The teapot and candlestick danced round the castle kitchen while the twins watched with their wide blue eyes.

I thought of Mum and Auntie Anne, laying the table so carefully next door, preparing a feast, a ceremony. I thought about how for a whole week I hadn't been allowed to see her, my mum and aunt fussing over what was best, when they should have just asked me and I'd have told them: what's best is when me and Abigail are together.

Now Uncle Robert leaned forward from the couch, slowly, as if not to disturb. To be honest, I'd almost forgotten he and the twins were there. 'Abigail,' he said. 'Your mum and I were thinking we could redecorate your room.'

Actually, I thought, that would have been Mum's idea. But of course Auntie Anne would have agreed.

'Some new wallpaper, or paint maybe,' he went on. 'What do you think?' He meant well, he always did.

Abigail glanced up at him. 'I don't mind. But you honestly don't have to.' It sounded like she was saying, I'm not sure why you'd bother.

I felt it again, that shifting between us, that shadow of something in the way. 'We *should* do it up,' I said, touching my shoulder to hers. 'It could be one of our projects, you remember?' Sticky tape, cardboard, crepe paper, glue. We'd made everything from dolls' houses to theatres. 'We'll get new cushions, we'll put up posters. I think I know just what you'd like.' Just the thought of it gave me shivers of excitement.

On screen, plates and soup spoons joined the dance. She still hadn't replied. 'Abigail, don't you want to?' I bumped her elbow.

She nodded then, her shiny hair swinging. *Yes*, and I exhaled with a wave of relief. I hadn't realized I'd been holding my breath.

I leaned right in to my cousin. 'All right then,' I declared. 'We will.'

Uncle Robert sat back on the couch, cracking his knuckles. *Be our guest*, sang the candlestick. *Be our guest!* Abigail shifted her position, curled her own leg up. Same as me. Matching. We sat like that, side-by-side, mirror images of each other, until dinner was ready and Mum called us through.

In the dining room, eight plates were laid out with clean, upturned faces, each set of cutlery aligned, eight glasses set twinkling clean. Our dining room had never looked so pretty. Mum stood at the head of the big table, directing the rest of us: Abigail to sit here, the twins to sit there. With our table extended, there was room for everyone. She pointed me to the seat opposite Abigail. Then my aunt and uncle on one side of us, Sam and Laurie on the other. Mum next to the twins at the head of the table and Dad, furthest from her, at the foot.

When Dad carried the food through, it smelled great. Pasta made with Mum's best sauce, garlic bread, a fancy salad. It looked like a feast when he set it all down. Uncle Robert stood to help dish up, and Mum was there overseeing it all. I noticed she'd even put placemats down, the ones we usually used only at Christmas. A proper special occasion then.

We passed the filled up plates round the table, plenty for everyone. 'Ow!' said Laurie as I set down his. I think Sam had kicked him under the table.

'Here,' said Dad to the twins. 'Here's your bread.'

'Lillian,' Auntie Anne said, 'this looks delicious.'

'It's an old recipe,' she said, 'but I believe Abigail used to like it.'

'No salad,' said Sam to my uncle. 'I don't want the leaves.'

As the plates were handed round, I realized what it looked like. Like one of those spreads in the magazines Mum read. *Beautiful Homes* or whatever they were called. I imagined all those journalists seeing us now. Maybe Mum had imagined the exact same thing.

'The hairdressers were so good,' she was saying. 'So professional and kind.'

Sam's fork scraped on his plate. 'Come on, Sam,' said Uncle Robert, 'you're a big boy now.'

'Ha!' said Laurie. 'You're being a baby.' I felt the jerk of his leg as Sam kicked him again. I shifted on my chair, suddenly uncomfortable, out of nowhere thinking, *they were there when it happened*. Tiny witnesses at nine months old.

'They even gave us the haircut for free.'

Sam pushed his salad leaves to the edge of his plate. Across from me, Abigail twisted a forkful of spaghetti on her spoon. She held her cutlery normally, neatly, no slips. So in all those years she'd had proper food then, not been made to eat like an animal, face first in a dish. Nothing like what they whispered at school. I shoved the ugly images away. 'We're going to do up Abigail's room,' I said loudly, looking at Mum. 'I've got loads of posters. I've got loads of ideas.'

'That's wonderful,' said Auntie Anne. 'That's great.'

'Does anybody want more spaghetti?' Mum was tilting the serving bowl, though our plates were still full. I took a big mouthful, tomatoey and rich. Dad was wiping his fingers from the bread. Mum added more to her own plate, more than I knew she'd ever eat, then picked up her glass. She looked like she was making a toast. 'Abigail. On behalf of all of us, can I say—'

Sam's knife shrieked on his plate. 'Sam,' whispered Auntie Anne, 'that's enough.'

'—we're so thankful you're here. We'll do everything we can for you. Whatever you need. Our family is so happy now and, honestly, Abigail, that's all we need to focus on. Whatever has happened in the past, however awful it's been, now it's over. The past doesn't matter, Abigail, only what we have now. And look, we're all here, just look at us, your family—'

Sam scraped his lettuce right onto the table. 'I told you! I said, I don't *want the leaves*!'

He shoved his chair back.

Mum's glass hung in mid-air. 'Lillian,' said Auntie Anne, 'I'm sorry!'

Someone was meant to tell Sam off, get him to sit up and unfold his arms, but instead a painful silence expanded around us, growing steadily queasier, like altitude sickness, the empty air too thin. Another moment and I felt like my eardrums would burst. Even Dad seemed at a loss what to say.

Then Uncle Robert's mobile rang.

He pulled the phone from his pocket and looked at the

screen. He glanced at my aunt, held out a hand – *enough now* – to the twins. 'Excuse me,' he said to Mum. 'I'll be right back.' He got up and went through into our kitchen. 'Robert White here,' I heard, before the door swung shut behind him.

Mum lowered her glass. Auntie Anne got up and quietly pushed my cousin's chair back in. Sullenly Sam picked the salad leaves back onto his plate. But nobody started eating again.

Instead we waited.

When Uncle Robert came back, he didn't sit down. He just stood opposite my aunt, holding the back of his chair. He stood looming over us, the ceiling light shining on his bare head and we all sat round, looking up at him, hearts thumping.

'Robert?' said my dad. 'What on earth is it?'

My uncle looked like he didn't know what to do with himself. I don't think he meant to announce it at the table, I don't think he meant to blurt it out to Abigail like that, but the news was so big, and we were all staring up at him, that I don't think he was able to hold the words in.

'The police have found him. Cassingham. They've brought him in.'

Auntie Anne let go of her fork and it rang against her plate. My uncle had put his hand over his mouth, but I thought it was perfect, us all being together, getting the news as a whole family at once. Because it was good news, the best news; wasn't it what we'd all been waiting for? I thought we should have streamers, should have champagne to celebrate this. Things seemed to move very slowly then: Mum clasping her hands together, like a victory gesture, her knuckles white, and Uncle Robert carefully sitting back down. The twins looking round at us, trying to make sense of what my uncle's words meant. Dad seeking out Mum's eyes, their gazes locking across the table.

And Abigail.

Abigail bringing her hands together, grasping at the shining plastic bangle on her wrist. She twisted it, dragging it up over the width of her thumb, drawing a dark rash across the skin.

She set the bangle down on the table, the plastic edge clacking sharp against the wood.

'Abigail?' My dad's voice was uneven with surprise.

She looked up at me, her eyes loaded, hooded. 'Never mind then,' she said, 'about the posters.'

I looked round the table, at all the clueless mouths. They had never been able to read her like I could. I could tell at once what she was thinking, as easily as knowing my own mind. That shifting thing in her now all made sense. I shoved back my chair and reached straight across to her, just like when she'd reached out to me in the dark on our first night. I locked my hand around my cousin's wrist, where only a moment ago my aunt's bangle had been.

'No. No! Listen to me, Abigail.' The skin of her arm was hot in my grasp, but I didn't let go. 'I'm telling you – it isn't like that. This is forever. You aren't ever going back.'

Chapter 11

ANNE

Robert lay beside me in the bed. I was exhausted but we were both awake. When cars passed by outside, growling up the road, their headlights swung beams across the ceiling like search lights.

'How, *how* could she think that?' I said. Our bed felt like a box, a coffin. I was still so stiff with shock. In the darkness, all the contours of our room seemed alien, filled with shapes and objects I didn't know.

For over a week, DS McCarthy had told us, their suspect had hidden out in the attics of the school where he worked. I couldn't stop picturing him, squatting, crawling around up there above the unknowing children. Then he'd tried to get away and escape out of London but a cleaner at Euston Station had spotted him. When he glanced at her, that face on TV had done its job; the cleaner left her bucket and mop in the middle of the concourse, went straight to the office and dialled the police, and they'd come and arrested him on the spot.

They'd arrested him, and then Abigail had said *that*.

'She was talking – ' I took a shuddering breath – 'as though he has a *right* to her. As though she is *supposed* to be living with him.'

And now I thought again of what the officers had told us at the start: that not once in the police station, even when she was safe, even when a dozen people were there to help her, not once did she mention us, her family, not once did she talk about wanting to come home. I'd assumed she was only overwhelmed, in shock; I had never, *never* imagined this.

'I know, I know,' said Robert. 'I can't understand either.'

The pain of it lay on me like an iron sheet. I sat up, trying to lift the weight, shook my head, pressing my palms to my eyes. 'Maybe ... I don't know ... is this what it's like? Hasn't this happened in other cases? Stockholm syndrome, isn't that what it's called?'

'I read—' said Robert and then broke off. He was always reading, always researching. We'd fallen out over that over the years. These other victims, I would tell him, they're not our daughter, how is some hostage article meant to help? But now I needed an explanation – any explanation – for what Abigail had said, so this time I needed him to go on.

He lifted himself up in the bed beside me, the springs creaking. 'They say kidnappers can be very good at those things. Mind games, brainwashing, creating dependency ...' It felt as though we both needed to believe this. 'And maybe because –' I winced as another headlight swept through – 'at the start, she was so young.'

He didn't need to add the other sickening details we'd learned piece by piece from DS McCarthy. Robert didn't need to say, *she was locked in his attic,* and I ignored the voice in my head that said, *yes, but not the whole time.* He didn't need to say, *you know he had sex with her.* He didn't need to list the ways this man had wreaked his abuse.

'All right then,' I said, lowering my shoulders. 'He frightened her, he hurt her. No wonder her world's been turned upside down.'

I heard Robert take a deep breath through his nose. He was silent for a moment, hesitating too long, and suddenly I felt more than ever the desperate longing for someone who could tell us how to manage all of this, how to navigate this territory that was so frighteningly strange. Someone who could explain the landscape we had found ourselves in – not some detective, not Lillian, but someone who could see right into my heart and know the truth and love that was there, who could understand Abigail and everything she'd been through, and see beyond all the muddled relationships of our family and tell us clearly, now, where we stood. But I had known from the start that there were no protocols for this, a missing child found alive after seven long years. So here I was with Robert in the darkness of night, trying our best, the blind leading the blind.

A noise from next door. Laurie or Sam.

'You're right,' Robert said at last. 'I'm sure you're right.'

'So what now? What do we do now?'

'Anne—'

'I know. I can hear him.'

'Wait.' In the dark I felt him grasp my hand. 'What if—'

'Laurie's calling.'

'Listen – Anne, what if there are other reasons Abigail is so confused, doubts in her mind that her abductor played on?'

It felt as though all the air had disappeared from the room.

His tone – I knew he didn't mean all that happened with Preston, he didn't mean how many times she'd moved house as a child. But the other thing – he couldn't know. How could he know? He wasn't there, he didn't see it, but what if someone, somehow had told him? I tried to pull away. 'Robert, Laurie's *crying—*'

'Anne, I'm saying, I should have been there, I never should have argued with you. The children were upset, *Abigail* was upset, I should have chosen to come with you. I never should have let you all leave on your own.'

I went still; my hand was still in his. For a moment, I wished he had blamed me instead. This was worse. This was a slippery slope and I knew what was waiting for us at the bottom. All Robert's remorse, all Robert's guilt; guilt that he had been left to carry because I'd never had the chance to shoulder my own. If only, if only at the start I'd been able to tell him, but Lillian was the first person I had been able to get hold of and when Robert arrived, hours and hours later, by then I was trapped, I had already lied.

Laurie's whimpers were louder than ever. 'Robert. Don't,' I said. He thought he was sharing to make me feel better, to make me see I wasn't the only person with regrets. I couldn't let him go down this track. I freed myself and snapped on the light. 'Why are we making this all about us?'

In the glare of the light, my husband's profile was like a hollowed rock. 'We're not.'

'Then why are you saying any of this?' My eyes were stinging from the lamplight. 'Listen, Robert. He did this to Abigail. He got into her head, we can't let him into ours. She needs us to be strong. We have to be *strong*.'

'I'm trying, Anne. What more do you want?'

I sat there in our rumpled bed, our son crying in the next room, and I wanted to say: *For you to love me to the ends of the earth and for nothing ever to break your love.* Instead I let my hand drop, feeling so cold in my thin nightdress and so exposed in the bright light. 'Just for us not to tear ourselves apart.'

Eventually I got Laurie settled and managed to get to sleep myself. Two, maybe three hours later, I woke to find Robert's side of the bed empty. The sheets were still warm, the mattress still dimpled. When I sat up, I heard a sound that I recognized: a heavy slide with the soft *thunk* at the end, out there in the street. But why now, in the middle of the night?

I pushed back the covers and got up quietly. On the landing, I listened at the twins' door. Silence now. The door to Abigail's room was open a little way; we'd taken to leaving it like that, and a low light on the landing, as for a young child. Her room was silent too, with no sound of sleep-talking; despite everything this evening, there was none of that to log in the notebook tonight. Downstairs, I heard the front door open and shut. In just my nightdress – Abigail still had my dressing gown; I'd forgotten to order her one of her own – I went down.

Robert was in the kitchen and the table was strewn with paintbrushes, paint trays, wallpaper scrapers, symbols of my life with him. Safe and loving and good and stable, a home and a family for Abigail. All I'd ever wanted for her. In that moment, as I stood looking at him across our shining kitchen, with the beautiful worktops he'd fitted for me specially, I was overwhelmed by the pressure of living up to his goodness, of not letting him down, of deserving his love and the happy family he'd given me. I stood there, fighting desperately to block out the thought: *you've still no idea of the mistake I've made.*

'Robert?'

He started at my voice. 'I didn't mean to wake you.'

'I was up anyway.' I surveyed the equipment he'd brought in from his work van outside.

He gave me a tired smile. 'I think it was a good idea of your sister's,' he said. 'It might actually help.'

I switched on the kettle and sat down in one of the kitchen chairs; no point in going back to bed to lie awake and stare at the ceiling. I lifted a paint-flecked scraper and ran a finger along its edge. Well, all right, maybe it would help and if there was any way to bring us all closer, then God knew we needed that now. There were bigger questions, bigger things I knew we needed to address: what to do about all Abigail's missed schooling, whether we should be organizing counselling, how on earth she would deal with any trial. Yet it only felt possible to take such small steps at a time and the risk of going wrong always felt so large. So if we could first just make it right within the walls of our home ... The tightness gave a little in my chest. 'I'm sorry about before,' I told him. 'And I'm up for doing this.'

Robert nodded. 'Something to try at least.'

The next morning, I woke Abigail early, her bedroom bright with clear June daylight. I sat down carefully at the end of her bed, ignoring the weakness I still felt in my limbs, the aftermath of last night's shock. We had to move past that, we had to look forward, and she had already agreed to this, hadn't she? I laid out our plan. 'We can use whatever colours or wallpaper you like ... You can make it completely your own.'

What better way to make it clear this was permanent? What better way of starting afresh?

The first job, once she was up and dressed, was to put all the knick-knacks and toys away. She didn't seem sad to see them go, though I kept the flopsy there on her bed. When the walls and surfaces were all clear, and the furniture covered with dust sheets, Robert handed us each a scraper, the twins too, and we brought the radio up from the kitchen. I was slow and clumsy to begin with, but it came back to me soon enough, my muscles remembering how to catch the edge of the paper and release it inch by inch with a steady shucking movement.

I took hold of a loose piece of yellow and peeled it away. In the motion, I was overcome again by a rush of memories, the history that wouldn't leave me alone, the path backwards through time, everything that for so long I had tried to ignore. The dingy flat in London with Preston, where walls stayed unpainted while the money went on other things. That flat that never felt like home, the flat where the three of us clashed time and again. My life with Preston, that misguided attempt at a family, it had brought out the worst in all three of us, all the worst sides of ourselves. We kept trying though, me, him and little Abigail. I knew he and I were young, but I'd always thought we could get there and, honestly, we tried so damn hard. But there was something in us we couldn't get past. It made fault lines that we could never mend and instead there was so much anger that kept building: his anger, my anger, and within Abigail too. Her crying, her tantrums, would go on for hours, so fierce that I could hardly bear to go near her, or else she'd turn so stone-cold silent it scared me.

In the mess, in the chaos, it felt like something was invading our house, bringing out the worst in all of us. There were times when I'd be so overwhelmed and upset I couldn't seem to keep anything straight. Things would go missing or I'd find them out of place – spare keys, my pocket diary – and I'd say to Preston that someone must have been there, invading our lives and tampering with our things, until I ended up sounding as though *I* was the one on drugs. And even after we stopped living together, for as long as we had contact, it was always the same. Those fault lines, that anger. Until Lillian finally got me to stop.

With Robert, though, it was different. Here, now, I held onto that. With Robert, it all got better; I saw her become her best self, a smiling, bright, contented child, the child I had always wanted her to be. There was laughter instead of anger; fun, silliness, easy-going joy. I remembered ballet classes, family days out, everything a normal family would do. Finally I felt like a good enough mother; finally I felt I was getting this right.

I remembered moving into this house only a month after we got engaged – a rush job all round and Abigail would have been barely five. It had been a fixer-upper, but I knew this time we would make a home to be proud of. And we did. We made a *family* to be proud of. In the new house, I got carried away, not waiting for Robert, and he was mad at me for pasting new paper straight over the old, but the vibrant yellow I'd chosen looked so lovely that he couldn't stay mad at me for long.

Across the room, Abigail fumbled her scraper and it fell with a clatter, cutting through the radio's adverts. Robert crouched and lifted it back into her grasp. 'Here. Turn your wrist a little. Do you see? All right then. Gently.' He was good with her. He had always been so good with her, this child who wasn't his but whom he loved like his own.

She jabbed at the wall, her grip firmer now on the scraper's handle, digging her way beneath the layers. Over time, the bold colour had faded and it was a paler yellow we were peeling off now. In the same way, in the morning's bright light, the events of last night seemed to be fading, no worse or more real than Laurie's bad dream. And look, here the paper underneath was pristine: plain white with a diagonal blue stripe.

'Abigail?' It seemed so important suddenly that she should see this. 'Abigail? Come here a minute.' I shucked away a little more of the yellow, separating the layers to show the design underneath.

'Abigail?' said Robert. Over the radio, she didn't seem to have heard me. 'Go and look for your mum.'

Clumsily, as though she'd forgotten how to programme her legs, she got to her feet. 'Look,' I said. 'Your room had this paper when we first moved in.' I could feel her standing right behind me, the heat of her. On my knees, I pressed a hand to the wall, smoothing the old pattern. 'You were so delighted that we were moving in with Robert. You were so excited that this would be your home.' I was so aware of my need to convince her: *we* are your family, *here's* where you belong; you and me and Robert and the twins, no one else. This is a place where you were *happy*. I felt her leaning down over me to look. 'Do you remember?'

But when I turned, her expression wasn't at all what I'd

expected. She was staring at the wall as though it would bite her, the scraper clutched in her hand like a blade. The words blurted out of her: 'That paper.'

I pushed myself to my feet. 'Abigail, what is it?'

'That paper. That wallpaper, it matches. I remember it now. I remember, I do.' But she looked as though she was going to be sick. She sat down hard on her covered bed, the scraper dangling. 'Please – I can't to do this any more.'

It felt like whole minutes that we were frozen like that: Abigail rigid on the bed, me looming like a shadow above her. It was Robert who stepped forwards, turned the racket of the radio down and gently released the scraper from her hand. 'It's fine,' he said, 'if you'd rather leave it for now. I can carry on here, with the boys.'

'Let's go out,' I said to Abigail. 'Let's go for a walk.' She needed sunshine, space, fresh air to bring the blood back to her cheeks. Anything to stop her looking like that. After all the confusion of last night, we had moved too fast. What had we been thinking? Before anything, we had to set her straight, get those distorted thoughts from her head.

I dug the trainers I'd ordered for her out of the wardrobe downstairs; they were still in their box and I had to thread the new laces through the eyeholes before they were ready for her to put on. They weren't quite the right fit, half a size too big, but with two pairs of socks she would manage okay. I watched her pull the laces tight, her fingers clumsy as she tied the bow. She followed me down the stairs with the trainers and a jacket on – her own jacket this time, finally arrived.

'Ready?'

Outside, it was gusty with a whipping breeze and the sky was grey again, the sunshine of the morning hours disappeared. The cars on the road bridge seemed faster than ever. I could tell she still wasn't used to the wind and I kept wanting to tell her to fasten her new jacket properly, not leave a gaping gap where, even in June, it might get into her chest.

I walked briskly as we reached the towpath, to try to get some strength to my limbs. Since I'd last walked out along here, the grass and trees and bushes had burst forth and now stray fronds and branches snaked across the path. 'Don't trip,' I said. 'Here, mind your feet.' The wind made my throat dry and the words seemed to get snatched away. As we walked downstream she kept her hands stuffed in her pockets. I realized now where I was leading her, along my familiar route towards the lock. I should have taken her the other way and let her walk with her back to the wind, but we had set off in this direction now and it would only confuse her if I suggested turning back.

I pointed out a mallard with a string of ducklings, paddling at the water, getting blown downstream. Abigail stopped and watched until the mother duck had shepherded her brood to shelter. But she hadn't come out here with me just to look at ducks; I'd known that from the moment we set out. She needed me to talk, to explain things to her but I was walking through a minefield of things I was terrified to say. But you have to, I told myself, you have to say something. You have to speak because you need to find a way to set this straight.

'I know how confusing this has been for you,' I began but trailed off because what did I know, really? I hadn't been there. I didn't know what he'd said to her, day in, day out, for seven years. The heel on my boot had begun to squeak. We were rounding the bend now, the canal lock coming into view up ahead. I let the wind fill up my lungs trying to think how to keep everything on track. As we came up the low incline, I could see that there was no one there, no figures in yellow, and the place looked empty and abandoned. 'Look,' I said, pointing at it anyway. 'This is what I mentioned last week. We're working on it, restoring it.'

Abigail hardly glanced up. She was right next to me but the space between us felt miles wide. She went on walking, one foot in front of the other, the two pairs of socks pulled up round her ankles. She tugged up her zip. At least, I thought, now she's sheltered from the wind. I tried to see in her the child I remembered, how she was in the years before he took her, when she was her best self, her happiest self, and I tried again. 'The detective said he claimed to be your uncle.'

She lifted her chin from the collar of her jacket and let a word out: 'Sometimes.'

Sometimes.

In the wind, her hair was whipping at her cheeks. Was there even any point in going any further? She didn't care about the lock and I only cared about putting her right. I turned to face her, feeling the wind shove at my back and she came to a short stop in front of me.

'He wasn't your uncle,' I said.

Did she think the police hadn't investigated every single relative? Did she think we would have left any stone unturned? Lillian had gone on and on about Preston's brother. She was convinced he was involved, convinced for some reason that it had to be him, but then Lillian had a prejudice against Preston's whole family.

'He wasn't your uncle. He didn't know you at all.'

Preston's brother lived happily with his own family in Scotland and the police had found not one shred of evidence against him.

Her hair blew across her face, catching in her mouth. She released a hand from her pocket to yank the strands free. 'He told me other things as well.'

We were head to head now, thick gusts of wind swirling between us.

'But these things he told you – you can't have believed them?'

Abigail kicked at the ground, scuffing the toe of her brand new trainer in the dirt. She'd become a parody of a surly teenager, angry with me, angry at the world. 'Abigail,' I said, 'please don't do that.'

'I don't know. It wasn't just about being my uncle.'

'What else then?'

She still wouldn't look at me. She stood twisting her shoulders as though she just wanted to go home. She went on with her trainer, kick, kick, kick, and I felt all my fears and anger from last night resurface.

'*Abigail.*'

She stopped. Beside us the reeds and grasses were bent over in the wind. She lifted her chin again and I stared at her, waiting.

'He said you could have come and got me if you'd wanted. He said you knew exactly where I was.'

The wind gusted like a punch to the back of my neck. I felt like I was falling over a ravine. I could barely control myself as I grabbed her by the elbow. 'Come with me.'

I gripped her so hard I was scared I was hurting her, but I needed her to come with me, I needed her to see. I marched her all the way back to the house, half dragged her into the kitchen. I yanked out a chair. 'Sit there and don't move.' Her face was chalk white.

I left her and went upstairs. I dragged the ladder down from the loft, ignoring the twins as they came out of her bedroom. I pulled the nearest box from the pile in the attic and wrestled it down, missing a step and scraping my ankle bone on the ladder. Downstairs, I upended the cardboard box right there on the kitchen table: piles of paper came spilling out, all the documents we'd cleared from Abigail's room. Pages and pages of information we'd pored over through the years, every scrap of anything we could find. I'd made Robert put all this away, but now I could see what a mistake that had been.

'There's another four boxes of this, Abigail. Seven years' worth – two thousand, six hundred and thirty-five days. *That's* how much we didn't know.'

This was all the evidence we had. I spread the papers out all over the table so she could see every detail of how hard we'd searched. I caught a flicker of realization in her eyes and a moment where her features softened. Surely looking at this, she couldn't doubt us.

And yet when she finally looked up at me, somehow it still didn't seem to be enough.

Chapter 12

JESS

When Abigail had pulled off her bangle and said that, it felt like losing her all over again. All the next day, I felt like a ghost. It frightened me and I needed to be okay.

That night, I went upstairs and brushed my teeth, then sat up in my room, still dressed. I heard Mum and Dad each go into the bathroom, then climb into their bed, the springs complaining. It took them a long while to settle down. When at last I heard their bedroom light click out, I waited a quarter of an hour more. Then I slipped back downstairs.

I felt my way through the hallway and kitchen and opened the door that led to the garage. The space was cold and full of the ticking hum of the old freezer that stood in the corner. The toolbox was buried under a pile of Dad's old dentistry magazines. My dad, the repairer of broken smiles. When I was ten, he'd fitted me for braces. I remembered his soft breath on my face, his quiet concentration, the way he wrote careful notes in my file while we waited for the plaster to set. Easy as that to fix my slanting teeth. Easy as that, I'd thought, to fix anything.

As quietly as I could, I opened the top of the toolbox, making all the little shelves and trays fan out. The screwdrivers were laid out in a neat row, their handles colour co-ordinated by size. I couldn't remember which one I needed, so in the end I took out all three of the smallest. Then I closed the box back up.

In my room, I took the chair from my desk and placed it at the foot of my bed. When I was younger, I'd have to stack my thickest school books on top to reach, but now I only needed the chair. I took off my socks so my feet wouldn't slip.

High up on the wall in the corner was a small air vent, its grill held in place by four grubby screws. When it was windy, it would whistle in the duct and clatter the slats. The first screwdriver was too thin, but the second one fitted fine. The screws were stiff, thickened with dust and black gummy dirt that stuck to my fingers as I twisted them free. With the movement, the chair shifted under my feet, clunking against the wall. From next door, I heard Mum murmur and turn over. She'd always been a light sleeper. I pressed my palms to the wall to steady myself and counted to twenty.

When the house fell silent again, I reached up and hooked my fingernails round the back of the grille. It stuck for a moment then lifted off. The wallpaper underneath was darker where the daylight hadn't faded it. Because of the angle, reaching up from below, I couldn't see inside the vent. But I knew what was in there. Mum thought I had thrown them away. Once I was ten, eleven, she said they were unhealthy. But I hadn't. I had hidden them in here. The concrete tunnel was gritty and I could feel cobwebs. For a moment, I fished in the air at nothing, my wrist scraping the edge. Then I hooked my thumb under the cardboard lid.

I inched the box towards me, black-speckled with mildew, biting down a cough and blinking the grit from my eye. Carefully, I climbed down. I sat on the bedroom floor, cross-legged, the shoebox in front of me.

Inside, as I knew I would, I found them all.

My clippings.

Abigail had always been everything to me; I hardly knew myself without her. When I was eight and she disappeared, overnight my world collapsed. At the school gates, I clung to Mum's hands, refusing to let her turn her back on me for an instant. When teachers tried to pull me away, I screamed.

The doctor called it *separation anxiety*. Well, Mum told him, can you blame her? She's frightened she'll be taken too. But it was worse than that. It felt like half of me was already gone.

In the beginning, Abigail was *missing*, and that meant she had got lost, the way car keys got lost, or a favourite teddy, or like when the school gerbil disappeared under the classroom cupboards. Abigail had got herself lost, but everyone was looking for her and sooner or later we'd find her, or she'd just turn up. I remembered holding the big hallway phone to my ear and hearing Auntie Anne's questions, endless questions, and Mum crouched alongside me telling me not to worry, I wasn't in trouble, but could I think of anything, anything at all? Abigail was somewhere in a city she didn't know, surrounded by strangers, separated from her mother. Did she have any favourite shops, favourite kinds of places where she might have headed to feel safe? I tried. I told Auntie Anne everything I knew about Abigail. But none of my answers helped.

In the days that followed, my aunt and uncle put up big

posters, like families do if their cat goes missing. Have you seen this girl? But days went by, then a week and *missing* didn't make any sense. At eight, you know how to say you're lost. At eight, you know how to ask for help. If she was only lost, surely she would have been found by now. Soon *Abigail is lost* turned into *Abigail was taken*. That was what *abducted* meant.

In my room, I lifted the lid and tipped up the box, spilling the pictures and stories across the floor. When Auntie Anne and Uncle Robert finally came home from London, their hollow faces had frightened me. It was everything I was frightened of in the world. In response, I hunted out every story I could find, cut pictures from magazines, tore whole pages from library books. Stories about happy endings, children who escaped, children who found their happy way home – I collected a whole storybook's worth of clippings, comforting fantasies about my cousin. Everything beyond that terrified me. This adult world, the real world, the world of growing up. If I took one step without her, who knew what would happen? Instead I would stay in the bubble we had made with our games, and I would stay there, unchanging, until she came back.

Now I pushed my fingers into the mass, until I found the printed photograph I'd put in here too. The last one taken of me and Abigail. I am eight and she is eight. We stand with our arms around each other, barefoot, our nearest legs pressed together, as if for a three-legged race or like conjoined twins. The photograph's been taken against the sun and our outlines are blurred, merging. If you look, you can see how our shadows make a single shape.

I laid the photograph face up on the floor. Then I reached over to my school bag tucked under my desk, and fished deep into the front pocket. I pulled out the creased sheet of paper, the page Lena had given me. I unfolded it and laid the article down, edge to edge, next to my own photo.

Abigail and me. Abigail and him. I stared at those two images, side by side, for the longest time. And it didn't matter how hard I looked; never, *never* could she belong with him. And I would never allow him into our lives. I took up the article with its ugly picture and tore it into pieces – so small he was nothing but pixels and scraps. Tomorrow I would throw the whole thing away.

I placed the photograph of me and Abigail on my pillow. And all night I slept with her beside me.

On Sunday, Mum said they'd begun redecorating Abigail's room. Soon as I could, I headed over with a fat roll of posters, ones I'd bought for myself on a rare shopping trip with Lena, but never got round to putting up. Well, now Abigail could have them all. I knew she would want me there, I had promised to help. I texted my aunt to say I was coming but I didn't ask Mum and Dad, just left a note. Mum hated me doing things without asking, but I was tired of always waiting for her permission.

The buses across town were hardly frequent, but I knew the timetable off by heart. I had to either take the bus or cycle to get anywhere. We lived on the north side, in a village that had been swallowed up by the town. Mum liked it because it was supposed to be the posh area, but to me that just meant there was even less to do. Abigail, the Whites, they lived on the south side. Kind of a more ordinary place.

It was sunny that day, summer finally deciding to get going, and it was hot in the bus on the way over, so hot I had to take my coat off. That's how I arrived, my bag with the tube of posters jammed in it bumping on my back, my coat dangling over my arm. The walk from the bus stop took me the back way, the way we'd come when we first visited. I let myself up through the gate in the back hedge and knocked on the whorled glass, like we'd done before. The bus, the walk had taken longer than I'd planned and I knew now that I wouldn't have much time – not if I didn't want to make Mum furious. But even half an hour together would be enough.

I stood on the decking in the shade of the Whites' house, my T-shirt cooling against my skin. I knocked again, stepped back and listened. Birdsong in the street and cars driving by, but no sounds from the kitchen, no shapes or movement. I hitched up my bag, went round to the front. No sign of my uncle's van on the street. I rang the doorbell to confirm what I already knew: no one home.

I felt stupid for thinking they'd all just be waiting for me, there in the house for my next visit. I sat down on their front step, my coat flopping over my knees. The sun was hot round this side and today there was no breeze. I stood the tube of posters up between my feet. It wouldn't be long before Mum would be calling me, blipping up my mobile with texts. Half an hour, an hour at most. But I would wait as long as I could.

From across the road, the shadow line of a lamppost moved round like a sun-dial. When the edge of it hit my shoe, I dug in my bag and pulled out a crumpled sheet of notebook paper and a pen. All right then, I'd leave Abigail a note, and the posters, so she'd know that I had been at least. The ink in the pen was dry and I had to shake it out before it would write.

Abigail,

I came to see you, but you were out. Thinking of you lots, and I'll come again soon. Love Jess.

I drew a heart at the bottom, then another one, their shoulders crossing. Two hearts: mine and Abigail's. I folded the paper up, just as I heard my mobile ping.

I was tucking the note in the flap of the letterbox when I heard the engine, Uncle Robert's van pulling up in the driveway. They were here.

The van door swung open and Abigail climbed out, a little awkwardly, still a little heavy. She stopped short when she saw me. The twins came tumbling out and then Uncle Robert from the driver's side. 'Jess?' he said. 'What are you doing here?'

Abigail, Uncle Robert, the twins. They stood looking at me like the bears discovering Goldilocks in their house. I held my note out towards Abigail. 'I should probably have called first. I just wanted to see you. And I brought the posters, like we said.'

She came forwards and took the paper from my hand. Read my message carefully, right down to the hearts at the bottom. 'That's really nice,' she said. 'Thanks, Jess.'

Uncle Robert closed the sliding door of the van.

'Where's Auntie Anne?' I asked.

A tiny shadow dipped across my uncle's face then he smiled, but a funny smile and his eyes didn't match. 'She's gone to yours.'

'To our house? Why?'

Uncle Robert put a hand on Abigail's shoulder, like reassuring her. Or singling her out. 'Oh,' he said. 'You know. Decisions.'

'We went to the big store,' said Sam, like he was explaining, 'but we didn't decide on anything.'

I couldn't work out what he was on about.

'But you brought the posters?' said Abigail. She looked tired, her eyes kind of sleepy.

I lifted up the tube. 'All here.'

'Are you coming in?' said Laurie.

In the summer sunlight, Abigail's hair was bright with its old golden glow. Something expanded in my chest, like a flower in time-lapse bloom. I shook my head. 'I can't. Mum's already texting.' And anyway, it was enough. Seeing her, standing next to her, giving her the posters.

'We'll get together again soon,' said Uncle Robert, 'don't worry.' He and the twins were ready to head in.

I hugged Abigail goodbye, little sparks passing between us. The feel of her stayed with me all the way home, like I'd absorbed it into my cells. Seeing her, holding her, even for a moment, it made everything, absolutely everything, okay.

When I got home, right enough, Auntie Anne was there, and the kitchen table was covered in strips of paper – rainbow shades, pale to dark, red, blues, pinks, creams. Tiny pots of paint lay scattered at one end, a dozen little dark blue tins.

Mum sat at the head of the table. I put my bag down and hung my coat carefully on the back of a chair. I didn't say anything about where I'd just been. Mum didn't even seem to remember I'd been gone. 'What's going on?'

Auntie Anne pressed her palms to the coloured strips and fanned them out across the table. 'Here, Jess. Come and look.'

Sam's words. *To the big store.* So that's where they'd been – choosing paint. But why had my aunt brought all of this here?

'This is for Abigail?'

Mum opened her mouth, but my aunt was faster. 'What colour do you like? What would you choose?'

There were so many, almost too many to pick from. I looked to Mum, but her mouth was closed now. I shook my head. 'I don't know. It depends.'

'Cream, do you think? Or is that too plain? Wait – what about – what colour is your bedroom?' Her voice tingled with anxiety. I tried to ignore it – the twisty feeling on the floor of my stomach that I so often got with my aunt.

'Well, what colour does Abigail want?'

Auntie Anne smiled at me, a sad kind of smile, strained at the edges. 'She can't decide,' she said. She gave a tight laugh. 'Or maybe she just doesn't want to pick!'

Her comment was shrill and I winced.

'Annie,' said Mum. 'All these options, you're overwhelming her.' Her voice was low. It went like that when she was holding back, when she was being very careful about what she said. It was a voice I knew not to mess about with.

'It's her bedroom. I want it to be right.'

'Then choose for her! It's just paint.' There was a scraping sound as Mum pushed back her chair. She got up and went to the sink, turning on the tap and running the water over her hands. I watched her fingers twist round one another. Before long I could see the steam rising.

'Mum,' I said. '*Mum.*'

She didn't look up, just went on standing there letting the water turn the backs of her hands red. I pushed past my aunt and turned off the tap. I couldn't make sense of what was passing between them.

Mum took a deep breath and pressed her palms down on

either side of the sink. 'Jess, don't you have any homework to do?'

I looked back and forth between them. Auntie Anne didn't say anything.

Slowly I picked up my coat and bag and climbed the stairs, pulling myself up the banister. I shut my bedroom door loudly, making it bang. But I stayed outside my room, on the landing. Silently, I sat down at the top of the stairs. They couldn't see me from here, but I could hear their voices. There were words I missed, gaps in their sentences, but I caught enough. It was the tone as much as anything. Like skating on ice, thin enough to crack.

'The way she is with me. I think she remembers.'

'Annie, she's traumatized. She's remembering all sorts of things. Why do you think it must be about that?'

'I can't help it. I look at her and I can't stop going over it.'

A pause. I slipped down a few stairs so I could see a bit of them now – my aunt's back in the chair, Mum's lower half by the sink. 'Somebody *took* her, Annie. What difference does the rest make now? Honestly, you can't keep bringing this up. You have to move forwards, you've enough to deal with. Robert, Abigail, they don't need this.'

Auntie Anne's next words were slow in coming. She was gripping the edge of the table. 'But I could have said something. I could have told the police at the time.'

'For what – so they could blame you? So our whole family could be in disgrace? Listen to me, Annie. It wouldn't have helped.'

I didn't catch what Auntie Anne said next. Her voice had

gone too quiet. Too quiet for Mum too, it seemed, because she was asking Auntie Anne to repeat herself.

'At least they might have been able to tell me.'

'Tell you what?'

'Whether it mattered. I think it matters, Lillian.'

I curled my fingers round the lip of the stair. I wanted to be sick in the silence that followed.

At last Mum spoke into the cold stillness. 'For Christ's sake, Annie, just be glad that she's back.'

Chapter 13

Wednesday 12th June:
Day 17

ANNE

The thing is, Abigail was always a difficult child. Those early years were filled with crying fits and tantrums that wore us both out, impossible to understand, impossible to deal with. I didn't seem to know how to make peace with her, only cold silence. Having Abigail and living with Preston made it obvious: I'd never known how to fix things myself. But now there were people, professionals, we could turn to.

The kitchen, our pretty kitchen, was full of sunlight, the morning rays streaming through open blinds. The surfaces were all clean, the breakfast things put away and the air was lemon-fresh from the plates drying in the rack. At the sunlit table, I scrolled through the websites DS McCarthy had given us. It would be preferable he'd said, to do this after the trial. But go ahead, he'd said, if you feel you can't wait.

'What about this one?' I said to Robert. 'She specialises in childhood trauma.'

He was pulling on his overalls to go out to work, the smell of sawdust homely and familiar. When I angled the laptop towards him, the sun from the window glinted on the screen, bleaching the image. 'If you want,' he said. 'If you think she'd be best.'

'But I'm not sure, Robert, that's why I'm asking.'

He was tugging on his jumper, leaving the overall sleeves dangling. He changed tack; there was something on his mind as well. 'I know it's only the initial hearing, but I think Abigail's family should be there, right from the start. Even if it's only one of us.'

'You want to be there when he's going to say *that*? You want to actually hear him claim he's not guilty?'

'Somebody should be there, Anne, full stop.'

Well, I'd always known, hadn't I, how responsible he felt? Because it was due to him that we had been in London and that I'd ended up on the Underground with the children by myself. We had gone down to visit his mother in Guy's Hospital, because this time, Robert said, she really was sick. We'd even brought the children to see her, though she didn't show any pleasure at them being there. And even when Sam and Laurie got tired and grizzly, Robert said he ought to stay on at the bedside of his mother who he'd never got on with, who had never accepted me or Abigail as her family, who could never find a single good thing to say about me and who even during that hospital visit had been cruel. I wanted to leave, Robert wanted to stay, and we argued because of it and I got so upset with him. In the end he stayed and I left with all our children and the buggy, to make our way back to the hotel on our own.

Afterwards, it was three hours before the police could reach him, his phone set by hospital policy to silent. Twenty missed calls before they sent a message through the hospital switchboard. And Robert had never forgiven himself for any of it.

My phone buzzed next to me, a call appearing on the screen. I recognized the digits: DS McCarthy. The thought of his cool grey eyes made my stomach clench.

'Aren't you going to answer that?' said Robert.

I should, I knew I should, but instead I switched the phone to silent and, drawing a breath, turned the laptop back towards me. 'I really think that Abigail needs this.'

This time, Robert stopped pulling on his boots and came to sit next to me. 'All right. Let me see.'

I opened the page links one by one. When we came to the therapist I'd picked out before, he pointed. 'That one.'

'This one?'

'Yes.'

'Okay.' We were agreed. On my mobile, the voicemail alert pinged.

Robert stood now, checking his pockets for keys. 'Anne, listen, about the hearing. I know they've told us he plans to plead not guilty; I know it will only last ten minutes, but—'

But I didn't need to argue with him. I understood, I did, why he needed this. 'It's all right,' I told him. 'If it helps, you should go.' When I looked up, I felt so much love from him.

'Thank you, Anne.' He leaned down to kiss me. 'Please tell Abigail I won't be home late.'

When he closed the front door behind him, the house fell silent. The boys were at school and Abigail was upstairs, still sleeping. I looked again at the profile on my laptop. In her photo, the therapist looked kind and wise and like someone who would do all she could to help. I imagined telling her everything I was afraid of. I imagined her finally setting Abigail straight. In the quiet, I let my tired eyes close and the sun from the window warm my cheek.

The shrill of the landline was like someone yelling in the silence. It went on ringing until I pushed my chair back from the table and lifted the receiver.

'Mrs White?'

'Yes?'

'It's DS McCarthy. I've been trying to get hold of you.'

I let the pause between us hang. I knew he had. 'What is it?'

'The Met detectives have been questioning him and now we need to speak to you again. Something's been bothering me. Do you think you can come to the station?'

'With Robert?'

'No, we don't need Robert. It's your statement. Can you come now?'

'Right now?'

'As soon as you can. And Mrs White? Please could you bring Abigail too.'

I went upstairs. I was wrong: Abigail wasn't sleeping. She was sticking posters to her unpainted walls, an array of pretty boys and punky girls, none of whom I recognized.

I let the door close softly behind me. 'Who are all these, then?'

She was using her teeth to tear off a strip of Sellotape. 'Jess's favourites, and I like them too.'

'We'll have to take them down before we re-paint.'

'I know.'

'Have you chosen, then?'

She didn't answer, just carefully smoothed the Sellotape onto the wall, securing a last corner. The sticky tape was going to leave marks. She stepped back. 'Do you like them?'

I nodded. They were nice posters.

'Abigail?' I said. 'I need to take you down to the police station. DS McCarthy wants to see you again.'

'Why? I've already answered all the questions.'

'I know you have. They just want … They want to speak to me too. Can you get ready? He waiting for us now.'

DS McCarthy was standing outside the station, clearly impatient, his long face pinched. He looked as though he had just finished a cigarette, or wished he had. We arrived at the station forty-five minutes after his call.

'Come in.' No *thank you for coming*.

Inside, he led us straight through to the rear, down a long corridor to a set of interview rooms. DS McCarthy stopped outside two doors. 'Abigail, you'll be in here. I know it's new to you – we haven't had time to show you – but I hope you'll find it similar, familiar from London. And Mrs White – Anne – you'll be in here.'

I stared at him. 'I should go in with Abigail.'

He shook his head. 'No. You don't need to do that.'

'She needs someone with her.'

'She'll have that. An appropriate adult.'

'But not me?'

'No. You're a witness. You can't be present.' He opened a door onto a room with soft chairs where a detective was already sitting waiting. 'Abigail?' He was expecting her to go in.

'Detective? What are you going to ask her?'

DS McCarthy's face was an unreadable mask. He crossed the corridor and opened the second door. 'Please, Mrs White. In here.'

In the room allocated to me, there were two more officers waiting, a woman in a pink blouse and a man with a beard. They both stood up as I came in.

'It's really just a formality,' said the man. 'Have a seat.'

When the three of us were sitting, the woman switched on the tape recorder. 'Not strictly necessary this time,' she said, 'but…' I remembered being taped before, years ago, when I made statements to police in London. I was thinking about that as they made their introductions.

'I'm DC Vickers and this is DC Neilson. Mrs White—'

'Anne.'

The woman in pink – DC Vickers – nodded. 'Anne. We'd like you to look at a picture of our suspect. This is the man we're questioning over the kidnapping of your daughter.'

DC Neilson opened the slim file that sat in front of them and handed the print across to me. I'd seen this already, every time it flashed up on the news but this printed image was crisper, cleaner, bigger. So this was him, his face life-sized, introducing himself to me. John Henry Cassingham.

'Have you charged him then?'

The detectives glanced at each other. The detective in pink began to speak, but her colleague cut in. 'The detectives in London are about to seek advice from the CPS. That's why this interview is so important. Please look closely at his picture and tell us whether you know this man. Whether you recognize him at all. Whether he is known to you in any way.'

I closed my eyes for a moment. I couldn't keep on and on staring at him or letting him stare at me.

'And are you showing this to Abigail too?' I asked.

'No. We wouldn't need to do that at this stage.'

Of course not. What a stupid question.

I looked again at Cassingham's face: wide jaw, pale eyes, that pale blond hair that framed his cheeks. Who knows, maybe if I had seen him in person and been able to hear his voice and see his mannerisms and gestures and breathe in the very smell of him, there might have been something there. As it was: 'I don't know him.'

I pushed the picture back across the table. DC Neilson put it back in the file. 'What about other people in your family? From the news – have they said they recognized his face or his name?'

Robert, Lillian, Fraser. No, no, no. I shook my head.

'For the tape?'

'No. You can ask all of them. She was lost and he took her. None of us knew him.'

DC Neilson nodded. 'All right.' He pulled something else from the file. 'Now. You will recognize this. The Met have sent it up to us.' He handed the sheets of paper across to me. 'A copy of your original statement.'

I stared down at the typed sheet, my own words and signatures staring back at me. *Around six p.m. we boarded a train at London Bridge.*

'Have a read through. If there's anything else you can add, let us know.'

There was a delay. People were pushing to get off while we waited.

'Where did he find her?' I asked. 'I never saw him, so where did he find her?'

The DCs looked at each other again. 'She says she met him outside the Tube station. No more than a dozen yards from the entrance.'

'You can see it then? On CCTV?' Footage, proof of the awful thing he did.

DC Vickers pinched her nose. 'We've tried, believe me, we've tried, but on the cameras, you can't see anything but water and umbrellas.'

The bubble of hope dissolved. Even back then, they'd never been able to find anything, no matter how many times Robert demanded they check. She'd been too small, lost in the crowd, a ceiling of umbrellas hiding her – and hiding *him* – from the lens. But how, *how* could still no one have noticed? '"Met him",' I said, 'and then – what? He just took her? And no one did anything?'

DC Neilson sat back in his chair, not saying anything. I looked back and forth between them. 'What does that mean?'

DC Vickers pressed the palms of her hands together. 'We were wondering that ourselves.'

Something in her tone made me stop. I'd felt only friendliness from her before but now there was a shift like a sudden drop in temperature and I was all of a sudden so aware of them looking at me, two on that side of the table and me, alone, here on the other.

'We checked all the old statements,' DC Vickers went on. 'Nobody reported a fight or a struggle.'

I knew that, didn't I? Robert had gone on and on about it – how nobody claimed to have witnessed anything. Yet in my mind I'd always pictured my daughter fighting like a tiger to get away. Now I was realizing that my picture had always been wrong and I had been entirely mistaken.

'You say he isn't known to you or Abigail,' DC Neilson said, far too slowly as though he was screwing each word into the air between us, 'but can you think of any other reason why your daughter would go *willingly* with this man?'

He let the question hang in the air, like a noose or a guillotine above me. I closed my eyes again, suddenly sick of all this. How did they know to touch this painful spot, this place that hurt from the slightest pressure? I could see her again, floating up that escalator, making her way out onto the London street, into the sodden sheets of rain, the crush of spread umbrellas. Opening my eyes, I fought with myself to keep my voice level and my thoughts clear, focused on what mattered and not spiralling down into that place where nothing good lay. 'Well, wasn't it the same with Tonia? Didn't he take her in exactly the same way?'

The detectives exchanged a look. Tonia. The little child in the garden.

DC Vickers tilted her head. 'It would seem so.'

'Then you *have* all the reasons. My daughter was lost, she was confused, she was *eight*.'

'Then we should only need to write a line or two,' said DC Vickers, 'if that's what you're saying. He didn't know her and you didn't know him. You've been shown his picture and attest you've never seen him.' She drew a blank, clean form from the file and I watched as she carefully turned the words into my statement.

Out in the rain, he saw her. Perhaps he was the only one who did, when everyone else was too wet and in too much of a hurry to pay any attention, crushed under umbrellas and gusts of wind.

'If you are happy with this as your additional statement, then you can sign it and we'll be all done.'

He saw her and she saw him. And then what? Then he leans down out of the crowd, through all those other people passing her by, and holds out a hand. *Little girl, why don't you come with me?*

It could be the straightforward answer to their questions. It could be as simple, as plausible as that. DC Vickers pushed the form across to me, the spaces for my signatures in black and white. For a moment I stared down at the declaration: ... *liable to prosecution if wilfully stating anything false.*

Then I picked up the biro she had given me, and signed.

DC Neilson got me a coffee while I waited for Abigail to finish. We'd been here over an hour and my ears were ringing and I only wanted to take Abigail back to the safety of our home. They had Cassingham and would charge him soon, and then the hearing, a trial and it would all be over.

The door down the corridor opened and I spilled a slop of coffee over my hand. I put my wrist to my mouth to remove the stain.

Abigail was coming up the corridor with DS McCarthy at her side and the appropriate adult – a brown-haired, plain-looking lady – following behind. Beside me, DC Vickers and DC Neilson stood up too and I saw a look pass between the officers, a tiny lift of DS McCarthy's eyebrows – *Anything?* – and a quick shake of the head from DC Vickers. *Nothing.* Then DS McCarthy's look again: *Are you sure?*

On Abigail's face was a look of something – anxiety, frustration? 'What's wrong?' I said.

'Nothing. She did fine.' DS McCarthy tucked a hand into his pocket as though he was doing all he could to look relaxed.

'What happened?' I asked again.

DS McCarthy cleared his throat. 'We were hoping she would make a victim impact statement. It's useful evidence. We'd like her to say, in her own words, how she's been affected by her abduction.'

I looked at my daughter. 'Can't you tell them that?'

'It's fine,' said DS McCarthy. 'We've plenty of time. Any time before sentencing.'

'And I don't have to,' said Abigail.

'The detective says it's important.'

'But I don't *have* to.'

I looked up as DS McCarthy. 'She's going to see a therapist –' I hadn't had the chance to tell Abigail yet – 'maybe that will help?' I wanted DS McCarthy to see that we were co-operating and doing everything we could to help. If there was something I didn't know, then I couldn't help that, but in every other way we were doing everything we could.

'Certainly. Perhaps.' He spread out his palms as though to say, *who am I to judge?* You are though, I couldn't help thinking, and I feel it with you every time, that you are looking at us and judging everything we do.

Behind her fringe, Abigail's face was dark. She rubbed at her eyes. 'Can we go now, please?'

On the drive home, she stared out of the window, swimming in a sea of her own thoughts even as I tried to paddle my flimsy raft towards her. 'I looked up all of them. She seemed the nicest, I think you'll like her and I think she will help.'

She half turned towards me. 'What? Help with what?'

'The therapist. With anything you need. Any questions you have in … in coming to terms with it all.'

My daughter released a deep sigh and I felt as though she had come to me for something and had been asking for years and I hadn't heard her once. I only just caught the words she mumbled, leaning her head against the car window and barely audible over the thrum of the engine.

'Why can't you just talk to me yourself?'

Chapter 14

Thursday 13th June:
Day 18

JESS

I couldn't stop watching Mum all week. I kept trying to read her face, her movements, for signs. I'd always known there was stuff she didn't tell me. Stuff – I'd assumed – that just wasn't my concern. Dad was the one always trying to talk, trying to *share* things. But now I'd seen something else entirely. I'd always known Mum could hide things. But now I knew that, maybe, she could lie.

On the surface she was the same as ever. She set my clean clothes on my bed same as always. Hassled me to tidy my room. She made the same face each morning as she clipped on her work badge – lead nurse at the GP practice. My mum, manager of everything.

All week she went on like that. Every day I thought she would say something, and every day, nothing at all changed. It made me wonder if I'd imagined it all. Maybe I'd misheard, or made the whole thing up. Or maybe I just had to ask her for the truth.

On Thursday night, Dad was at his late clinic. When I came

home from school, it was just Mum and me. A whole evening of the two of us. No one else, no distractions. I went upstairs and got out of my school clothes. If there was ever going to be a time, it was now.

Mum had changed out of her work clothes too. I helped her with dinner, setting the table. Just two plates, two knives, two forks. When dinner was ready – a healthy thing with vegetables in it – we sat down opposite each other. She was so composed, so careful as I watched her eat. *Nothing* showed. I was sure she must feel it, my eyes on her, my questions floating like huge bubbles between us. What did my aunt want to tell the police? What was it Mum claimed couldn't make any difference? I wanted Mum to say something, but I couldn't bring myself to ask. If I dared bring up what I'd heard, I'd have to admit I had been listening. Creeping about, eavesdropping, and I knew she could turn that back on me. But the longer she sat there without saying anything, the angrier I got. I wasn't a kid, I wasn't eight anymore. Wasn't I old enough now to know what was going on?

Mum ate her last mouthful and put her knife and fork together, even though there was no one but her and me to see it. 'Finished?'

I could have said something right there. *Just ask*, I could hear the voice in my head saying. *Just ask*. And I was about to, really I was – but then my phone rang, right at my elbow. Lena. Lena, who I'd hardly spoken to all week. Lena, the only real friend at school I had. Now she was calling, and if I didn't answer—

Mum waved her hand – *it's fine, go on*. She was already standing up, her empty plate in her hand. My phone was flashing, Lena's pixie face showing. And, swiping to answer, I couldn't ignore my relief.

I went through to the living room, sat down carefully on the big sofa. 'Hello?'

It had all been so awkward since she'd had a go at me in the park. Now I knew she was holding out an olive branch. Probably we'd stayed friends because one of us always did – I tried to catch up with her or she tried to slow down for me. This time it was Lena who'd reached out. She was calling with an idea, a plan she'd come up with. The annual music festival was on this weekend. Why didn't Abigail and I both come? It wasn't hard to read between the lines. Lena was giving me a chance to prove myself. Giving *Abigail* a chance. Invite her out, Lena was saying, show me, prove to me that she's fine. I swallowed down all my reservations. I said yes almost at once.

'I'll call her,' I told Lena. In the kitchen, I could hear Mum washing up. The background noise helped drown out my other thoughts. 'I'll ask her right away.'

And I did. I rang the Whites' house there and then. Abigail was quiet when she came to the phone – like she'd just woken up – but once I explained it all, it wasn't hard to get her to agree. And then Auntie Anne and Uncle Robert said it would be okay too. So now everybody had said yes.

When I felt Mum touch my shoulder, I jumped. I'd turned the TV up so loud that I hadn't heard her come in.

'Everything okay?' She put a cool hand on my forehead, the way she used to when I was younger, smoothing back my hair. It was a wonderful feeling. I'd always loved it. I turned down the TV and let myself lean into her palm. 'Abigail and I are going to meet Lena on Saturday.'

I expected Mum to question me, to object until she'd extracted all the facts. There were so many rules and strictures with Mum, sometimes living with her made it hard to breathe. It would have been like that too, I thought, for my aunt when she and Abigail lived with us. Two whole years under Mum's rules.

Instead: 'That sounds wonderful,' she said. 'Abigail will be able to make a new friend.' Her gentle hand went on smoothing. The anxiousness in my chest softened. I thought of the help she always gave me with my homework, pushing me till I got everything correct. My ironed school blouses, not a wrinkle in sight. The meal she'd cooked tonight from scratch that, despite the vegetables, had tasted so good. So what if there were things I didn't understand? So what if there were things she kept from me? What did I know about how it worked with adults, what being a grown-up really meant? Mum had her ways – it was how she looked after me. It was how she'd protected me my whole life.

After that, I made myself stop thinking about what I'd overheard. I wouldn't ask, I wouldn't mention it. It was up to Mum and Auntie Anne to sort it out. Better to think of Abigail only. Better to make sure this all went okay.

On Saturday, Uncle Robert dropped my cousin off at ours with a duffel bag full of clothes. Upstairs in my bedroom, when she unzipped it, I saw it was stuffed with trousers, jumpers, skirts. Most still had their tags on. I sat down on my bed. 'These are all yours?'

'Yes. My mum's been buying them.'

'There's a lot.'

'I know. I wanted you to help me choose what to wear.'

I went to my wardrobe and opened the door wide so Abigail could see herself in the full-length mirror. She pulled off the plain blue T-shirt she'd arrived in, showing a white cotton bra underneath. She picked up a red checked shirt, tugged it over her head. She stood up in front of the mirror and pulled the shoulders this way and that. 'It's pretty,' I said.

Abigail rubbed her bare arm where she had her nicotine patch, then pulled the red shirt off again. I reached down into the bag and lifted up a yellow top, summery and soft. 'Why don't you try this one?' It was far nicer than any of the clothes I owned, and I knew it would look lovely on her. When she put it on, the shop tag made a little lump in the back. She did up the tie, pulling it tight at the waist. We both looked at her reflection. With the light jeans she had on, she looked pretty, girly. An ordinary fifteen-year-old.

'You should wear that,' I said, a bit too loudly. 'It really suits you.'

Instead, Abigail picked at the knot she'd tied, unravelling it to take the top back off. She pushed it into the bag, pulled out something else – a tight black jumper. The rolled neck came right up to her chin, the sleeves right down to her knuckles. The static made her hair messy and fuzzed. She looked gawky, a pale scarecrow.

I didn't want her to wear an outfit like that but she didn't take it off again. I went to my dresser and handed her my brush. 'Here.' She could fix her hair at least. 'Tuck it behind your ears.' I showed her how. With the weight pulled back like that, you could make out her cheekbones and the soft angle of her jaw. She looked at herself, then found my eyes in the glass.

It would have to do. I smiled. 'You look great.'

The music festival took place in the big park at the north end of town. Local acts, plus food shacks, craft stalls, all that kind of thing. Mum and Dad used to take me when I was little. It wasn't far to walk from our house and it was sunny, the upwards rise of summer. I'd found pairs of sunglasses for both of us, and they helped make her outfit look less strange. After all the changing, we were running late and the park was already full by the time we got there. I could feel Abigail tense at the sight of the crowds. Only three weeks in – was she really ready? But I refused to let my own nerves rub off on her.

Within the grounds there were toddlers, parents; I scanned the little groups and knots of families, friends. At first there was no sign of Lena; just me and Abigail on the edge of this whole crowd. What would happen if Lena didn't come? What would happen if Lena changed her mind and dropped me? At school, I didn't have other friends, I didn't know where else I'd fit in. Then I saw her, holding the hand of a little red-headed girl, tugging her to keep up as she came hurrying across the grass. I recognized the kid – a neighbour that she sometimes had to babysit.

I pointed, for Abigail's sake, and waved. 'There she is.'

Lena came up. 'Sorry,' she said. 'There was a bit of an emergency next door, they needed me to take Kayla.'

'It's all right,' I said. 'Doesn't matter.' Really it didn't. Not now she was here.

I took a deep breath. This was such a weird moment, one

that meant so much to me. Here she was, my cousin, whose absence had always fallen like a shadow on our friendship. The playmate Lena could never quite replace. Lena had stopped believing that she would come home. But now here she was, returned. Real.

'Lena,' I said, 'this is Abigail.'

For moment my best friend didn't say anything. She was still trying to catch her breath. Then she smiled. 'Abigail. It's really good to meet you.'

'Hello, Lena,' my cousin replied. And smiled back.

'Abigay! Abigay!' shouted Kayla. Lena gave her arm a tug. 'Yes, yes, hello to you as well.'

Kayla grinned.

I looked about me, able to breathe properly now. 'This looks fun.' A horseshoe of stalls fanned out across the grass, and the marquee stage was set up at the far end. I could hear the music from here.

Lena curled her loose hair into a knot at her neck. 'Tom's band is playing in a few minutes. I thought we could watch.'

Abigail crossed her arms straight out in front of her, clasping her hands in a funny kind of stretch.

'Only if you want to,' I said, quickly.

'Sure,' said my cousin, letting her arms drop.

Kayla was leaning out from Lena's arm, her weight a momentum. 'Come on then,' Lena said, 'let's get a space at the front.'

We leaned on the railings they'd set up, metal barriers hot from the sun. When they came on stage, I pointed out Tom for Abigail. He was a year older than us, popular, part of the cool crowd from the boys' school down the road. I only knew him and his friends because of Lena. Since Abigail came home, I was realizing that more and more. It was only because of Lena that I'd ever really fitted in.

Lena swung her hips. She had a way of moving, this way of twisting and tilting her body. Unpractised, like she'd just grown into it. I saw how Tom looked at her when she danced like that. A way no boy ever looked at me. I moved myself a little closer to Abigail as Lena linked her fingers with Kayla's, swinging her whole body from side to side. Whenever she stopped, Kayla shouted, 'Keep going!'

'They're great!' I shouted across to Lena. I wanted her to see me enjoying myself. I wanted her to know that I could like what she liked. So what if Lena had Tom in her life now? I was willing to like him too, and he had always been nice enough to me.

'They're good, aren't they?' I said to my cousin. 'And I'm really glad you can get to meet my friends.' Because I was, of course I was. Glad Abigail had said yes and Mum had agreed and that, even in her odd outfit, my cousin didn't look that weird. Because this way, I told myself, squeezing the hot railing, this way, maybe, I could have both. My friendship with Lena and everything that brought, and the magic of my world with my cousin.

Tom's band finished their song, started a last one. Their singer was saying thank you into the mic. Kayla was tugging at the hem of Lena's T-shirt. Lena bent down, said something I couldn't catch. Kayla shook her head, her bottom lip thrusting out. Lena straightened up. 'She needs the toilet.' She shook her head. 'Tom won't want me to miss his last song.'

I glanced at Abigail, leaning on the railing. 'I can take her,' I said.

'Could you?

'Abigail? You'll be okay for a few minutes, won't you? If you stay with Lena while I take Kayla?'

Of course she could do it. Lena was so ready and willing to be friends. 'Okay,' said Abigail, after a moment.

Lena pushed Kayla forwards. 'Here, Jess will take you. You can go in the café, she knows what to do.' Kayla gave a skip, happy now. 'Thanks, Jess,' Lena said. 'And thank you, Abigail.'

We headed to the café, Kayla hop-jumping beside me. 'Tom is Lena's boyfriend,' she said.

'I know,' I said. And thought, *please don't ask if I've a boyfriend too.*

There was a queue, but a lady let us go in first. 'Can you go by yourself?' I asked Kayla. 'Don't lock it and I'll stand right outside.'

Through the door, I listened to the rustle of clothes and the little sing-song words she mumbled to herself. In the summer warmth, I grew fuzzy and relaxed. Abigail and Lena and Tom and the music. All of my misplaced nerves dissolved. I heard the flush and the bang of the lid. 'All done?'

Kayla came out and I lifted her up to wash her hands.

When we came back outside, Tom had come off stage. He was down by the railings, with Lena and Abigail. It was hard to make them out against the sun's rays. At first I was glad to see them together, but then it looked like something weird was happening. I pulled Kayla's hand, hurrying her up.

By the time we got to them, they'd all stopped talking. They weren't saying anything. Just a screech of feedback from the speakers and a flush on Lena's cheeks. 'What is it?' I asked. 'What's happened?'

Lena began, 'Abigail—'

But Tom shrugged off the moment, stage-buzzed, smiling. 'It was nothing,' he said. 'Honestly, everything's fine.'

In the summer sunshine, I smiled back. 'Great.'

Afterwards, Abigail and I walked Lena and Kayla home. Kayla hung from Lena's hand, taking little jumps through the air, landing two-footed, slap on the tarmac. Lena stooped down and whispered something to her. For a while Kayla went on taking jumps by herself. Then she reached out and slipped her hand into my cousin's. Abigail startled, surprised at the touch. Then she looked down at Kayla and I saw her shoulders relax. Lena smiled across at me.

'Do you know what to do?' she asked, and Abigail nodded. Our slim shadows flickered ahead of us.

'One, two, three,' Lena counted and together they swung Kayla into the air. Kayla shrieked and kicked her heels. A perfect moment. My cousin happy and normal as anyone. I could have freeze-framed that second forever.

We said goodbye at Lena's front door, and Abigail and I walked back to my house together. As we crossed the playing fields, my cousin pointed into the high blue sky. 'Is that a swallow?'

I stopped and looked up, following her line. The bird flickered above us in a dip-darting flight. It was a sparrow, and the season was way off, but in that moment what did it matter?

'Definitely,' I told her. 'First swallow of summer.'

Chapter 15

Thursday 20th June:
Day 25

ANNE

On the laptop at the kitchen table, I typed his name into the search bar: Detective Sergeant David McCarthy. I could hardly explain the urge or what it was that unsettled me. It was only the way his grey eyes always looked at me, at my family, as though *we* were the only ones under suspicion. But he couldn't know what I'd done, *surely* he couldn't. There had to be another reason, I had to believe that; I only needed to find out what it was.

The cursor blinked as I clicked the search key and the page flipped over to a list of hits. There were so many it was hard to focus. His name seemed to crop up everywhere, but it was never him; there were other Davids, other people called McCarthy. I kept opening the links and clicking back, still unable to find what I was looking for.

Nothing, nothing, and then something: on the second page of hits, I found him. When I clicked on the link, the screen half froze, then the story appeared.

I hadn't heard about this case. Despite all the research

146

Robert had done during those years when Abigail was missing, I hadn't come across this poor family. Perhaps because the child's disappearance had only lasted a matter of days, not months or years. It had happened in Leicestershire though; only the next county over.

DS McCarthy's name was all over it. A child, his grandparents, and a line of enquiry other officers refused to pursue. The truth discovered one day too late.

'What's that?' Abigail came looming up at my shoulder and I jumped. I hadn't heard her come down the stairs.

I swiftly closed the laptop. 'Nothing. Are you ready?'

Today was Abigail's first therapy appointment. She was dressed for it like an ordinary teenager, in jeans and a rose-pink T-shirt. All her clothes had arrived by now, almost too many. She tended to wear the same outfit day in, day out; I had to remind her to put them in the laundry basket. These jeans and that T-shirt were a case in point; four days in a row, at least, she'd been wearing them.

In the car, I checked the address on my phone and put the postcode into the sat nav. It was spotting with June rain and the air outside was humid and muggy. I knew Abigail needed to talk; I knew there were questions she needed answering, but what good could my own words be to her, little more than a catalogue of regrets and failings? On her website, the therapist had looked so much like someone who could help and knew how to resolve all kinds of problems. She admitted on the phone that she'd never had a case quite like this before, but Ms Coulson's voice was so gentle and kind that I knew without doubt that I'd made the right choice.

I looked over at Abigail now, sitting crookedly in the

passenger seat. 'It's fine if you don't like her,' I said. 'Just see how you feel, we can try different people, find which one works for you.'

She gazed out of the window. 'You need to turn here.' The arrow on the sat nav pointed clearly to the left. I braked a bit too sharply, turning without my indicator and the car behind beeped.

'Sorry,' I said, to Abigail, to the other driver, and anyone else who needed an apology from me. 'Look out for the house number,' I said. 'The even numbers are on your side.'

It was a nice street on the west side of town, rowan trees with berries in bud and little garden gates in neat hedges, and hardly any distance really from our house. The rain-spotted wheelie bins, put out at the edge of the kerb, had house numbers painted on them. Very proper.

'Here,' said Abigail. 'Number 26.'

There wasn't much room on the street for parking and it took me a while to squeeze into a space. The tall gate at the side of the main house squeaked as we opened it, and it took me a couple of goes to replace the latch. We rang the bell of the little annex at two minutes past the hour.

She didn't look quite like she did on her website. Her hair was longer, and she was wearing glasses. But her eyes and smile matched the kind voice I'd heard. 'Ms Coulson?'

'Yes. You must be Abigail and Anne.'

She opened the door wide for us, and I waited for Abigail to step in first. Inside, the annex was like a cottage with a neat waiting area and the therapy room behind.

'Come straight in,' she said, 'and please call me Jenny.'

In the therapy room proper, we sat in two dove-grey chairs

facing her. The room was small, intimate, calming pictures on the walls and a soft rug on the floor, unobtrusive tissues on the table and a little clock that ticked on a shelf.

'It's a pleasure to meet you, Abigail,' Jenny said. She used her thumb to push her glasses up on her nose and went through how she worked: the bounds of confidentiality, the exceptions to that rule. '…And you've given a full statement to the police already? That's always best, when there are legal proceedings.'

Abigail hesitated. I noticed that she hesitated.

'Yes.'

This wasn't the first appointment we had taken her to. Three days before, Abigail had been seen by an educational psychologist. Another recommendation, another way of knowing where we stood. She hadn't been to school since Year Four; she'd been a bright child then, but what about now? It was seven years of education she had missed.

We'd had to travel to Newark to see the psychologist, Dr Hallam, and in the car on the way home, Abigail had described the pictures, cards, puzzles, the stopwatch. She'd had to calculate numbers, remember things, solve problems. She remembered especially the little plastic cubes, their sides red and white, that she'd had to match to geometric designs. Dr Hallam wouldn't tell her if she was getting the questions right or wrong, just said, that's fine, keep going, do your best.

I mentioned that now to Ms Coulson – Jenny.

She lifted her eyebrows and smiled at Abigail. 'Police interviews and an IQ test too? What a lot of assessments you've had.'

Abigail smiled back from under her fringe. 'Yep.'

'So, what's your understanding of why you've come here?'

Abigail's fingers began picking at each other, gently at first, then harder. 'I was living—' said Abigail, then stopped. 'A man … John Henry … took me to live with him in London.'

'All right.'

'But now they've told me he shouldn't have done that. Now I'm … home again. At my dad Robert's house.'

The therapist nodded. 'Now you're home.'

I felt the muscles along my shoulders ease the smallest bit.

'And how,' the therapist went on, 'would you say you're doing with that?'

Abigail went on picking with a fingernail at the skin of her thumb. *Pick, pick, pick.* I waited but she didn't say anything. I waited for Jenny to ask another question but the therapist was sitting there silent as well. The little clock on the shelf ticked along, precious seconds that we'd paid for in advance.

Finally Abigail spoke up. 'Everyone in my family's very happy. Everyone says they're very happy that I'm home—'

'We are—' my voice cracked. '*We are.*'

'But I keep getting a feeling.' Abigail's hand fluttered up at her chest.

'Can you describe that?' Jenny's voice was so soft.

'Like burning. Or – like squeezing.' Now Abigail pressed the flat of her hand to her chest.

'All right. Like burning or squeezing. And what brings that on?'

'It's because … because all we talk about is that I'm home, how everything is happy and *safe* for me now. And I just keep thinking – how can any of this be real? Because here, inside, it doesn't feel like that *at all.*'

I didn't move. I couldn't move.

The therapist drew a slow breath in through her nose. 'It would be natural,' she said presently, and I felt the knots in my shoulders let go, 'to feel intense emotions. The sensations of anxiety, you can feel them in your body.' She tapped her fingertips to her own chest. 'Tightness, that can feel like burning. And it's not uncommon,' she went on, 'for children who've been through trauma to feel the world is unreal. Or still unsafe. There can be so much to process. It can take a while for the brain to catch up.'

Abigail still didn't look directly at the therapist but her fingers stopped picking at least. As the therapist sat observing her quietly, I had such a strong feeling that this woman understood.

'It makes sense,' I said 'you're right – everything you've said ...' I said, fumbled for my handbag on the floor, my hands clumsy with relief. 'There's really been quite a bit of confusion and it really has been hard for her to adjust. I brought along – ' the zip snagged then growled as I wrenched it – 'this notebook. I've been keeping notes.'

I smoothed out the corners where it had got crumpled in my handbag and flipped through the pages to let Jenny see. I'd written as neatly as I could, all my observations about my daughter since she came home. The foods she liked and didn't, the things she knew and the blanks in her life. What seemed to trigger her changes in mood, habits she'd developed, preferences and routines. The sleep talking.

'... Everything,' I said. 'I wrote all of it down.' All these weeks since she came home. Hours listening on the chilly landing.

I held the notebook out to the therapist but she wasn't looking at me. She was watching, intently, for Abigail's reaction. It was tiny, tiny, but I could see that my daughter was shaking her head. I saw myself suddenly through Abigail's eyes, skulking round the houses, spying on her and I knew at once that I'd made a terrible mistake.

The notebook went slithering off my lap, bouncing on the floor to lie on its side like a bird shot down.

'I'm sorry, I don't know what I was thinking. I thought it would help us. Abigail, I'm sorry.' I picked up the crumpled pages.

'It's all right,' said the therapist. But I knew it wasn't. I couldn't bring myself to look at my daughter.

I knew what the therapist was about to say and I got the words out before she could. 'It'll be easier if I wait outside. I'm not helping, I know that. It would be much better for Abigail to talk with you alone.'

The therapist stood up as I did, holding out a hand to make me pause. 'Abigail, what would you prefer?'

I longed for Abigail to ask me to stay, even as I pushed the notebook back into my handbag and even as I told myself, Anne, stop expecting.

'It's all right,' she mumbled, 'if you prefer to go.'

For the rest of the hour, I sat in the tiny waiting room outside, feeling like such a terrible failure. I'd left, and how could I know that's what she'd really wanted? The look on her face when she'd said I could go. Why hadn't I been brave enough, strong enough to remain there? All I could think now was that I should have stayed.

The silence felt like a great breath I was holding and the notebook sat like a lead weight in my handbag. When my phone rang, the jangling ringtone was like an insult in that quiet space. I knew who it was; I still recognized that string of numbers and my heart lurched at the sight of them. I scrabbled to press the cancel button as the door of the therapy room opened, and Abigail came out. Her face was relaxed, and the therapist was holding up a diary.

'Can we make another appointment?'

A wave of relief washed down me. It hadn't been a failure then, after all. I stood up, my legs shaky but able to smile and show Abigail I was proud of her, that she had done so well in agreeing to come. We booked another session for next week, plus a whole series more for the weeks after that.

On the way home, Abigail put the radio on, and I let her turn the volume all the way up.

That same evening, Dr Hallam the educational psychologist called us. She had the results of Abigail's IQ test. 'She's very bright,' Dr Hallam said. 'Really, she has quite a brain.'

She was calling from the train on her way home. 'Your daughter' she kept saying instead of 'Abigail'. Confidentiality in public, of course. Her voice was crackly on the line – my mobile on speaker-phone laid out on the low table in the middle of the room so that both Robert and I could listen. 'It's not just her natural intelligence,' Dr Hallam went on. 'She knows things. She's learned a lot.'

'What do you mean?' There was a pause, or a break in the line. 'Hello?'

The line cleared and Dr Hallam's voice came through

distinctly. 'Your daughter's IQ is 127 – well above average. But it isn't just that.'

Through in the kitchen, I could hear Abigail on the landline, talking to Jess, little bubbles of excitement in her voice.

'What then?' I asked.

'Mrs White, Mr White... I gave her GCSE exam papers. Maths, Physics, Chemistry, History. She understood them and was able to answer. Abigail hasn't missed any schooling at all.'

For endless seconds I couldn't speak, I couldn't look at Robert. It was as though the world upended all over again. She'd been held captive in a house for years. She'd had no friends, she was kept secret from the world by a man, a complete stranger. But now we were learning that he'd educated her, given her books, learning. Given her all those things we would have. I couldn't hold it straight in my head. The line between black and white was blurring. What did it mean that he'd done this for her, cared about her in this way, as though she was his own child? Out of all the children in London, why, *why* did he pick Abigail for this?

'Be grateful for small mercies,' came Dr Hallam's voice faintly.

But if he gave her these things, if he was *good* to her, how much more damaged must her loyalties be? What if, living with him, she'd been *happy*, and was longing now for everything she missed? What if it wasn't that she didn't understand – what if she understood the difference completely, and it was simply that she would prefer to go back?

My stomach turned over and over. If *he* was good to her, and if I ... if I ...

What had Abigail said to Jenny, how much could she

remember and how far back would they have gone? They had seven whole years to cover. Had they gone from the end – or from the beginning? And the same with the last interview Abigail had given to the police. That statement, the one I'd made right at the very start, when I'd described how exactly we got separated. Had they shown my words to Abigail as well? Could she have read them and realized that I'd lied? And if she had, how could I ever, *ever* explain?

When Robert hung up the phone, I covered my head with my arms, unable to say a word. I could picture every wall around me crumbling, flaking beneath her Sellotaped posters, ceiling plaster splintering, beams crashing down.

How desperately I'd been trying to hold them up.

Chapter 16

JESS

When the last bell rang, Lena and I took the back exit from school. A week and a half on from the music festival, she and I were close again. Maybe she'd appreciated me making the effort – to go out with her and Tom, and bring Abigail too. Maybe she'd seen that Abigail could get along with people. In the summer sunshine, I felt my heart lifting, imagining a future when all four of us were friends. Lena and Tom, me and Abigail, all of it clicking and me never having to choose.

Instead of taking the bus home, I was going to walk with Lena part-way. Her route home was on the way to my cousin's, and I was going to visit Abigail straight from school. I had something I wanted to give her, a present I'd been carrying about with me for weeks. As we weaved past the teachers' cars, late June sunlight striped with shade, I paused, hopped, flicking my foot. I could feel a stone lodged in the tip of my shoe, a crumb of gravel digging right into the sole of my foot. 'Lena, stop a minute.' I crouched down.

'What's up?'

'I've got a stone.'

I unlaced my shoe and wiggled my foot out. My school sock was bunched and wrinkled round my heel. I hopped again, trying to keep my balance.

Lena crooked out an arm. 'Here.' It was easy between us now. Natural.

I held onto her elbow and tipped my heavy shoe up. I could hear the stone rattling but nothing came out. In the heat, kids shoved past us, eager to get home.

'So,' said Lena. 'When were you going to tell me?'

'Tell you what?' The stone still wouldn't come out.

'You know. About Abigail.'

'"About Abigail"? What do you mean?' A piece of grit came finally tumbling out. How could something so small have caused all that discomfort? I let go of Lena's arm and crouched down to shove my shoe back on.

'That's she's coming back to school.'

Crouched there on the hot concrete, I froze. 'What?'

I could feel Lena above me. Her shadow hung right over me. 'Well, isn't she?'

Very slowly, I straightened up and made myself look right at my friend. She was staring at me, waiting for my answer. I shook my head, made myself laugh. 'Yes,' I told her. ''Course she is. I was just surprised that you already knew.'

It was because Lena's mum was on the school council. That was the way that my best friend had heard. And as we headed down the lane away from school, I had to pretend I'd known all along. A plan for Abigail to return to school? Why hadn't my cousin said anything? In fact, why hadn't *anyone*? Auntie

Anne would have told Mum, and Dad would have asked, but no one had ever said anything to me.

I thought about the snippets of conversation between my parents. Like, just the other night, Dad asking in front of me, *hasn't anyone heard from Pres*— and Mum cutting him off, making a face: *shhh*. Even though I already knew who Dad was talking about. I already knew all about Abigail's real father, about the fight, the panicked phone call from Preston's brother. About how it was my mum who came to the rescue. Dad had told me all of it years ago because he always wanted to *explain* everything in our family, always wanted everything shared. Mum was different, refusing to talk. Mum kept things back, hid things, I knew that now. So how much was there that I had missed out on?

'So – I mean, do you think she's ready?' Lena had started to walk a bit faster. She was tall and her legs were longer.

'Sure,' I said, hurrying to catch up. 'Why not?' Okay, so it had come as a surprise, but the truth was, it was a good thing, wasn't it? It said how well she was doing, if Abigail was thinking about school. But there was Lena always questioning things. Why couldn't she ever just let things be good? I hitched my bag back onto my shoulder.

Lena shrugged. 'I don't know. It just seemed so hard for her to know what to say to people. You know – like, to me, or Tom, at the festival.'

I stopped short, a squeezing pressure filling up my chest. Now my own voice was loud, defensive. 'She was *fine* with you at the festival! You saw her, playing with Kayla!'

But I had left her alone with them, hadn't I – Lena and Tom? And hadn't something gone wrong between them?

Lena stopped too and turned to face me. I couldn't read her expression. Maybe she wanted to push me – challenge me again like she had at the play park, make me see things the way she saw them. Maybe she also just missed the way we used to be friends. In the end, I saw her shoulders drop.

'Listen, Jess,' she said. 'Do you want to come back to mine? Mum won't mind, you can have tea with us, we can do our homework, watch TV – whatever.'

I was grateful to her and I wanted to, really I did. But now there was Abigail and I had promised to see her. Now there was Abigail, and it seemed I still had to choose.

Despite the heat outside, it was cool and shady in the Whites' house. I found Abigail in shorts, cross-legged on her bed, a soft blur of hair on her legs. She didn't shave, I realized. Or didn't know how. Another weird sign of difference between us. I turned my gaze to her room instead. 'But you still haven't painted it.'

The peeled walls were smooth, Uncle Robert must have sanded them down, but they were still stained and blotched between the posters.

Abigail uncurled herself from the bed and stood up. 'I don't really feel like being inside today. I've spent days in here. Why don't we go out?'

Now I thought about it, it did feel kind of stuffy. 'All right, but where to?'

I should have known her answer would be the railway; I should hardly have needed to ask. Here was something that hadn't changed in all this time – this strange pull that she'd always had, ever since she had moved into this house. She had tried to explain it to me once – her fascination with the violence of it, the roar. There's a roaring in me sometimes, she'd said, and it's like the trains let it out.

I didn't want us to go there now, but how could I bring myself to argue? She remembered this so clearly from childhood and I didn't want to spoil that. We left a note: *gone for a walk*. I took my bag with me and we headed up the path at the end of her road, pushing through the line of scrub and bushes. In the summer heat, the leaves were thick, but someone had cut the branches back, clearing the path and it wasn't hard to make our way through. We came out onto the rough blanket of grass above the railway tracks – the sloping embankment.

At the sight of it, I hesitated. I couldn't help it. It wasn't just all my aunt's warnings. It was this weird connection my brain had always made. How the shelf of grass was like a platform. The railway line kind of like the Tube. I'd always thought this had been part of it, that maybe something had come over her in that Tube station, her instinctive fascination snatching her attention, making her disorientated, distracted.

'This'll do,' she said. 'Here.' She'd found a space on the grass and was already sitting down. I dropped my bag beside her.

The grass was dry and warm to sit on. From here, we could see the struts of the thick workman's bridge a little way up the tracks, the one no one was allowed to go on but which everyone knew local teenagers sometimes climbed. We sat looking down over the railway line, with its low, loose fencing, and into the back gardens of the houses on the other side. Someone had put their washing out on a whirligig: big yellow sheets that billowed in the breeze and a line of baby socks, each one held up by a blue clothes peg. In the sun, I could feel the bridge of my nose turning pink.

The dusty grass was speckled with daises, a least a dozen within reach of my hand. I took one of the furry stalks and pulled it from the ground. With my thumbnail, I pinched its stalk then pulled up another to thread through. I held the linked flowers up to Abigail.

She searched for the name. Found it. 'A daisy chain.'

'Why didn't you tell me you were coming back to school?'

She shrugged. 'It isn't all decided yet. It wouldn't be till after summer anyway.'

She picked a daisy of her own, snapping its stalk, and drew the slim white petals off one by one. *Loves me. Loves me not.* Was she thinking that, did she even remember the rhyme? And if she did, then who was hers for?

I pulled up another flower and added it to my weave. 'Well, do you want to go?'

She hesitated, scratching at her cheek where a fleck of pollen had smudged. She wasn't wearing the pink bangle any more, I noticed. 'I don't know. I can't tell yet what I want.'

Far off, a train hooted. 'But I mean, it would be good, right? If we could go to school together?'

I'd finished my daisy chain and held it out to her. She looped the flowered bracelet over her hand. The daisies were wide open, limp in the heat.

'You make it sound so simple.'

'Well – ' I thought of the teachers welcoming her, my class-mates finally getting it – 'it doesn't have to be complicated. I mean, if your parents think it would be best. And like, I dunno, if my mum thinks it's fine.'

She had one petal left on her single daisy. She pulled it off, unsticking it from her fingers, and let it scatter in the wind. 'Maybe. But how do you know whether to trust them?'

'What?' I looked across at her, the bridge in the background. 'Who?'

'Your parents ... Mine ...'

I felt something crawl along the bottom of my stomach. I thought of what I had overheard with my aunt. I thought of my parents behind closed doors.

'Of course I do, Abigail. They're our *parents*.'

She leaned forward, pressing her forehead to her knees, hard enough to make red marks. 'All I want is to know what's real. I'm trying to separate it out, Jess, but it's so hard. All the stuff he said. What actually happened? What he told me, is that how it really is?' Her hands were fists against the ground. 'It's so tangled in my head, Jess, but I need to know so all I can do is keep trying to remember.'

I had no idea how to answer that. I had no idea what I was meant to say. I didn't recognize my cousin like this. I pinched another daisy stalk, squeezing the flesh against my nail, pulling it from the ground. She was home, we all loved her and that was enough. He was simply a monster but we'd got her away from him. She was sitting here, with me, in the sun. Why couldn't she let that be enough?

'You remember *us* though, don't you?' I dropped the flower and reached over for my bag, digging in the side pocket. 'Look, I brought this to show you.' The photo I had salvaged from the shoebox. I pulled it out for her. Abigail wiped the pollen from her fingers and took the photograph by its edges. The thumbprint she made on it merged with mine.

'It's us,' I said. 'From before. The day I lost my sandal in the stream.' From a distance, I could hear the clatter of the train approaching. It would hoot again as it came under the bridge.

Whole seconds slid past as she looked at the picture. Then she pointed to our bare feet, our naked toes. 'You fell in the water,' she said, 'and skinned your knee.' It was like it was coming back to her. Like she could see and feel our reality again. She turned the photograph over, as if hunting for some clue on the back. The noise of the train grew louder, the steady rumble.

'My sandal got washed clean away,' I said. 'We searched for hours though and in the end we found it. Then you gave me a piggy back all the way home.'

She looked at the picture again. Her face was softening, her shoulders relaxing. Rounding the corner, the train hooted like I knew it would, and the clattering sound of the wheels rose up.

'It's my favourite photo of us,' I told her, lifting my voice up over the roar.

She laid the picture down in her lap and pressed her hands to her ears. I did the same. She was saying something but the roar of the train blurred her words. 'What?' I shouted as the sound buzzed in my chest, vibrating through the ground. 'What?'

The train hurtled past with the knock and whoosh of each carriage. She was mouthing something to me, her words lost amidst the roar and rumble, but I could make out something, the shapes on her lips.

The very last carriage swooped by and the heady silence covered everything over again. The impossible words had been sucked away by the train. I couldn't bring myself to ask her to repeat them. They were so impossible, so wrong.

He had pictures of me from before, too.

Chapter 17

ANNE

For days I'd tried to decide what to do and finally I had decided on this: a gesture to show that, no matter how Abigail felt, in my mind she was home, finally where she belonged. It's just paint, Lillian had said, and how many times in my life had she been right? Why else did I trust her the way I did, taking every piece of advice she gave? So many times, she'd had the answer. Now it seemed Lillian was right again and this would be the one thing to help us move on.

From the living-room window, I watched them go, towels tucked under their arms and the straps of Abigail's new black swimming costume peeping out from under her shirt. I had told Robert they should take their time. Go swimming, take the longest session, take them for ice-cream before you come home. It would be good for her, anyway, to spend time with the twins, all of them together as siblings, getting better at playing with them. So I knew I had two hours at least, and if I made no mistakes that would be long enough.

I watched Robert help the twins into the van and waited

for Abigail to fasten her seatbelt. I listened for the sliding slam of the door and the growl of the engine fading up the street. I waited out the minutes until I could be sure they wouldn't turn back. Then I went upstairs, into Abigail's room, and took down each of her posters from the walls.

The Sellotape came away furred and crumpled and left marks as I had told her it would. I rolled up the posters into a thick heavy bundle and took them into my and Robert's room. When I came back, the walls were as blank as a stare. I pulled out her bed, her desk, her dresser, then went down to our garage where I knew I'd find dust sheets. They smelled of Robert, of all his work with plaster, paint and wood, and I had to stop a moment, overwhelmed by how much this family meant to me. Overwhelmed by the thought that I could still lose it all.

In her room, I dragged the sheets over the furniture until there was almost no trace of her left.

For a moment I stood in the silent space with my heart thudding; from exertion or anxiety I couldn't properly tell. Then I closed her bedroom door behind me and went downstairs into the utility room, the tiny space that led off from our kitchen, where there was a sink and the washing machine and dryer. Inside the machine, the clothes were dry. I pulled them out and sorted through them: Robert's overalls, the boys' socks. Mixed up amongst them was what I was looking for: the rose-pink T-shirt she had worn day in, day out these last couple of weeks. She'd finally given it up for washing and now it was clean and dry and ready. I ironed it, as though that mattered. Then I folded it up in a plastic bag.

I took my handbag and keys, and the T-shirt. When I stood

on the front step locking the door, the day was so still that it felt as though the whole world was watching.

I don't know what I had been thinking the first time. Lillian had been right: the choice had been overwhelming. We had taken her to the huge warehouse on the outskirts of town, with every colour under the sun. How could we have expected her to choose?

Now, at the mixing stand, I held out the T-shirt. 'I know she likes this colour,' I said to the kind man who took it from me. I couldn't believe how easy it was. You wished for a colour and there it was. Robert had already made the calculations for how much we'd need, written out in pencil. Two standard tins, ten litres each.

The paint cans were heavy to carry back to the car and they banged my legs, bruising my thigh so that in the shower the next morning I found the blue marks. I set them in the well of the passenger seat, along with the brand new tray and roller I'd bought. Back home I carried the paint upstairs and opened the window in Abigail's room. There was still no breeze but it would let any fumes out.

I prized the lid from the first tin and poured a shallow dribble into the tray, enough to coat the length of the roller. Once I started it would be hard to go back. But wasn't that what I had done since she came home? Hesitate, shy away? Wasn't this what she needed instead? I got up and stood face to face with the wall. Lifting the roller and gripping it tight, I made the first mark, right across the wall above her bed: a rose-pink rainbow. A stark, wide, bright streak.

I lowered my arm and stepped back. All right, so now the

easy part was done. Now came the rest. I pushed the roller and tray into a corner and went back into our bedroom. In the drawer of the dresser was the notebook I'd so foolishly presented to the therapist, all my efforts to help her, all those scribbled words and phrases, my clumsy attempts to understand her. I lifted out the abandoned notebook with a painful tightness in my chest. Through the window I could hear a bird singing, celebrating summer. To its song, I tore out the used pages, all the ones I had written on, picking out the shreds of paper left in the binding until there was nothing left but unmarked space.

I carried the blank notebook back into Abigail's room. Then I sat down on her bed, and waited.

Just as on that first day, I heard them arrive home, though this time it was Abigail who was first up the stairs. She came up alone, just as I'd hoped, and when she pushed open her bedroom door she started.

Her hair was still wet from the swim, dripping onto her collar, and her skin looked dry and flaky from chlorine. She stared at the gaps from the posters, the paint-speckled dust-sheets, the pink streak on her wall.

'What's going on?'

I stood up. 'I thought you'd like this colour. If you really don't, it's okay, we'll change it, but it's a pretty colour and I think it will work.'

She stayed in the doorway, her chest rising and falling. 'Where are my posters?'

'Just next door. I didn't want them to get splashed. Here.'

I handed her her T-shirt. 'I took this to get the right colour. I know it's a beautiful colour on you.'

She was breathing more slowly now. I should have realized that it would give her a fright, at first. 'And what's that?' I knew she would recognize the notebook.

'Come in. It won't bite.' I opened the notebook for her on her bed. Like a wary creature, she sidled closer.

'Forget about what I wrote in there before,' I said. 'I've taken all of that out now.' She came up to stand right next to me. 'I thought, while we painted ... if you have any questions—' I found myself stumbling and pushed myself to go on. 'I didn't give you a chance before. All the questions have been us asking you. If you need to, you can write any answers I give you down in here, so that you know it's the truth and you won't be confused.'

As though moving in a dream, she turned over the blank white pages, then looked up again at the arc on the wall. 'You want to paint right over it?'

In her face I could see so many expressions: anger and hurt and hope and fear. It was a battle with herself, I knew that: whether to let it all go and trust me or whether to break me apart in her pain. I could see the child I had so struggled with and the child I'd so loved, her worst self and her best self and all the selves in between. For a moment I had to close my eyes and lower my head, ready for if it all went wrong. When I opened my eyes again she was kneeling up on the bed, the roller in her hand, touching her fingers to the shining streak of paint.

In the end, she chose not to ask me anything and we put the old blank notebook away. Afterwards, work-tired, we sat out in the garden and upstairs the windows of our house stood open, letting out the rose-pink fumes.

'It really is,' she said to me then. 'My favourite colour. I didn't realize it before, but it is.'

Chapter 18

Thursday 25th July:
Day 60

JESS

After summer term ended a few weeks later, I went to stay with Abigail, just for a few days. Then a few days turned into a week, and before we realized, I was practically living there.

My aunt and uncle were happy to have me, they knew that I was always good for Abigail. It was Mum who objected, but she always would, and by then I was sick of the tensions in our house. At my aunt's, it had always felt easier, not rigid and stuffy and walking on eggshells. So I told Mum and Dad it would only be three days. But once I was there, I stayed much longer.

Like that very first night, I slept in her room, on the fold-out camp bed in a thin sleeping bag. The walls of her room were rose-pink now, finally painted. We woke up lazily to the sunshine each morning. Summer was at last properly here. She was a sleepyhead, slow to come around, and I made sure not to rush or jolt her. I still remembered that first night. Those bruises on my arm. The twins would already be up; sometimes we'd hear their voices in the back garden, the bump of a ball being kicked about, sometimes a shriek. They were warier now of asking her to play. Uncle Robert always left for work early. We'd come down to find his coffee mug on the draining board. If Auntie Anne was out or busy, we got ourselves breakfast. By now Abigail knew where everything was in the kitchen: bowls, teaspoons, the handle for the grill pan. Over cereal, or toast, or bacon and eggs, we sat across from each other, still in our pyjamas, hardly different at all from when we were eight.

We could do anything we liked and Abigail still had so much to catch up on. We bought magazines, binged on soaps, on TV box sets. Piece by piece, I told Abigail all the stories of our family, from those years when she had been away. They were *her* stories – this was her family. I made her listen, made her remember them, until she could tell them like they were her own. And I talked to her about the photographs. What she'd claimed.

'A picture of you from the newspapers?' I asked. I was trying to understand.

'No,' she said. 'It was like a proper picture, from when I was little. He said it was sent to him.'

'But it couldn't have been. Sent by who? How would that even be possible?' It was silly the way we kept going round in circles. 'I mean, what did the police say when you told them?'

But then she'd go quiet, stop answering, like I'd caught her out. Eventually she admitted she'd never told the police. It was obvious to me then that she just couldn't accept it. The fact that he'd lied to her. Cut some picture from a magazine, said it was her.

In the end I'd just forget it, put another TV box set on.

I don't know who first suggested it, but at the beginning of August we took a trip to the coast. A night or two away like we used to. When Abigail and I were little, our families had taken holidays together all the time. Why not do the same again now? There were still all kinds of camping spots around Whitby. All right then, said Auntie Anne, let's get away. Let's book a couple of caravans by the sea.

The August sun was hot in the sky as we drove there – me travelling with Mum and Dad, and the Whites in their own car in front. Lincolnshire was so flat it made the sky above huge. A big, baking blue over the fields. We had the windows down to let the sea breezes in and the temperature on the dashboard read 29 degrees. It was a thick, sticky heat that got everywhere, into every corner and fold. Mum forecasted thunderstorms and it was true we could feel the crackles in the air. I closed my eyes against the flickering sunrays and hung my hand out of the window, trailing it in the air streams as we headed up the coast.

The caravan park was a mile or two inland. It was peak season and the best rentals – the ones right by the sea – had been snapped up months ago, but Uncle Robert had found us two smart caravans side by side, sleeping four each. Two little homes away from home.

We drove slowly over the grass between the pitches, looking out for the number that marked ours. Dad had stopped for petrol on the way, and the Whites had got there ahead of us. It was the twins I spotted first, waving at us, their hair shock-blond from the summer sun. Then the figure of Abigail in the doorway of the caravan, barefoot in her shorts and checked shirt. Seeing her at a distance, I noticed how much thinner she was now.

The two of us helped Mum and Dad unload the car and put the food we'd brought away in our little kitchen. Just like when we were little, Abigail would sleep in our caravan, enough room for everyone. Outside, Uncle Robert and the twins were setting up a barbecue and through the little windows in our caravan and theirs, I could see Auntie Anne next door, dressing a salad. I waved at her and she waved back.

We unfolded the deckchairs Dad had dug out of the garage back home. Some of them still had cobwebs on them, we hadn't used them in so long. The adults wanted to sit in the shade of the awning Uncle Robert had set up between the caravans but I dragged two chairs out across the grass for me and Abigail. We sat with the charcoal smoke blowing through our hair and I let the grass tickle my bare feet. You could hear the chatter of other families nearby, the ring of plates and click of plastic cutlery. A dog dashed past us, a ragged ball in its mouth, jumping in a little circle when Abigail reached out a hand, then bounding on.

I shifted in the sloping deckchair, turning my shoulders so I could look at her. 'It's nice, isn't it? Being here like this. We used to come to these places all the time, remember?'

She leaned back in the deckchair, stretching out her legs. It had got easier and easier with all the time we spent together. Ever more relaxed, more open, more talkative. 'Sort of. There're still bits I remember and bits I don't. I remember living with you in London. I remember when Mum and Robert got married.'

They came to live with us after the big fight. We moved to Lincolnshire six months after that. I pictured the wedding, three years later. Free of tantrums. All that got so much better, once Mum made my aunt cut ties with Preston. Before that, Abigail was always getting so upset, so angry.

By the time the food was ready, I was starving. We heaped our plates and balanced them on our knees. We sat leaning forwards, elbows almost touching.

'Did you see the posters when you drove in?' I asked.

'What posters?'

'For the fair. There's a fair across the way tonight. Look, you can see it from here.' I pointed so she could make it out – a cluster of lorries, coloured stall-tops, the long arm of some ride that swung in a high arc. They brought back memories too – the whirl of waltzers, the pulse of music, the melting sweetness of candy floss. It had been years since I'd been to a fair.

Abigail shook her head. She sawed with her knife to cut her hot dog. It made a sharp squeak across the plate. 'We must have come another way. I didn't see them.'

Still, I felt the idea fizzing in my fingertips. 'We should go,' I said.

She laid her knife down. Her fringe had almost grown out by now, I realized, and she had that section of hair clipped back, though a few strands had come loose. 'To the fair?'

'Yes. Why not?' I glanced over my shoulder at the grown-ups. 'Let's ask them.'

Abigail pushed some stray hairs off her forehead. 'I'll ask,' she said.

She lifted herself out of the deckchair and headed over to Uncle Robert and the twins, by the barbecue. I twisted round in my seat to watch. The twins were jostling each other. Play-fighting – or fighting – so close to the flames. They stopped though when Abigail came up, Laurie rubbing his arm, their eyes suddenly hopeful. I couldn't make out the words but I could see Abigail's lips moving. Uncle Robert nodded, though his eyes flitted over to Auntie Anne, sitting at the plastic table in the shade of the caravan. I put my plate down on the grass and went over too, the ground warm on my bare toes. I stood myself next to Abigail.

'And what about you boys?' Uncle Robert was saying. He half turned to speak to Sam and Laurie. 'That would be fun, wouldn't it?'

Abigail reached out and caught his shirtsleeve, pulling him back round. 'I meant just me and Jess.' I saw the moment of hurt on Laurie's face. She never really wanted the twins with her, I realized. Like there wasn't room, like she was always trying to shove them out the way.

Uncle Robert looked at my cousin. 'That's what you want? You and Jess on your own?' She didn't say anything, and neither did I. A film of sweat prickled on my top lip. He looked like he had a spirit level in his head, trying to decide how to weigh this up. 'All right,' he said slowly. 'Let me speak to the others.'

He headed over to where the rest of our parents sat by the caravans. He put a hand on Auntie Anne's shoulder, looked at Mum and Dad, said something to them all. Auntie Anne got up and went inside. Uncle Robert followed her in and I could hear their voices, a tiny bit raised. Not an argument. Just anxiety. It was a lot for us to ask of them – to let us go out there, on our own. Mum half stood up like she wanted to push in after them. Dad stopped her with a hand on her arm. *Not now, Lillian. Leave it alone.*

We waited.

Eventually, Uncle Robert came over to us. He reached into his trouser pocket for his wallet and pulled out two ten-pound notes. 'For the rides.' Sam and Laurie turned back to the barbecue, their shoulders sloping. 'All right, don't sulk,' Uncle Robert said. 'You can choose something tomorrow.'

'Is it all right then?' I said. 'Are we allowed?'

Uncle Robert nodded. 'An hour and a half then come straight back. Jess, keep your phone to hand at all times. Call us at once if anything happens.' He was so serious. I felt my heart constrict. This wasn't going to be just some ordinary teenage fun, I realized. This was going to be a test for us all. I swallowed as I took the two notes from him, folded them and pushed them into my jeans.

'Hang on a sec while I get my shoes.' I'd left them in the Whites' caravan earlier. I darted away up the steps to the open doorway and stopped short. Auntie Anne was still standing at the little sink, folding and refolding a tea towel. The skin looked red round the corners of her eyes. I didn't know what to do. I was about to step away when she turned round.

When she saw me there, she smiled, but her smile was wobbly, like she was winching it up onto her face. I smiled back, keeping the rest of my face still. 'I just came to get my trainers.' They were lying kicked off under the little pull-out table.

I shoved my feet into them, yanking at the loose laces.

'Auntie Anne?' She was still standing at the sink. 'I'll have my phone and we'll only be across the way. I promise that we'll be all right.'

'Of course. I know. She's so good when she's with you.' The words hung in the air, thick with adult feeling.

'OK,' I whispered, suddenly frightened of the promise I'd made.

We set off across the fields behind the campsite, our shadows tall puppets on the ground in front of us. We walked in rhythm, our arms bumping. Sunset was maybe an hour away and behind us the sky was growing pink, but the heat still hung thick in the air. Through its shimmer I could hear the thump of music, the garbled roar of the DJs, the muffled shrieks of the riders.

Soon we were on the edge of the showground. We crossed the threshold of it together, stepping in tandem into its world. A world of lights and giddiness and fun. At the steps to the bumper cars I held out one of the notes to the skinny man who circled the track, his eyes squinting for customers. We clambered into a car and I gave Abigail the wheel. As we looped the scratchy belts around us, I looked up to see the blue crackle of electricity across the ceiling. My tummy thrilled. I wanted to share it all with Abigail. I'd put so much on hold while she was missing but now she was back and we could do anything we chose. Abigail gripped the steering wheel, the coloured lights chasing themselves over the whites of her knuckles. The man who'd taken our money stepped up onto the back of our car, offering us a pile of grubby change. He leaned down to murmur into the space between us. 'Ready, girls?'

I looked across at Abigail. 'Ready?'

She looked back at me, her pupils wide. Ready.

'Three, two, one—' shouted the man in the booth and we lurched forward as the current flipped on. I gripped the side of the car as Abigail wrenched the wheel left and right and we were hurled against the rim. I let out a shriek as I was flung sideways, holding up my arms to let them fly too. She twisted the wheel so we flew backwards, heaving into the knot of cars behind. The impact jolted us forwards and laughter tumbled out of me as we plunged and our hair flipped into our eyes.

We rode and flew and it was all over too fast. When the lights went dim and the power dried up we coasted to a stop, breathless. Abigail's hair stood out around her head. 'Do you remember?' I panted. 'Remember?' We were burning brighter than ever. I imagined that if I touched her, I'd receive a fizzing shock.

Outside, the air smelled of peppery fat from the burger and hot-dog vans. At a bright pink stall, a woman whipped sugar into towering piles and we bought two giant rolls, bigger than our heads. Far away, on the horizon, was the flicker of lightning – the storm Mum had predicted. I pointed it out for Abigail just as the faintest shudder of thunder moved through us. As we ate, our teeth grew pink, stained with sugar dye.

We stood by the candy-floss stall and watched the people and the rides. And I noticed the two boys standing near the steps of the waltzers, who were watching us back. We didn't make eyes at them or toss our hair the way Lena might. But they went on watching us all the same, as we bit into our pink clouds.

Then I tossed my bare candy-floss stick away, breaking the connection, and we were off again, running towards the space catapult. We paid our money and clambered into the little cage. When they pulled the lever, we hurtled into the air, the soles of our feet pressed against the sky. It was like spinning in an endless tumble, element after element, and despite all the sugar we'd eaten, I didn't feel sick and neither did Abigail, and we just tipped our heads back as we spun and whirled, our hands clawing the sides of the cage, our hair flying out like Catherine wheels. The whole thing was a thrilling adventure. That's what I wanted, I realized now. Both of us in this adventure together.

When we returned to earth the two boys from before were still there, looking at us across the muddy grass. The sun was sinking now and they were almost silhouettes in the glow. Abigail dropped the sticky candy-floss stick she was still clutching into a bin. Even now that the tumbling had stopped, I was still dizzy with the adrenaline racing in my veins.

As we passed by them, the taller of the boys, the one whose hair was short and spiky, nodded at Abigail like there was something understood between them. The other one – the tall one with curly black hair – carried a motorbike helmet under his arm. As we headed across the grass towards the arcades, they came meandering after us, the tall one and his spiky-haired friend who walked with his hands deep in his pockets. They couldn't have recognized Abigail, I was sure of that. They wouldn't have been so casual if they had. To them we were just two girls, teenagers like them, having a good time.

By the arcades, zinging with lights, the curly-haired boy came up alongside me. He wanted to win me a prize, he said, on the water-gun stall. I giggled, glancing at Abigail, then grinned at him too so he'd know I wanted him to do it. Up close, I could see the stubble on his chin. He slung an arm round my shoulders and the smell of aftershave waved over me. I wondered what Lena would say. If she'd be impressed. Now it was like he was trying to lead me away from Abigail and his friend, like they meant to separate us. I giggled again and twisted back, ducking out from under his arm.

At the water-gun stall there was a long, sticky queue. The

four of us stood with the jangling, clanging music swirling round us. Spiky Hair was digging in his jacket pocket, pulling out a pack of cigarettes. He offered Abigail one, twitching the bright white box. I didn't catch how she reacted – the curly-haired boy was talking to me, and grinning like he'd made a joke. I hadn't heard what he'd said above the music, but I laughed anyway.

He leaned closer. 'Do you want to then?'

'What?'

Curly Hair held up the helmet. 'Ride the bike.'

Right then, it seemed so obvious to say yes. What else was it but the next part of our adventure, after the dodgems, the candy floss, the whirl of the space catapult? 'Abigail?' I said. 'You want to – go see the bike?'

In the crowd, someone bumped her as they came pushing past. Against the chiming of the slot machines, her voice seemed muffled, hesitant or – something. 'Okay.'

Well, she'd said okay. I gave Curly Hair a wide smile.

I tucked my hand in Abigail's arm, gave a half skip as we weaved between the stalls, out to the fields beyond the fairground. The sky was liquorice-coloured, the sun had nearly set. Curly Hair had parked his bike at the edge of the fields and crouched down now to unlock the chain. He swung a leg over the saddle in an easy movement, his hips tilting as he settled himself astride. 'All right then,' he said. 'Who's first?'

I don't think till that moment I'd really intended to get on. I hadn't stopped to picture this. But now I thought, what harm can it do? It was only another ride, another way of having fun, hardly different from the ones we'd paid for. And what had we come here for, but to have fun?

'Jess—' said Abigail. But before I could change my mind, I hitched myself onto the saddle behind him, my jeans squeaking on the hot leather. Out of the gloom came the spark of a lighter, Abigail leaning away as Spiky Hair offered to light her cigarette. Curly Hair gunned the engine, making me shriek. I shouted out to Abigail, but the racket of the engine ate up my voice. I gave her a wave instead, grasping his shoulder as we jerked away.

He didn't go very far or fast, but it was still the most fun I'd had in ages. I squeezed my arms around his waist, squeezed with my legs too, taking in deep breaths of his smell. Is this what I'd been keeping back from? Well, no one could say I was holding back now. Not Lena, not Tom, not anyone. I tipped my head back, sent a shout up to the sky.

After just a couple of minutes, we coasted back to them. In the little light that still glowed in the sky I could make out their figures, shadowy, and the dancing point of a cigarette. Closer now came a spark of lightning and after a period I couldn't measure, the growl of thunder. Something wet on my forehead. The first spatter of rain.

I climbed off the bike, legs a bit shaky, the insides of my thighs feeling a bit bruised. I couldn't stop smiling though. 'You want a turn?' I said to Abigail. 'Have a go, honestly, it's brilliant.' I wanted her to ride the bike. I wanted for us both to have done it. Matching, breath for breath. Curly Hair wiped his tongue along his lip, his mouth turned up in a crooked-looking smile.

Abigail dropped her unsmoked cigarette into the mud. 'I don't think so.'

My heart dropped. I'd so wanted both of us to have had

this fun. We'd always, always done everything together. 'You just have to hold on tight,' I told her. 'Trust me, once you're on, you'll love it.

'You just have to hold on,' Curly Hair said, like mimicking me. Spiky Hair's expression was impatient, almost a sneer. The rain was coming down harder now. Abigail stood there, her hair darkening in the wet and I felt something grow hollow in my stomach. I wanted to say now, *but don't if you don't want to*, but already she was lifting her leg over the seat. Her face in the darkness was so grim, so set. Curly Hair twisted round sharply to look at her. 'I said, hold *on*.'

She closed her arms around his waist. With her cheek flattened against his back, I couldn't see her expression. Curly Hair gunned the engine and yelled out something I couldn't hear. As the bike went ripping away across the field I thought I saw him put his hand on her thigh.

Then Spiky Hair and I just stood there. We were a long way from the fairground and you could hardly hear the music any more through the rain. The sound of the bike had faded too. They'd ridden so much faster and further than I had. I looked at Spiky Hair, close up now. I'd thought the two of them weren't much older than us – seventeen, eighteen maybe. But now I could see he was much older than that. Both of them were so much older than us. He tilted his head back and blew smoke at the sky. 'You'd better hope she enjoys herself,' he said.

It was a long, long time before they came back. At last, I could hear the bike's roar and smell the petrol hot in the air. I rushed up to meet them as the motorcycle veered sideways, the back wheel skidding so the bike tilted and wobbled. Curly

Hair gave a laughing whoop and Abigail came sliding off in a graceful slow motion as Curly Hair skidded away in a show-boating circle.

In the warm rain, my cousin's shoulders shook with hiccups, that way she laughed and the effort to catch her breath. I landed on my knees beside her, giddy with relief and laughter too.

But when I reached out for her, she knocked my hand away, pushing herself up to her feet.

'Abigail!'

She was haring away and I stumbled after her, the rain falling in great strips now, so I could hardly see. When I caught her up, managed to grab her, she whirled round. I saw her hand come up, a white flash, and felt the explosion of pain as she drove a stinging slap across my cheek.

I tasted the iron of blood in my mouth. 'What's wrong?' I was in shock.

Her words almost disappeared in a crash of thunder, just her mouth moving and her face contorted in the dark.

'You think I wanted to get on a bike with *him*?' Behind us I could see the boys – the men – grinning, scornful. 'We don't know them, they're complete strangers!'

'So why didn't you say anything? You should have *said* you didn't want to go on!'

'Really, Jess? And you would have listened? You don't see it, do you, you've no idea. It's all just playing games to you. We're not eight anymore, we're not eight. But you've been safe, haven't you, your whole life, how could you ever imagine anything different? How could you ever know what it's like to be in danger?'

For a moment I couldn't move, only stand like a statue as

the thick rain battered down on us. It was true, everything she said was true. How could I possibly have done that to her? How could I have been so naive, so blind?

She sank to a crouch, like I'd punched her in the stomach. 'You act as if I mean everything to you, but you've really no idea, Jess, how I feel.'

They were the most painful words she could have said. I got down on my knees in the soaking mud. I would have lain down there if she'd asked me to.

'Abigail – please! I'm so sorry.' I would have done anything for her, anything in the world. 'I was so stupid, but I promise – I'll never let you down again.'

Chapter 19

ANNE

I stood the wine bottle on the flimsy worktop with a clatter. It was so humid outside the caravan, worse now that Robert had let down the awning sides against the rain. The close air was like someone breathing down my neck and I was glad I'd been given a reason to duck inside.

I wiped my arm across my forehead. The rain drumming on the roof sounded like an avalanche, hard pebbles hurled from above. I fumbled with the bottle opener, trying to lever out the cork. It was a fancy wine that Lillian and Fraser had brought but the wooden cork had swollen in the humidity and my hands were too damp in the heat. The opener slipped as I twisted it and the cork flaked.

I didn't want to go back outside where Robert and Fraser and my sister were all waiting. We were all here on a family holiday, and wasn't this everything I had wanted, yet I felt caught between two parts of myself: one part in here, on my own and uncertain; the other part who was supposed to be out there pouring wine, pretending I was as together as Lillian.

I thought I'd found a steady place with Abigail; when we'd painted her room, something had seemed to resolve. But now again, I felt things crumbling, splitting. I pushed the corkscrew in again, twisting it deeper into the crumbling wood. Inside, the dark wine looked almost black. Four glasses, one each; if we didn't finish it, Lillian would say it wasn't worth keeping. But I didn't like the taste, I honestly never had. Even the smell of it caught at my throat.

In my pocket, my mobile blipped, another voicemail alert, another message like the others I'd deleted without listening. Or after only listening to half, words that didn't even make sense: *Please call me, listen, he seems so familiar …*

I could feel myself so pulled in both directions, drawn to the past but so frightened of it too. It felt sometimes as though I had been split right down the middle, never having dealt with the mistakes of long ago, only burying them somewhere and sealing it over, trying to become a new person entirely. I had drawn a line and now was trapped on one side, except when something couldn't help breaking through.

My phone buzzed again, ringing, needing me, and I was right on the verge of answering this time when I saw them coming back across the fields. Abigail and Jess, black against the sunset sky, picked out by the low lamps of the campsite. They were walking shoulder to shoulder, so close I could hardly tell them apart. Jess and Abigail. They were safe, they were happy, they were coming home. With the relief came the strangest clarity and I seemed to know, quite clearly, what I had to do.

The sky was ink-black now, barely a few streaks of light on the horizon where the storm hadn't yet reached. I pulled the flaking cork free and threw it, useless, away in the bin.

For a moment, the two girls disappeared from view, winding their way between another row of caravans. In those stolen few seconds, to the number of the last missed call, I wrote one message, as simple as I could: I'm sorry. I can't. Please leave us alone.

Chapter 20

JESS

After the trip, back at the Whites' house, Abigail and I went to sleep together and woke up together, just like before. The sun rose each day, slipping across the rose-pink walls of her bedroom. I'd wake first and lie listening to her breathing, the heat of the bedroom like a cocoon. In the mornings, we'd go out and sunbathe – beach towels, sunglasses, iced glasses of juice.

In the late afternoons though, my cousin would ask to spend time alone. I'd see it happening, soon learned to spot the point when she would ask to be excused. It was like something gradually fizzled out in her and a look of blankness would appear. 'Go on then,' Auntie Anne would say. 'Up you go.' I'd watch her climb the familiar stairs, her hand sliding step by step up the banister.

Once, I crept upstairs after her, pretending I was only taking clean towels up for Auntie Anne. From the landing I could see into her room – she'd left her door just a little bit ajar. I'd expected her to be napping, lying in bed but she wasn't. She was at her desk, hunched over, writing something. I must have made a noise, creaked a floorboard because she turned round. When she saw me standing there, she got up off the bed, crossed the room until she was right there in front of me. Then she shut the door, right in my face.

Had something shifted since that night at the fair? I knew I had hurt her, that I'd let her down, but I refused to believe that that changed things forever. I just had to wait, be patient, till it came right. Till then, I'd be there for her, same as always. And I would never make that same mistake again.

In the evenings, anyway, she'd be up and about again. We'd sit watching TV, my legs stretched out across her lap, while the twins played some noisy card game on the floor. She liked comedy programmes, PG films. She didn't like shows with swear words, sad endings or fights. While the TV flickered, I'd watch my aunt and uncle in the kitchen, one washing the pots, one drying. Each time Auntie Anne handed a pan over, holding onto it a second too long, it was like she had words she wanted to hand over too. But nine times out of ten, she never said anything, and otherwise the words were only about everyday things: packed lunches, trips to the park, the Asda shopping list. Sometimes, when I watched them together, their little gestures of kindness, I'd hear fragments of my parents' voices echoing in my head:

– *Robert blames himself, can't you see that?*

– *And so should we blame Anne instead? For a mistake, just a stupid mistake ...*

– *We can't keep doing this, Lillian, we can't ... I'm telling you, we have to say something.*

– *And I mean it, Fraser, don't you dare.*

An argument – from now or from long ago? I couldn't tell,

I just tuned it out. Instead, I'd persuade Abigail to join in with the twins. We'd play their card game, hand after hand, and I was always careful to make sure she never lost. Once the kitchen was clear, my aunt and uncle would come and join us, Uncle Robert putting his big feet up on the sofa. Everything felt totally normal then, and come bedtime, it would be just me and Abigail once more. Old playmates, sleeping side by side.

One night I dreamed we were playing *Do-you-trust-me?* We had jumped, thrown ourselves, leaped into thin air. Abigail was tumbling, falling, her back to me, hair covering her face. But I was there, falling with her. I was there, and I reached out and caught her. I knew then – when I landed, woke up – that everything was going to be okay.

Middle Saturday in August, I took Abigail to the cinema. They'd finally opened the new complex in town and I wanted Abigail to come see a film with me.

In the warm summer evening, we could have easily walked to the cinema from the Whites' house, but Mum and Dad insisted on picking us up; they'd decided to watch a film too, some revival of a Seventies classic they wanted to see. 'But we won't get in your way,' said Dad. 'Just pretend like we're not there.'

It wasn't Abigail's first trip to the cinema – I remembered going to the old theatre when we were little – but it was the first since she'd come home. She wore the yellow top, the one I'd tried to get her to wear for the music festival. She'd picked it out for herself this time and she pulled her hair into a low ponytail. It looked nice.

Mum and Dad's film started before ours so they went in first, leaving us alone in the foyer. I took Abigail up to the sweets counter to buy popcorn, two big boxes, one each.

In the theatre, we found seats near the back. I waited for my eyes to adjust to the tall, wide screen, and my ears to the booming sound. 'You okay?' I whispered to Abigail, and she nodded. Her face was softened, relaxed. She was okay. We were okay. As the lights dimmed, I felt myself sink down into my seat. I loved the cinema, its cosy, enveloping feel. You could shut out everything in here, surrounded by the pictures and sounds. My blood grew warm. Abigail wriggled in her seat, her shoulder coming to rest against mine.

When the film ended we came out, ears ringing, blinking into the bright lights of the foyer. I was light-headed from the popcorn, the darkness and the heat. The foyer had a strange atmosphere. People stood in clumps, their faces serious. And where were my parents? Their film had finished half an hour ago. I stretched on my tiptoes, scanning. There. I saw him. Dad. He waved, came over.

'Where's Mum?' was the first thing I asked.

'Just outside, getting some fresh air.'

'Has something happened?' The lights felt super-bright.

'It's nothing. Nothing to worry about.'

'What do you mean though?' It was only now that I caught sight of the lights outside – blue, flashing.

Dad scratched his chin. 'There was an elderly lady having breathing problems. They called an ambulance, just as a precaution. Your mum took care of her until it arrived. Her nurse training, you know.'

'What about the lady? Did they make her okay?'

Dad hesitated. 'She's in the best hands.' Maybe not so good then. 'Come on,' he said. 'Let's catch up with your mum.'

The ambulance set off as we came out, its lights going, its siren now too. We found Mum in the car park. The sun was going down, nearing that time when your eyes keep struggling to adjust. The big neon sign on the wall of the cinema was blinking on and off, pasting a pink sheen on everything. People straggled past us, bleary-eyed from the dark, making their groggy ways home.

'What did I tell you?' Mum said, out of nowhere as we came up.

Dad stopped short, so short that Abigail bumped right into him. I knew that tone in Mum's voice. I'd heard it a million times – through walls, up stairs, behind closed doors. 'What did I *tell* you?' she said again.

I saw Dad bristle, glancing at us, his shoulders rising. 'What you always say: don't mention it, don't say anything.'

I realized she must have seen it in our faces. We must have come out looking all grave, not like we'd just tumbled out of a film on a popcorn high.

'So you *were* listening,' said Mum. I felt the blood emptying from my legs, all the warmth from sitting in the cinema beside Abigail.

'We saw the ambulance,' Abigail said.

'Don't,' I tried to say.

'I always listen,' said Dad, his voice more brittle the louder it got. 'But they asked a simple question and I gave them a simple answer.'

'Worrying them and making a drama—' A group of other

193

teenagers wandered past, turning their heads and one of them pointed.

'All I've done is tell them the truth.'

'Yes, and in doing so you've spoiled their whole evening!' Mum's voice went bouncing off the cinema walls, the tarmac, the cars. One of the passing girls snapped her gum, watching us like we were some kind of freak show. *This* is spoiling it, I wanted to shout. The two of you yelling at each other in front of everyone! About nothing, about some stupid, tiny thing!

'The girls could tell,' said Dad. 'It was obvious to them that something had happened. Do you think if you don't mention things, they don't exist? It doesn't work like that, Lillian, it never has!'

I wanted the ground to swallow me up. I felt exactly like that. An argument escalating out of nowhere, both of them acting so out of control. My parents argued, I knew that, but always in private, so I could pretend not to hear. Never in front of me. Never, *ever* like this out in public. I was so angry I wanted to cry, but it was Abigail's expression that I could hardly bring myself to look at: her face like a ghoul's every time the neon flashed. What must she be thinking – finding herself in the middle of this, these adults, her own aunt and uncle, so angry with each other?

Perhaps it was Abigail that brought them back to themselves. Mum blinked, looked at my cousin, shook her head. 'I'm sorry,' she said. Her smile looked like it hurt to make. 'Just ignore us. Both of you, please just ignore us.'

Dad was still breathing quickly. I wanted to shake him. Shouting like that in a car park at Mum. It was horrible, like a bad dream. In that moment, he hardly seemed like Dad at all.

'Come on,' Mum said, her voice the only thing still working it seemed. 'I think we all need to get some food.'

After dinner in the burger house up the road – a stifled, stupid affair – Mum and Dad dropped me and Abigail off at my aunt and uncle's house. I could hardly manage to say goodbye to them. I could hardly look at them. I just wanted them to go.

Auntie Anne welcomed me and Abigail inside. She smiled at us, but then her face dropped. She could tell something had happened. I didn't say anything, just said we were tired. Let Mum explain it to her, I thought.

'I'm sorry,' I said to Abigail as we brushed our teeth before bed. 'I'm sorry if they upset you. I've no idea why they were acting like that.' We were a family. That was supposed to be the glue that held us together.

Abigail spat a blob of toothpaste into the sink, the whitening toothpaste she always used. My own mouth was stinging, raw from Listerine.

'It's fine,' she said.

But it wasn't. Because now the glue was twisting, breaking; cracks were showing and I didn't know why.

Or – I thought I didn't.

Abigail straightened up and wiped her mouth with the back of her hand.

I swallowed. 'It wasn't about you,' I said.

Chapter 21

Sunday 18th August:
Day 84

ANNE

My sister called first thing the next morning. I think she wanted to apologize for what had happened at the cinema, although with Lillian it was never really an apology because that would mean admitting she'd done wrong.

'Everything's fine, really,' she told me over the phone. 'It's just that sometimes Fraser and I clash.' She gave a short laugh. 'Neither of us are perfect. But trust me, everything's fine.'

I don't know what else I'd expected her to say.

'Anyway,' she went on, 'have they set a date for the trial?'

'Yes,' I told her. 'September the twenty-third.'

'The twenty-third? So close to Abigail's birthday?'

'I know. But it isn't as though we have a choice. There's something else though.'

'What?'

I hesitated.

'Annie, what is it?'

With her question, I felt the full weight of concern on my shoulders, a weight I had been trying to ignore for weeks. I should have told Lillian earlier and asked for her help before now. 'It's all going to play out differently. Because of Mrs Dillon.'

'Mrs Dillon?' Lillian took a moment to place the name. 'Tonia's mother? The other little girl? Why – what's she done?'

I told her everything, all in a rush, and explained what DS McCarthy had told us. There'd been a case conference. Tonia's mother was refusing to testify. She'd told police she wanted the charges relating to Tonia dropped and had signed a statement saying so. She was no longer speaking with police and the neighbour witness now wasn't talking either. *No comment* was all either of them would say.

'She doesn't want Tonia associated with Abigail.'

'"Associated with Abigail"?' said Lillian.

'She means, with the Abigail White case.'

Abigail White. Mrs Dillon would have known the name. She would have remembered the campaigns Robert waged, week after week, and then every month, every year. I understood the horror she would have felt when the full story came to light. So much worse than she could have imagined.

'But why?' said Lillian.

'She has her reasons,' I said slowly. 'She's going through a custody battle. There are accusations of neglect. She's worried a trial like this will only make her look worse.' I thought of the photograph I'd seen, a paparazzi shot, stuck up on a website. In it you couldn't see Tonia's face, only her small form, backwards-facing to the camera, Mrs Dillon pushing through a crowd of journalists with Tonia's legs wrapped round her waist. Her expression is hard and focused, her mouth a straight line. She's holding a hand up, palm out, to the camera – a stop sign, keeping everyone at bay.

In the silence on the line that followed, I could sense my sister gathering her thoughts. 'So the whole trial will be focused on Abigail now? She won't be just a corroborating witness?'

'Yes.' I stayed silent, waiting for the meaning of it to sink in. I waited for Lillian to ask the next question. 'And what about you then? Will they call you to testify?'

'They haven't yet.'

'But they might?'

'Yes.'

'And if they *do*, Annie – will you tell them what happened?'

'I—'

'Even though it won't make a difference? Even though it can't possibly help?'

'Lillian … I honestly don't know.'

After telling Lillian, I stopped talking about the court case. What mattered was that he was going on trial. DS McCarthy and his colleagues had done their job and now it would rest in the hands of a jury. They had my further statement, that form I had signed, legally attesting: *I don't know this man.* There was nothing more my testimony could add, nothing that would help the case and nothing – Lillian had assured me – that would change the outcome anyway.

So when three days later the phone rang, and Robert picked it up and I read at once from the look on his face that it was DS McCarthy, I thought he was only calling to say everything was on track. Even when he told us we had to come to the police station, it didn't cross my mind that anything was wrong.

We left Abigail at home with Jess and the twins, playing

another complicated card game. DS McCarthy had said he'd only need us for half an hour at most. At the station, he was waiting for us at the front desk and it was only when I saw the hardness in his eyes, that same hardness that had been there from the start, that I felt the flicker of unease in my stomach.

The room he led us to was hot and close – no windows. I hadn't been in this one before. There were no files, no papers, nothing on the table, only two chairs laid out – waiting for us. We both sat down.

'What's this about?' said Robert. He sat on the edge of his chair, as though ready to get up again at any moment.

DS McCarthy's grey gaze fell on us both. 'Something is bothering me. Something in my mind still isn't adding up. I want you both to listen very carefully to this, then afterwards tell me if there's anything I should know.'

My heart slipped in my chest. 'Anything, like what?'

And Robert said: 'Listen to what?'

But the detective didn't answer, just clicked a button on the tape player and I jumped at the sudden creak of static. A hum, a hiss, then disembodied voices burst into the room, two men talking, questions and answers. He didn't explain anything, he didn't ask for our consent and I realized something about this was all wrong; this was something underhand and unofficial. As the noise filled the room, DS McCarthy leaned back in his seat, as though the sounds were nothing to do with him.

And your hours of work?

Mondays to Fridays, 6 a.m. to 10 a.m., and 3 p.m. to 6.

Only? So on this particular Saturday, you weren't working?

No.

It was like a radio play, the voices back and forth, a strange, meaningless conversation. 'What is this?' said Robert. 'What are we supposed to be hearing?'

'Keep listening,' said DS McCarthy. 'You'll see.'

What were you doing instead that day, at – say – four in the afternoon?

I was at home.

At home? Are you sure?

Or maybe I went out driving.

Which is it? Home or driving. At 4 p.m.

I froze.

I was out driving.

Uh-huh. And while on this drive, you met a little girl.

I curled my hands around the underside of my chair, letting the metal dig into my palms, the sting an anchor as the dizziness rose up.

She was playing outside. We got talking. She wanted some of my sweets. It was drizzling. Her coat didn't have a hood.

You got chatting, gave her a sweet; it was wet, you thought she was underdressed.

I knew what this was. 'The interview.' My voice was barely above a whisper. 'This is his police interview.'

'That's right.'

'But you can't play us this,' said Robert. 'It isn't legal to play us this.'

DS McCarthy's voice was steely. 'Please just keep listening.'

Then what?

I said she could come and get dry in my car... so we did that. But she wasn't really drying. The heater only really works when the car's going. So we drove around a bit.

You drove off with Tonia. With no one's permission.

Tonia, Tonia, everything about Tonia. I couldn't understand why the detective was doing this. What was it he thought we could possibly know? The recording hissed on.

All right. What then?

We drove round the block. But she'd got too wet. So I took her to my house. So that she could put her clothes on my radiators.

You could have taken her back home. To her home.

I told you. It was raining. She'd have been back in the garden, outside, getting wet all over again.

All right. You drove her to... 15 Martins Road, your own address? How did Tonia seem then?

I don't know. The cold was making her cry. She hadn't liked the car. She'd stopped talking to me by then.

You don't think she might have been scared, that maybe she wanted to go home, that she wanted her mummy?

'We don't want to hear this,' said Robert. But neither of us moved.

There was nothing for her to be scared of. I made sure she had her seatbelt on. And her mum had put her outside in the cold and wet. She was better off with me, at my house. I kept her indoors.

For two nights.

I was waiting for the weather to pick up.

Uh-huh. But she tried to get out, didn't she? There was a struggle.

I don't remember that.

She has bruises.

I covered my eyes with my hands, trying to block out the images his words conjured up.

'Keep listening, please.'

I don't remember.

Fine. Let's skip forwards a couple of days. Why did you run off and hide when you discovered Tonia gone from your house? Why didn't you go out looking for her?

Because I'd realized what had happened. Because I realized Abi was gone too.

I let go of the chair. My hands had gone limp at the sound of her name.

So what did you think had happened?

I didn't think, I knew. She's such a good girl, Abi. She found a twenty-pound note once, one of the rare times I took her outside. It was just lying there on the pavement. She told me we should hand it in to the police. To the police – twenty pounds! Who taught her that? But that's the way she thinks. So I knew that's what she'd done with Tonia. Gone to hand her in.

Robert would have taught her that, good citizenship, a tiny instruction that in the end had saved her. But I was struggling to breathe. 'Turn this off,' but I was speaking the words down into the table; I couldn't seem to look up at the detective.

'Not yet.'

And Abi ... Abigail is your... daughter? Niece?

Not exactly.

Then what exactly is your relationship with her?

You can say, I take care of her. In a way I've been watching over her, caring for her, her whole life.

His voice was so bizarrely unconcerned, dreamy, it made the hairs on my neck stand up.

Oh yes?

When she came to me, it was like a miracle. At the station steps, I'd thought that was it. I was simply wandering outside in the rain and then suddenly, out of nowhere, there she was. Well, after that, I gave her everything. I played with her, read to her, I made her a room just like her own...

And Abigail's family? What about them?

Her family? Do you know, I think her own family meant for me to have her.

'Stop the tape.' I should get out of this room right now, I thought. 'Stop the tape!'

A button clicked. The sound cut off. The room echoed with the silence. When I eventually raised my head, those grey eyes of DS McCarthy's were boring straight into mine and I couldn't look away because if I did, what he would read into that?

'You told us that you didn't know him.'

I shook my head. *No no no.* 'We didn't, we don't. Even Casssingham didn't say otherwise, did he? On the tape, that isn't what he claims.'

'So why does he say it? That you meant for him to have her? That he made her a room just like her own?'

'We don't know. *We don't know.* We've told you we don't know who Cassingham is.' Robert took my hand in his. 'You shouldn't have done this. You had no right making us listen.'

My legs weren't my own but I managed to stand. I leaned on Robert and let him lean on me.

DS McCarthy stood up, opening the door for us. We were too shaken and too stunned to argue or challenge him. The detective nodded as we passed, as though he was on our side again, sharing our pain.

'But like I said: if there's anything else.'

Outside we sat in the car park for the longest time. I felt sick; in the van the smell of oil and engine grease turned my stomach in a way it had never done before. Beside me, Robert was white and silent. I tried to read what he was thinking, what he'd made of those sickening words.

'Robert. That man – Cassingham – he was living in a dream, a fantasy. DS McCarthy can't see that, but it's true.'

Robert let out a long exhale. I had to show him that it wasn't about us, that DS McCarthy had this all wrong. The detective seemed determined to prove we were complicit, that we were hiding something, that our family was to blame. But whatever I had done, whatever mistakes I had made, I needed Robert to know it was never like that.

I kept thinking of how Robert and I had met: Abigail and I stuck on Steep Hill, her new scooter broken, a stone jammed in the wheel and me loaded with shopping bags from Lincoln's department stores, unable to fix it. A stupid mess we'd got into – who takes a four-year-old on a scooter up Steep Hill? Then Robert appeared, crouching down, unjamming the stone, walking up with us, helping Abigail wheel her scooter to the top. That day, and for so long after, he'd been there for me and Abigail and now, more than ever, I needed him at my side.

'He must have breached all kinds of protocols to do that,' he was saying. 'We should report him. I'm going to report him.'

I was afraid that would only make things worse though. I tried my very best to steady myself and for once be the one to stabilize our world. 'I think I know why he did it,' I said.

'I never told you before, but I think it explains why he's so suspicious of us.'

I leaned my head back against the rough covering of the passenger seat. 'There was another case he worked on in Leicestershire. A boy went missing from his grandparents' house. People had seen a man in the area, hanging about in all the wrong places. DS McCarthy wasn't convinced.'

'DS McCarthy was involved?'

'Yes. It was a few years ago.' I had pieced together the scenario by reading the statements the Leicestershire force had released, the forum threads, the blogs.

'Well, so what happened?'

'They arrested the strange man and spent days questioning him. All that time, DS McCarthy suspected someone else. He suspected someone within the family. When they found the child, it proved he'd been right.'

'The grandparents?' said Robert.

I nodded. 'Grandmother. But by the time they found him, the little boy was dead.'

Chapter 22

Wednesday 21st August:
Day 87

JESS

When they came home, Uncle Robert got tea ready in silence. I heard the shower running for ages upstairs. When Auntie Anne came back down, her make-up was washed off and her whole face looked bare and defenceless. Abigail and I had planned to stay up with a movie that night, but in the end we all went to bed early.

I didn't hear her go back downstairs, even though she must have passed our bedroom door. And it was only because of the heat that Abigail and I slept with the window open and I caught the smell of smoke. I mistook it for cigarettes at first – I pictured my cousin smoking. But she was there, asleep, next to me. The fire was outside.

She had been careful, my aunt. She'd set up a space on the decking and she was using the barbecue grill – the one that had stood there since the caravan holiday, still waiting to be cleaned. The flames didn't burn so high and the crackle and pop was strangely comforting. For a while, I watched her from the bedroom window, half mesmerized.

When I went downstairs, I felt the current of night air that streamed through the ground floor. The glass double doors of the living room stood open onto the back patio. The thin white curtains billowed, curling back on themselves in the cooling breeze. Inside, the living room glowed blue. On the low table in the middle of the room, my aunt's laptop lay open, lit up like a ghost. The blue-white glow of the screen, the fire outside – like the moon and the sun, circling together through the night.

The smell of smoke was stronger now, and through the shifting gaps in the curtains I could see the low flames, orange and gold. My aunt stood with a heavy box-file cradled in her arms, in her pink quilted dressing gown, the one I always associated with her. One by one, she pulled papers from the file and laid them on the little fire. I recognized the box-file, recognized those pages. They were all the cards and letters my aunt and uncle had received over the years. So many condolences, so many offers of support. So many reminders that Abigail was missing. It was like my aunt was letting go of them now, one by one.

Against wisps of the grey-smelling smoke, the open laptop shone up at me, quietly beckoning. I don't remember walking forwards, I don't remember sitting down in front of it. But I must have done, because I remember the screen right in front of me, glowing large.

The screen showed an email account – my aunt's – and an email. Written to fraserbrady1974@gmail.com. To my dad.

An email. And a quiet little box, blocking the words, asking, **Delete draft or continue?**

Ahead, through the curtains, my aunt went on placing sheets

of paper into the fire, without turning, without seeing me. Snowflakes of ash spiralled up into the air. I watched my aunt watching them, her back to me. My hand reached forward and pressed on the mouse pad. I clicked on the message box, pulling it to one side. I held it there, the tip of my finger turning white. Text filled the preview pane.

Fraser, I don't know who else to turn to. I've tried to speak to Lillian but she doesn't understand or doesn't want to hear. But you've always believed in facing the truth, and you know as much as Lillian does what happened. It was just one moment, one stupid moment on that train, but now every time I look at her, I'm more convinced than ever that it matters. She seems so angry, Fraser, and I don't think it's just about what he did, is it? All along it wasn't just about him. It's about us, her family and what I did.

Fraser – I know you believe that too …

Something in the fire outside crackled and snapped. I let go. The text box sprang back to the middle of the screen, covering the text. The file in my aunt's arms was empty now. She must have caught my movement as I stood up, seen my outline as I ducked out of the room.

'Jess?'

But before she could be sure, I was gone.

All the next day, I must have seemed so distracted. Whenever Auntie Anne asked me anything, I kept answering 'What?' and then she would look at me with a strange look on her face. I didn't know what to do. From the bedroom window, there was no sign of the barbecue, no ashes, just the sun-dried decking and thin brownish grass. If I'd wanted to, I could have pretended even to myself that it was nothing but a dream.

Instead, in the afternoon, when Auntie Anne had taken the twins to the play park and Abigail was curled in her bed, asleep, I took a scrap of paper from my cousin's desk and wrote a note. Then I quietly let myself out.

It took me half an hour to walk there – Dad's practice was on the outskirts of town. It was hot, the sun pulsing. The hottest it had been all summer, it felt. A familiar figure was coming out as I reached the entrance, pretty smile and brisk gestures as she dug out her sunglasses, squinting in the glare. Shelley, the receptionist. 'Hi there. He's nearly done for the day,' she said. 'You can wait for him upstairs if you like.'

I climbed the steep flight as the door banged shut behind her. Upstairs, the waiting room was empty, only a clunky fan whirring in the corner. I sat down in Shelley's swivel chair and stared at the box of stickers that she kept on the desk to dole out to the kids that wriggled and squealed when my dad poked their gums. Dad always said he found that the hardest part of his job. You can't explain to them, he'd say, that you're not a bad man. The stickers though, Shelley would say, made up for a lot.

At last, the door to the consulting room opened and out he came, dressed in his normal clothes, no smock or mask, just Dad. His eyebrows jumped when he saw me. 'Jess – what are you doing here?'

He looked so tired, so care-worn. I hadn't seen him since that night at the cinema. I felt my shoulders drop, all bark and no bite. 'I'm OK. I just need to talk to you.'

He looked at me, his face serious. 'All right, come on then. I'll need to lock up here, but come down with me to the car.'

I waited while he set the alarms and turned the keys in the inner and outer doors. We headed down to the car park together. When we got into the car, it was like a sauna. I clambered into the passenger side, but I didn't put my seatbelt on and when Dad got in, he didn't start the engine. We sat there, doors closed, windows up, in the heat.

'We've been missing you, Munchkin. The house feels kind of strange without you.'

I didn't say anything to that.

'Go on then,' said Dad. 'What is it?'

But I hardly knew where to start. It was all so confused: what I knew and what I didn't. What I had witnessed and what I was never supposed to have seen. 'I've heard you arguing. You and Mum ...' I tried to put my words together, speak about these things I'd blocked out for so long. 'And Mum and Auntie Anne, too.'

Dad pressed his palms to the steering wheel. His hands looked swollen from the heat and I could see where his wedding ring made a dent in his finger. 'Grown-ups argue, Jess. They just do.'

'I know but—' It wasn't just that. 'There's something – something happened, didn't it? Back then, before, to do with Abigail. I found something – a message.' My throat closed up, like it wouldn't let me go on. I wanted to know and at the same time I so didn't.

'A message?' Dad's voice was confused. So my aunt never sent it. I pushed myself to name my worst fears, the worst thing I could think of.

'Was it an affair? Was that it? You and Auntie Anne, or Mum and—?' My words were coming out now in a rush. 'I'm old enough, you know. You can tell me.' Surely it had to be better to know.

'An affair?' Dad gave a laugh that sounded like a bark. He leaned forward and turned the key in the ignition. The windscreen wipers made a sudden leap across the dry glass. 'No, Jess. It was never anything like that.'

'What then?' My voice was high. 'What is it? I know there's something nobody's telling me.'

Dad stilled the wipers and gripped the steering wheel, hard and tight. I noticed suddenly the smudged circles under his eyes, the deeper lines across his forehead. He didn't answer. And at that my chest went very, very tight.

'Why can't you talk to me?' I said, my voice a small whisper. It had never been like this with Dad. He was the one always prepared to tell me everything. Always so *keen* to tell me everything.

Dad's voice was muffled. 'Because I agreed. Because I promised. Jess, please would you let it alone?'

I stared at him. I felt so hollow, so helpless. Before he could say anything else, I reached out and pushed open the passenger door.

'Jess—' Dad's hand pressed my arm. I stopped, one foot already touching the hot ground. 'You're right, you really are. We should be able to talk about this. But not yet, will you give me some time? I'm sorry about the arguments. Sorry we've upset you. But I'll speak to her, I will. I'll sort this out.'

I turned back. 'Speak to who? To Auntie Anne?'

A strange expression crossed Dad's face. 'No,' he replied slowly. 'To your mum. It's only ever been her—' He broke off, passed a hand across his eyes. 'Look, I will. About – everything. I'll sort it.'

I wanted to believe him, wanted to stop worrying and trust that he would fix this, whatever it was, the way once upon a time he'd fixed my jumbled smile. *Can you though?* I thought. *Can you?* And a picture flashed through my mind – a memory. Sitting at the kitchen table, knife and fork clutched in my eight-year-old hands. Mum lifting the telephone out of Dad's grasp, Auntie Anne hysterical on the other end. Dad stepping aside. Saying nothing. Doing nothing. Turning away.

The sun was scorching my arm and leg as I balanced there, half in, half out of the car. Dad's hand on my arm felt so heavy, yet strangely frail, like all the grip had gone out of him.

I got out of the car. I was going back to Abigail's. And despite the heat, I ran the whole way.

Four days later, I hugged Abigail goodbye. My bag was packed: my clothes, toothbrush, hairbrush, everything. We'd arranged this with my parents weeks ago. I was to return home this Monday evening, a week before school restarted.

'You'll be all right, won't you?' I said to Abigail. 'You'll be okay?' These last few weeks together had remained full of sunshine – warm, lazy sunny mornings. But that shadow was still there across our relationship. Like a faint dark shape in the corner of your eye.

'It's fine,' she said.

Was it though? Was it really? Me leaving her like this.

'You can text me, call me whenever.' I held her hands tight and was sure I felt her squeeze my hands back. 'And it's hardly any time till we'll be together at school.'

Outside, Uncle Robert loaded my bags into the back of his van, then I clambered up into the high passenger seat beside him. I waved at them through the smudgy window: Auntie Anne, the twins, and Abigail.

'Got your seatbelt on?'

I nodded. As my uncle pulled away, I rested my head back in the seat, suddenly exhausted. I was glad of his solid presence beside me as we drove. It was only with him, I realized, that I didn't feel the sense of undercurrent. There was a straightforwardness to him that I drank in like water.

'Uncle Robert?'

'Yes?'

'It's going to be OK, isn't it? School and the trial and everything after?'

'Yes, Jess,' he said and his voice was so steady. 'Eventually, it will.'

We pulled up outside and Uncle Robert helped me carry my bags up the path. The house seemed strangely dark – no lights, and when we got to the front door, it was locked.

'They must both be out,' I said, digging for my spare key at the bottom of my bag, trying not to show the dragging shock in my chest. 'They must have just forgotten. Dad has an evening clinic on a Monday and Mum is probably out at the gym. I should have called. I should have reminded them.'

Uncle Robert stood on the step, uncertain. 'Do you want me to come in, keep you company till they're home?'

I shook my head. 'No, it's fine. I'll text them now. I'm sure they definitely won't be long.' I was pretending to him, shrugging it off, but standing there in front of the dark, empty house I couldn't help thinking – what if it had been me? What if I'd been the one to go missing? Would I have come home and found myself forgotten, like this?

'All right then. If you're sure.' Uncle Robert squeezed my shoulder. 'Let us know if they're not back soon. And thanks again for all you've done for Abigail. I've seen how she is with you. You're patient with her and I know that helps.'

I looked up at him. 'Do you think?'

He smiled back. 'I know it.' Those three words meant everything to me.

I watched the tail-lights of his van disappear, then closed the front door quietly behind me. The house felt so hollow, as if these past few weeks no one had been living here at all. I turned the lights on in the sitting room and kitchen and stairs.

In the kitchen, a yellow Post-it note was stuck to the work-top by the sink, printed with Mum's neat capitals, left there for Dad.

There's lasagne in the fridge. Back 9.30 approx.
L.

Her initial was thick where she'd gone back and forth over it with the biro, its lines heavy, its corner sharp. Underneath, in small letters like an afterthought, she'd added *PTO*. I peeled the paper square off the worktop and turned it over.

The bathroom tap is working now, thank you.

I stared at those words. It was like a note between passing flat mates, distant colleagues. The Post-it sat there, its edges curling up. I pressed my hand down on top of it, flattening it out as if I could push it right into the wood.

I shouldered my bag and climbed the stairs, homesick even though I was home. From the landing, my parents' door stood ajar and I could see into their bedroom, just enough to make out in the gloom the ruck of covers at the end of the bed. Opposite, our spare room door was a little way open too. On some strange instinct, I pushed the door wide. Inside, the bed was rumpled, the covers turned back. One of Mum's work blouses hung from the wardrobe door and a pair of tights dangled over the back of a chair.

She was sleeping in there; it was clear as day. It felt like the floor was caving in under me.

While I had been living entangled with Abigail, my parents' marriage had fallen apart.

Chapter 23

ANNE

Three weeks before the trial, we took the train from Lincolnshire down to London. We were going to visit the courthouse, meet a woman from the Witness Support Service, all steps in preparing Abigail. On the direct train, only an hour, I watched as my daughter leaned her head against the window, letting it rattle against the glass. It amazed me that she could do that and not mind the juddering against her temple. But then I was learning that there were things that didn't affect Abigail in the way I'd expected, and other things – things we couldn't always predict – that did. Robert sat next to her, in the aisle seat, and I sat opposite them both. While Abigail stared out into the cloud-heaped sky, Robert and I found ourselves looking at each other.

For both of us, this journey felt like a test, forcing us to return to where everything once went so wrong. Abigail sat with us, but the ghosts of the past sat with us too. She had been worse since Jess left, I could say that for sure. She had withdrawn into herself again, like now, sitting with her head turned away. I had so often envied that bond of theirs that no one else could penetrate. I was Abigail's mother, but when my daughter came home, it hadn't been me that she turned to. There could have been a thousand reasons why. Or there could have been just one.

I was glad it was the fast train. I don't think I could have managed with the stops: Peterborough, Stevenage. We were running straight to King's Cross, and from there we would take the Tube to Tower Hill, where there was a station walking distance from the courts. Soon our train was rushing through the north of London: Alexandra Palace, Finsbury Park. I stood up to pull our coats down from the rack, and Abigail turned her gaze to follow me. All this that we were doing now was designed to help her. I knew we were asking a lot of her, but what choice did we have? Tonia's case had fallen apart. It was down to Abigail now. Main witness. Main victim. I handed her her jacket and she hugged it to her, like a blanket. She looked as though she wasn't sleeping properly again, or barely sleeping at all; dark circles under her eyes alongside a jitteriness, the energy of adrenaline or caffeine. Now her eyes were closing again and her head tilted back towards the glass pillow of the window.

'Abigail? We're almost there,' I said.

King's Cross wasn't as crowded as I'd expected and I was gratefully relieved at that. I had planned this journey far in advance, finding a way to avoid the Northern Line, because even if the courthouse was right next to London Bridge, how could I ever bear to go back there? We'd take the Circle Line and then, walk across the river from Tower Hill and arrive that way. But this yellow line was running jam-packed and that was enough to get me remembering. No buggy, I had to keep on reminding myself, no hospital and Robert is here. This is not history repeating. Still, that didn't stop me reaching out for Abigail as we pushed our way on board. I wanted to take hold of her, grip her tight but she slipped her hand away from my grasp, reaching up instead for the yellow pole above her head.

We rode through one tunnel after another and I watched Robert's eyes, scanning every platform. He was getting it, I knew: the needles of *what if, what if.* He was looking for her: a blonde-haired, bewildered eight-year-old girl, and he was needling himself: *I should have been there.* He had lifted the weight off me in saying that; slung it heavily onto his own back. Now he kept scanning the platforms, but there was no point because she hadn't stayed on the platform, that was the problem. She had burrowed her way away through the crowds, turning heel, disappearing and I couldn't pretend that I didn't know why.

I made myself reach out and touch Robert's arm. No words, but I was saying, *Not your fault.*

Caroline met us at the entrance to the Crown Court and introduced herself with her Witness Service badge. She smiled at Abigail the way everyone did: sympathetic, admiring, kind.

Because it was a Saturday, the courthouse was empty, all the cases wrapped up for the week. Its hallways and spaces were free for us to view; she would show us the witness waiting rooms first. As we made our way through that sombre building, the feeling crept up on me again. In a matter of weeks, everything would converge in this courthouse. I should have felt glad that he would be put on trial and held accountable for what he had done. Instead, it was a low sickening sensation I felt, beginning as a chill in my hands and a hollowness in my legs.

The witness waiting rooms were non-descript. 'You'll be in here until it's your turn to give evidence,' she told Abigail. My daughter took in the soft chairs, the low coffee table, the efforts made to put victims at ease. 'You shouldn't have to wait too long and straight afterwards, you can leave as soon as the judge agrees.'

The waiting room seemed like a safe place. It would be all right if Abigail was in here.

'And not see him?' she said.

Caroline hesitated. Instead of answering, she beckoned us to follow her. The door of the waiting area closed behind us, shutting us out of that protected space. She led us back along the corridor to the courtrooms. At number three she opened the door wide. 'This might not be the one that your case takes place in; in fact the chances are that it won't, but all the rooms are similar and this is just to give you an idea.'

It was smaller than I'd imagined. Much more intimate. The chill in my hands rose up through my arms.

'He'll be in here?' I said.

'The defendant?' Caroline nodded. 'Or in one just like it.' She leaned towards my daughter, pointing for her sake. 'He'll be in the dock – do you see this area here? The judge will sit here, the jury over there. And people can watch from the gallery here.'

I saw again the tension in Abigail's face. 'Who will be watching?' she asked.

'We will,' I said quickly. 'Me and Robert. We'll be here for everything.'

'And Auntie Lillian and Uncle Fraser?'

'If you want them. We can ask them to come.'

She answered almost before the end of my phrase, her words clipping the heels of mine. 'Yes.'

'There will be reporters too,' said Caroline, 'and members of the public.'

'And Jess.' It was a statement, not a question.

I looked around the courtroom again. Dock, judge, jury, gallery. 'And when Abigail testifies, where will she sit?'

Caroline was taking a leaflet from her bag. 'That's what I wanted to confirm with you now.' She held out the shiny fold of paper. The leaflet explained the special measures – the screen, the TV link, the recorded testimony – all of which were available to Abigail. As Caroline pointed out each one, guiding Abigail along the words with a neat finger, the chill in my arms and legs eased. It wasn't going to be how I'd imagined, her and him pressed together under one roof. We could keep her well away from him.

Abigail had that scraping restlessness again in her fingers, cravings still, at times, for nicotine.

'Yes. Thank you,' I said, speaking over Caroline, indicating the leaflet she held. 'Of course she must have something like that in place.'

Caroline nodded. 'Although ultimately, it remains up to Abigail,' she said as though it wasn't obvious from every element of my daughter's stance what she needed. Abigail took hold of the wooden bench-back in front of her. She was breathing so hard all of a sudden that I was afraid she might faint.

'Abigail?'

'I don't want to do any of it.'

Caroline's face became a well of empathy. She would know, it must happen all the time – a witness overwhelmed; it was what she was here for. Robert stepped forwards to lay an arm around Abigail's shoulders. He let Caroline murmur gently to her, telling her how important her testimony would be, how he might get away with everything he had done without the evidence she could provide. '… And listen. The judge has already agreed to these measures, given these circumstances, and your age and everything. Don't worry, you're going to have all the support you need.'

Before Abigail could say *no* again – and I swear that's what it looked like she was about to say – Robert pulled her close and hugged her. Just like that, straightforward. He could do that for Abigail, ignoring all the complications, all the mess of things in between. He had always been able to overlook all of that, such a straightforward person, my husband. It was one of the greatest reasons I loved him. Abigail let him hold her to him, as she always did, as she so rarely did with me, but this time I could see her fingers, held down against the side of her thighs, plucking a loose thread on the hem of her jeans as though trying to trigger her own escape.

When we got home Abigail said that she didn't want tea. Just a sandwich would be fine. But I knew she needed to eat, and the twins were starving; staying at Lillian's they probably hadn't been allowed any snacks. We were going to sit down, as a family, and eat a proper meal. The boys needed it and whatever she said, so did Abigail. In the beginning, anyone might have said she'd had weight to lose. But not now. Now she was looking far too thin.

I gave them each a packet of crisps to keep them going while I prepared a tray of sausages. We were back to using the oven again, now that the worst of the summer heat was fading. Robert scrubbed potatoes while I prepared broccoli, the one vegetable Sam and Laurie would eat without fuss.

'Do you think she'll manage it?' he said to me at one point, quietly, so that our children wouldn't hear.

I lined the sausages up so that they fitted neatly, perfectly filling the tray. 'She has to.' I washed the oil from my hands.

Sam and Laurie, with their crisps, were excited. At the Bradys', Jess had taught them a card trick and now they wanted to show Abigail. I watched as Laurie dealt out the cards. So often Abigail would push the twins away, as though their playfulness and exuberance was too much for her, as though it antagonized her seeing them that way.

When the cards were laid in their piles and rows, Abigail looked down at the spread and gave a sharp laugh. 'I already know this one,' she said. 'I taught this trick to Jess years ago.' It was cruel of her. She could have pretended, thought of their feelings. As I leaned down to open the oven, I saw Laurie's face fall.

'Never mind,' I said over the clatter of the tray. 'Why don't you play a game instead? Racing Daemon, isn't that your favourite?'

Abigail knew that card game too, she'd learned it when she was little, and now she was older than they were, faster. She played with a grim determination, winning hand after hand until I could see the frustration building in Sam's eyes and the flush building on Laurie's cheeks. Her hardness, this ruthlessness, I knew where it led, I knew how it hurt. When Laurie missed yet another card, I saw Sam raise a fist, as though to punch his brother.

'Sam!' I dropped the serving tongs with a clang. He froze, then lowered his arm. Laurie shoved his brother away.

Abigail scraped her chair back from the table; for a moment I thought she was going to bolt from the room. I stepped forwards, palms raised like a gesture for peace and found the courage to lay my hands on Abigail's shoulders. I felt her still under my touch. 'That's enough, you three,' I said. 'Dinner's ready for you all.'

Robert and I sat up in bed again that night. Abigail wasn't the only one losing sleep. Robert could hug her and ignore the rest; his straightforwardness meant he could pass right over things, cut straight through to what really mattered. But I was so worried about my daughter and so, so frightened of what was wrong.

Robert ran a hand over the shaved dome of his head. 'You can't expect her not to find things difficult. Not to be upset or stressed. This is the worst phase. Let's see how she is once the trial is over.'

That felt like decades away. 'She's supposed to be starting school next week.' We'd been so caught up in preparations for the trial, we'd hardly even talked about that.

'I know.'

I pressed the heels of my hands to my eyes, the headboard hard against my back. 'Have you looked at her, Robert? These last few weeks, have you really *looked* at her?'

I wished I could tell him everything I was afraid of: the fact that my phone was ringing again and wouldn't stop; the way I kept dreaming of DS McCarthy's eyes. Instead, I lay down flat in the bed in the dark, picturing all those lines I had drawn, all those lines Lillian and I had defended. As Robert beside me whispered goodnight, I tried not to think what would be unleashed if they broke.

So that night, again, I dealt with her on my own. Robert had fallen deeply asleep, anchored down in unconsciousness. He didn't wake up at the sound that woke me.

I sat up in the darkness. Robert had engineered it well and the sliding ladder could be unfolded with barely a sound. I heard it though, and I recognized the swish of metal on metal.

I pulled on my dressing gown and made my way out to the landing. The trap-door above me was open; cool air was seeping down, filling the house. She had pulled down the ladder and climbed up into the loft above. She hadn't found the light switch, but she had taken a torch from downstairs; I could see the bouncing light glancing off the walls and beams. I wanted to get back into my bed, climb in beside the reassuring bulk of Robert and pull the warm covers over my head. I didn't want to confront my daughter; I was so endlessly afraid of what might be said.

The rustling sounds above me stopped, as though some sly creature up there had gone still. I kept picturing her, hunkered up there. Then: *stop it*. It's your daughter, I told myself. Go and see what is wrong.

'Abigail?' I whispered. 'I'm coming up.'

The hem of my dressing gown caught on the ladder and I

had to stop halfway up to unhook it. The metal rungs were rough against my bare feet. I never went up here; it was Robert who had clambered up and down this ladder, bringing her belongings down, taking them back up.

She almost blinded me with the torchlight when I reached the top; I don't think she meant to, she was just trying to see. 'It's only me,' I said. 'Can you point the light away?'

She set the torch down on its end so that it made a column of white light to the low beams above. I pulled my feet up the last few steps of the ladder and knelt on all fours. I could feel plywood splinters and flecks of fibreglass under my knees. 'What are you doing up here?'

'My clothes. Aren't they up here?' The way the torch was shining, I couldn't see her face properly, only a white circle with black holes where her features were supposed to be. She was wearing a dark T-shirt, a dark pair of shorts and her white limbs stuck out from them at odd angles; I couldn't tell how she was sitting.

'Your old clothes?' I asked. 'But why do you want those?'

'I need to see – to check… Are they up here or not?'

I couldn't understand what she was after, only sense her agitation and I didn't know what to say, I had no idea what she needed to hear.

'All right,' I said. 'Hang on, let me show you.' I didn't know how else to calm her. I edged my way to the three black bin bags we had stored up here. 'Angle the torch,' I said as I untied the first. I could have switched on the lights, bathed us both in an orange glow, but for this strange task she was set upon, I sensed she needed us to be in the dark. The whole thing felt dream-like as though I'd been swept up in some sleep-walking mission of hers. She was awake though, I was sure. I lifted out a bundle of clothes, grey and white in the dim light, their colours lost to the darkness. Little jumpers, dresses, skirts, no doubt she would recognize them. These were the eight-year-old clothes I had stupidly filled her bedroom with when she first came home.

She yanked at the bag with her free hand, spilling out more items in a slippery avalanche. 'No, not these ones. These are all too big.' She tugged at the second bag, picking at the knot with her blunt fingers.

'Here, let me.' In this sack were her winter clothes: woollen socks, hooded coats, thickened vests. As soon as she saw them, she pushed them away, grabbing for the third bag, the beam of the torch swinging erratically. I drew a breath in through my nose, my lungs itching from the dust we had disturbed. In the third bag – all of her had fitted into just three bags – were her party dresses, crisp, shining things. She pawed through them, then let them slide messily to the floor.

'Where are the rest of them?'

I thought I could hear her teeth chittering, whether from chilliness or agitation I couldn't tell. 'The rest? This is all of them.'

'No! My other clothes, from when I was even smaller. These are all from when I was eight.'

I had to steady myself with my fists pressed to the splintered floor. What was this? Something else entirely. I was so out of my depth – her trauma, her psyche, I could find no way to grasp what she needed.

'I had dungarees, didn't I, red, can't you remember? I had other clothes, you know I did, when I was four, five.'

I'll ask her therapist, I told myself. I can call her first thing tomorrow. For now, I did my best to steady myself – and her – with simple facts. 'Dungarees? Maybe, yes – you could have. You had lots of clothes, honestly so many. But Abigail, ones from that age, you would have outgrown them.'

'So?'

'So … so we would have thrown them away, passed them to neighbours, given them to charity. Abigail, stop a moment. What is this about?'

I saw her withdraw into herself then, curling away from the mess of clothes between us, letting the torch slide from her grip so that its light spread like a staining puddle across the floor.

'*Of course*. Of course you did,' she said, an echo of my own words and there was such a bitterness in her tone. 'But I *saw* it, didn't I? Jess said I imagined it, but I didn't, I couldn't— ' I couldn't make a shred of sense of what she meant, only hear the wrenching in her throat, as though all her walls had suddenly crumbled. Agonized, I reached for her, biting back my own tears. What on earth was I supposed to say, how on earth was I supposed to help her?

'Am I going mad?' she said. 'I'm remembering, and trying to remember, and sometimes I feel I'm just going mad!'

My fingertips finally found hers. I laced our fingers and drew her towards me, like hauling something up from the sea, right up from the deeps, hand over hand. She came slithering into my lap and allowed herself to curl against me. All I wanted to do was hold her; it was all that I could do *to* hold her because there *did* seem something half-crazed in her at that moment.

I held her tight and rocked her, saying, 'It's all right, Abigail, you're just exhausted. You haven't been eating, you need your sleep.' I chanted the words like a shielding mantra. 'It's all right, Abigail, you just need to sleep.'

Chapter 24

Tuesday 3rd September:
Day 100

JESS

Summer was over. The holidays had wound up.

I'd said nothing more about my aunt's email. Coming home to find my parents' lives like that, I couldn't do it. It felt like I'd already risked too much. See? I told myself. That's what happens when you start asking questions. That's what happens when you try to pull things apart. I had to forget about it, I had to trust Dad. Had to believe my parents still knew what they were doing.

My alarm clock shrilled at 7:15. I hadn't woken up this early in weeks. *After the summer*, Abigail would say when I was staying with her. It was a phrase she used all the time then, like some kind of spell. There are things I'll need, for *after the summer*. I'll be getting up earlier, *after the summer*. I'll be out every day then, *after the summer*. She made it sound like that time marked a boundary, after which everything would be all right. Sometimes the phrase would modulate and blur in my ears, and it would sound like a place, some mystical and far-off country, a promised land. *After the summer*.

I imagined her now, waking in her own bed, the clock on her nightstand shrilling out the same time as mine. As I stripped out of my pyjamas and climbed into the shower, I imagined Abigail standing under her own warm stream. I had seen the uniform that they had bought for her, hanging in slippery see-through plastic bags in her wardrobe. The kilt, the blazer, the crisp white shirt – all identical to mine. Mum had ironed my uniform for me last night, and the wool and cotton was comfortingly familiar as I pulled them on.

I ate breakfast, ignoring the way Mum and Dad slid past each other like ghosts. I turned my eyes and ears off to them, the only way I knew how to cope. Instead, I imagined Abigail yawning over her own plate of toast. Smeared with cherry jam, her favourite.

I made the bus just in time, and all the way there, I pictured Abigail on her own route, riding in the car with Auntie Anne and the twins. First, they would drop off the boys at primary, Sam and Laurie landing kisses on their sister's cheeks as they scrambled out. Then she and my aunt would head on to our high school. Maybe Abigail would be feeling a bit anxious, such a big step for her, such a big new thing. Perhaps she would have to keep wiping her damp hands down the wool of her skirt. I pictured her craning out of the front window to catch sight of me at the top of the school lane, where we'd always agreed that we would meet. I pictured her clambering out of the car, waving goodbye to Auntie Anne. I saw myself coming up beside her, linking arms with her, the two of us walking into school just like that.

My bus reached the school road at 8:25. My legs were shaky as I climbed down. The sun was supposed to be out, but it kept disappearing behind blankets of cloud. I hitched up my school bag as I headed down the lane, still imagining my cousin hitching hers.

Lena was waiting for me by the school gates, like she'd done so many times before. With a jolt of déjà vu, I remembered meeting her here that very first time after Abigail came home. She looked a little bit taller now, since the summer. Taller than ever compared to me.

I'd hardly spoken to her all holidays. I'd been so wrapped up with Abigail instead. Now I wished I'd gone to see her, even once. She could have come with me and Abigail to the cinema, but I hadn't even thought to invite her. I hardly knew what she'd been doing all summer, only that she'd spent most of it with Tom.

By the time I reached her, the first bell for registration was already ringing, high and shrill, more like an alarm. As I stopped in front of her, pulling tight the straps on my bag, her eyes went flitting past me, searching. I knew exactly what she was looking for.

I tried my very best to act casual. I shrugged one shoulder, looked off somewhere in the distance.

'Well?' said Lena. 'Where is she?'

The whole pretence of my morning dissolved, falling apart like the daydream it was. I shook my head. 'She isn't coming,' I said.

I'd hoped up until the very last minute that the adults would change their minds. But they just kept saying she wasn't ready yet, even though I kept telling them I would look after her, I would be there, I would make sure she was fine.

I could read the look on Lena's face, even if she wasn't saying anything. I knew what she was thinking. *Told you so.*

'It's not like that,' I said. 'They just want to get the trial out of the way first. It only means she'll start a few weeks later, after half term, maybe even before then.'

Lena began walking, heading for our form room. 'Whatever. But we'll be late if we don't hurry up.' I followed her inside and along the corridors. Did she have to walk so fast?

'Honestly, Lena, my aunt and uncle are just being overcautious, and anyway, she just needs a bit more time.' I could hardly keep up with her. 'Lena, slow down.'

She stopped and turned for a moment to face me, then she was climbing the stairs to our form class, taking them two at a time. 'I wanted to invite you along to a party,' she said.

'A party?' I hurried to keep up.

'It's one of Tom's friends. You should come. Bring Abigail too, if you want.'

She pushed her way through the landing doors, turned the corner to the next flight. The doors swung awkwardly, almost trapping me between. I tried to imagine it: Abigail at a party, amidst boys, amidst booze.

'So will you come?' Lena said to me over her shoulder.

'When is it?'

'Next Saturday.'

I came to a halt, and she stopped too. I was about to say yes, of course I would come. Of course I wanted to hang out with Lena, with Tom, with all of his friends, because I did, I had never wanted to be left behind. And of course I was glad she'd invited Abigail too. But then I remembered. A week on Saturday.

'What date is that?'

'September the fourteenth.'

My heart sank. 'I want to, Lena, I really do. But it's Abigail's birthday. We're going out to celebrate.'

Now the second bell rang, a shrill racket. Lena carried on climbing, but slower now. 'So you don't want to.'

'Of course I do, Lena, but—' Why, why, did I always have to choose? 'Wait. *Wait.*' I grabbed for her arm. I was breathless from all the trying to keep up. I tried to organize my thoughts, work out a plan. 'Can't we do both? I'll go to dinner first with Abigail, and afterwards I'll come to the party, with you.'

Lena turned and looked at me. 'And what about Abigail?'

'What do you mean?'

'Aren't you going to bring her to the party?'

I felt my cheeks burn. She had caught me out. A slip of the tongue; I'd left my cousin out, unable to picture her in that place. I went on holding onto Lena's arm. I tried to tell myself that Lena was jealous. The only reason she would be saying all this. Testing me, tripping me up. I'd gone off with Abigail for the whole of the summer, barely spoken to Lena, that's what it was.

'I'll bring Abigail, if she wants to come.'

Lena had nothing but scepticism in her face. Behind her, up the corridor, I could see a group of our classmates lingering by the form room doorway. Girls who had done stuff like Lena, tried things, laughed about it, had the marks and scars to prove it. 'You don't know, do you, what happened with us and Tom?'

With Tom? I couldn't understand.

'You remember. At the music festival.'

I let go of her arm. I felt everything inside of me go cold.

233

'We were all talking about you, how happy Abigail must be seeing you again.'

I remembered them standing there, not speaking, almost frozen. 'What?' I said. 'Go on. Tell me.'

'I was telling your cousin how much you loved her …'

'And?' The awkward smile on Tom's face, the flush on Lena's cheeks.

'…*Yeah, but sometimes I hate her*, was what your cousin said.'

Chapter 25

ANNE

When it came down to it, she wasn't in any kind of state to go to school. On that first day when she should have gone, her uniform stayed in the wardrobe and she slept in late instead. She wasn't awake to wave Robert and the twins off, and the house felt far too quiet when they had gone.

It was close to midday when I finally managed to rouse her and get her dressed and down to the car. We weren't going to waste the day, I'd decided, and even if school was going to have to wait, there were other things that couldn't be put off.

We could have gone into Nottingham, or down to London even, and we would certainly have found something there, but the thought of the train journeys and the crowds and how long a day it would make it, meant I chose to drive her to Lincoln instead. Not the best, but I hoped it would do.

We found somewhere to park – £3.50 for four hours – and walked there together through the early autumn streets. We came in on the ground floor, through the section that sold wheelie suitcases and travel kits. 'We need to go up a few levels,' I said.

On the escalator under all the bright lights and the air-conditioning, I saw how washed out Abigail looked. She hadn't wanted anything but coffee when she woke up – black, no sugar – and though I'd taken her up a banana, she hadn't eaten it. I checked the directory and took her right up to the top floor. 'Before we start, we're going to have lunch.'

We'd arrived well after the midday rush, so the café wasn't full; I handed Abigail a tray and pointed out the options, as though she couldn't read them for herself. As though she wasn't able to read just fine. 'You can have quiche,' I suggested, 'or a baked potato.' I was hovering and even annoying myself. *Stop now, or you'll do that thing when you start going on and on and don't know how to stop.* Abigail shrugged, her eyes on a salad. I ordered for the both of us, quickly: quiche, with chips because she could really do with the calories, and a slice of crumble each for dessert. Piled up all together like that on the trays it looked a lot.

When we sat down she pushed her food around her plate until I told her, come on. Then she gripped her fork like a shovel and started eating, in quick, gulping bites. 'See?' I told her. 'You were hungry after all.'

In all the dozens of clothes I had bought her, nothing had seemed suitable; I had flicked my way right through her wardrobe, rejecting everything, all the skirts, the T-shirts, the expensive pretty tops. She needed something smarter, less frivolous, I didn't know what exactly. I just knew the impression I wanted her to make.

Abigail's fork squealed against her plate. In the end, she had eaten everything, even the crumble. I looked down at my own food, hardly touched, and made myself take three solid bites.

'All done?' The quiche sat heavily in my stomach. She pushed her plate away and nodded. I smiled at her. 'Come on then.'

There were two whole floors of womenswear, everything from beachwear to bridal. I was glad now that we hadn't gone anywhere bigger. It was only once we began walking round, passing display after display that I realized: no teen section. Children's clothes, yes, but hardly anything for a fifteen-year-old girl. The dresses and suits we saw were boxy, frumpy things; whatever I held up she shook her head at, and she was right, they were all wrong for her. She clicked through the racks with a sullen look on her face and with each click of a hanger I could feel my heart tighten another notch.

'Need some help?' A sales assistant, her head cocked.

'Yes ... please. We're looking for – a formal outfit, something that might suit my daughter – here, Abigail, come here.' I presented her to the assistant like she was a doll we were going to dress.

'For anything special?'

'My birthday party,' said Abigail.

A puff of air escaped me in a laugh. 'Well, yes, her birthday, but she also has ...' All right, what? What was I supposed to tell this kind assistant, who hadn't – God knows how – recognized Abigail, and who would only become embarrassed and awkward if I said. I pushed my hair back behind my ears. 'My daughter has an interview,' I said. And Abigail didn't correct me.

The assistant's face brightened. 'Got you,' she said. 'Follow me.'

She took us to an area that we'd missed, where the clothes were young and smart and just what we were looking for. 'Yes,'

I told her, 'this is much more like it.' I could see from the look on Abigail's face that she was also happier now, hopeful of finding something.

'Great,' said the assistant. 'I'll leave you two to it. Good luck for your interview!'

'Better?' I said to Abigail.

'Better.'

I thumbed my way through the racks leaving Abigail to do the same. It wasn't hard to pull items out now: this one could work, and so could this. I lifted out a cream blouse with a button-up collar, a blazer and an outfit that looked like a suit. And for her birthday too, why shouldn't she pick out something special? It was her sixteenth and it was her first birthday since she'd come home. And then I realized, counting the dates. The girls, always so close for that reason too: their birthdays only two weeks apart. Now Jess's would fall the week of Abigail's trial.

'I've got some.' Abigail was at my elbow, a handful of items folded over one arm, the straps of one already slipping off the hanger. I looked down at the pile in my own arms and smiled at her. 'Me too. Want to try these on?'

It took us a while to find the changing rooms but when we did there wasn't a queue. Inside, I helped Abigail hang the clothes in her stall. They barely squeezed onto the hooks. 'I'll be right out here,' I told her. 'Try them on and come out and show me.' I sat down on a soft, low chair, just outside.

I could see the flicker of her shadow under the stall door and a clatter and a flash of blue when she dropped one of the blazers. She scooped it up again from the floor.

'Have you got one on yet? Can I see?'

When she stepped out, in one of the shirts she'd picked out

for herself, I shook my head right away. It was far too big; it swamped her. 'What size did you get?' I stood up to check. 'Twelve? You're not a twelve.' Could she not tell how much weight she'd lost? So much, too much. 'I don't think it's right anyway. Too casual.'

Abigail turned to look at herself in the mirror. The sullen look was back on her face and the door of her stall banged a little too sharply when she went back inside.

That look. I knew it so well: one of the parts that came from Preston. Nothing changed the fact that she came from him. I remembered the one time he'd broken down and told me the reasons for all his anger, for his bad habits and all of his problems. The mess of his childhood, his mother's drinking, the stint in foster care at the age of fourteen, split from his brother, because for a few months his mum had lost it completely. All Preston's anger had such good reasons and I'd had so much hope of making it right.

The stall door clicked and Abigail came out again, this time in one of my choices, the cream-coloured blouse. It had looked good on the hanger and it was smart and modest, all the right things to wear at a trial, and it fit her just fine, only ... the colour. Pale cotton with her pale skin. It was too much; she would look like a ghost. 'Try the blazer on top of it,' I said. She reached into the stall and tipped it off its hanger with a jerk. When she shrugged herself into it, it rucked up the sleeves of the blouse.

'What do you think now?' The blazer gave some definition and was better against the pale of her hair.

She stared at herself in the mirror. 'It's fine.'

'Well, have you tried the other ones on? Is there something that's better?'

'This'll do.'

'Are you sure? We can keep looking.' I couldn't put my finger on it but the proportions were off somehow, or the cut on her, I didn't know, but something.

'This'll *do*.'

'I think it's because you're wearing it with jeans. We'll try it on at home with those grey trousers you've got. I think then it'll be just fine.'

'All right.'

But I had annoyed her and I didn't know what it was I had said; whether my words had sounded like criticisms, whether she'd wanted to be left alone to choose. The tightness in my heart spread to my stomach and I could feel it between us, that old, old wrenching.

'What about for your birthday then? Did you pick out anything you liked for that?'

'A dress.' Now her voice was sullen too.

'Okay then. Can I see?'

She closed the door of the stall again, banging it deliberately this time. I glimpsed her bare toe, the back of her foot as she twisted in the small space. I heard her clatter the hangers and something else dropped to the floor. She didn't bother to pick it up this time.

'Abigail?'

No answer. My nose was running; I fished into my handbag for a handful of tissues. Now it had gone quiet in the stall, no flicker of her shadow, just that silence that to me was worse than anything: the silence in which she was cut off from me completely. I didn't know how she would be when she came back out. Which Abigail – the child of tantrums and inconsolable rage, or the child who smiled, who let herself be loved? Now my eyes were running too, like an allergic reaction, but I knew it wasn't. She was my daughter and the rest shouldn't matter, but I couldn't stop thinking of how it had once been, when she was her best self and I was her loving mother, and I so wanted that daughter, I so wanted it to be that Abigail who'd come home. I found a tissue and pushed it against my mouth, trying not to make a sound.

The stall door opened. I wiped away my tears.

'What about this?'

I bought myself a second by blowing my nose. Then I looked up. It took me a long time to take it all in. It was as though I could only look at her in stages. The material was dark, a deep blood red, and it pinched her tight around the waist. It had no sleeves and the capped shoulders left the pale thinness of her arms exposed. The skirt flared and didn't even reach her knees, but the collar was high, circling her neck and highlighting the sharp line of her chin. Her stomach, from the full lunch, made a curve between her hips. All over the dress fitted her so closely I thought I could see her heart beating through it.

'Well?' She reached up and pulled the weight of her hair back from her face.

I let out a long, shuddery breath, so glad of the figure who stood before me. 'Abigail, it looks beautiful,' I said.

'Let's wait and make it a surprise,' I told Abigail on the drive home. 'Keep it hidden until your birthday do. Then everyone will see how lovely you look.'

When we got in, Robert was preparing tea and the house swam with the aroma of roast chicken. I kissed him in the kitchen, in front of the twins. 'Everything smells delicious,' I told him. We didn't show them what we'd bought but Robert could tell the trip had been a success – he could see it in my face. With clothes like those, I thought, she would do just fine. From here on in we could manage anything.

Later that evening, I heard the shower running, so I knew she hadn't yet gone to bed. She hadn't eaten nearly enough at teatime and she must surely be hungry, hungry enough for the glass of milk and the biscuit I was taking up for her, a caffeine-free snack to settle her for bed. With the glass and the plate, I climbed the stairs; the shower was still running and when I pushed open the bedroom door, inside there was only the smell of her: a cloying note from the deodorant spray she now used. I set the milk and biscuit down by her bed.

The room with its pink-painted walls seemed strangely empty. Despite the posters pinned to the walls, it still felt as though no one lived here. I sat down in the chair at the desk and, not thinking, I pulled open the right-hand drawer. Inside was a ruler that could be folded in half, a pink eraser and a dusting of tiny paper circles where a hole punch had leaked. In the left-hand drawer was a blue paper-clip, bent.

It was as I was sliding that left-hand drawer closed that I saw the bin at the side of her desk, a folded wad of paper stuffed deep into it. Scattered on top were scraps of the blue and white wallpaper we had stripped from her walls months ago, though why she had those I had no idea. I pulled out the folded papers, shaking them free of the wallpaper dust and flakes. The stack of single sheets was covered with her handwriting, joined up letters so neat and pretty they almost looked old-fashioned. At first, I thought perhaps they were from her therapy sessions – weekly exercises, homework – but when I opened them out I realized they were something else entirely.

On some pages there were two, three sentences, on some pages only a few broken phrases and on one, just three words: *What he did—*

And at the top of each one she'd written the heading: *Abigail's Victim Impact Statement.*

My heart climbed right into my throat. I smoothed out the page at the back of the pile. Here at last, her writing had filled the whole sheet; the garbled words made my scalp crawl.

What he did was wrong everyone says it but it was never wrong with him nothing seemed wrong in the beginning, only later on once the kisses – but now everyone says the whole thing was bad, so then who is bad, am I bad? In the beginning I was lost now I'm back home and everyone is very very happy, Mum especially says everything is all right now but is it? What don't I know, what aren't they telling me? Are we meant to be a perfect family, how perfect, but perfect isn't him on me jerking on the pillows and it isn't Mum unable to look me in the eye and to Sam and Laurie I'm just like a toy to play with, and Dad, Robert I wasn't properly ever his, so what if they meant it, what if everyone in my family meant it, and never knew it would turn out wrong what if they meant this to be, the whole thing, but I don't care anyway I do miss him that's the truth because he said he was mine and said I was his and he would never let me go, never, and everything was true from the very beginning because he knew, he knew, he knew me.

I didn't register that the shower had stopped running. I only registered Abigail standing over me, wrapped in a towel, her wet hair darkened and dripping. I stood up so fast I banged my knee. 'I'm so sorry, Abigail. I should never have read them.' And yet she'd left them somewhere so easy to find, as though part of her had wanted me to look.

She moved slowly, coolly, and to me that was worse than if she had been angry, furious and had torn them from my grasp. Without saying a word, and without meeting my eyes, she reached out and took the pages from my hand; it seemed such an immense power she wielded in that moment.

The towel hitched up to show the bony ridges of her thighs as she dropped the pages back into the bin. I felt myself go very still; her next words were like a straight punch to the head.

'And you still want me to write that fucking thing?'

Chapter 26

JESS

On the Wednesday before Abigail's birthday, I arrived home before either Mum or Dad. The house was quiet and empty. I changed out of my school clothes and sat in the living room to wait for them. As soon as I heard Mum's car in the drive, I filled up the kettle and put it on.

She came in looking exhausted. Her make-up had rubbed thin and there was a mascara smudge under one eye.

'How was work?' I asked.

She gave a smile that looked more like a grimace. 'Honestly, Jess, you don't want to know. How was school?' she asked instead.

I made sure to smile. 'It was fine.' I wasn't going to talk about anything. 'Do you want a cup of tea?'

She sat down heavily at the kitchen table and prised off her shoes. 'That would be great.'

When the kettle had boiled, I made it just the way she liked – strong with only a tiny dribble of milk – and I made sure to wipe up where the teabag had dripped.

'Aren't you having one too?'

I shook my head. 'I'm okay. But listen, Mum, can I borrow your laptop?'

She took a sip of her hot tea, almost scalding herself. 'Why? What's wrong with your phone?'

'Nothing. It's just that you have all the photographs on there.'

She was too tired, I think, to ask more questions. She waved a hand. 'It's through in the sitting room, charging.'

'I know,' I said. 'I just need the password.'

I left her in the kitchen, drinking her tea with her eyes almost closed. The laptop was fully charged by now, and the screen opened up when I typed in the characters she had given me. I'd had this idea for weeks, and on my way home from school today I'd bought the album. In the shop, I picked out the best one; a broad, thick book of beautiful pages, just waiting to be filled.

I refused to believe what Lena had told me. What she'd said had happened at the music festival. She'd lied, or else she was mistaken, probably she had simply misheard. Or if Abigail had said it, she just never meant it. Because my cousin could have never meant that. I loved Abigail – we loved each other – and nothing Lena said could ever change that.

Now I just needed to collect the right pictures. Along the bottom of Mum's laptop screen was a row of icons: calendar, notepad, Internet, photos. Mum's photos. She had hundreds of them stored on here: our official family archives. I remembered, years ago, her saving them all. After Abigail went missing, we rarely looked at them, too sad, but everything was different now.

Here was a copy of the picture I'd given her: me and Abigail from that day by the stream. I think Dad must have taken it when we got home – wet and laughing, one sandal hopelessly soaked. And here were other photos of me and Abigail, of Abigail and her family, and Abigail with us. The 'last opened' dates on them were so old. I scrolled through them; there were memories and moments even I had forgotten, me who thought I remembered everything.

Distractedly, I heard the front door slam, Dad getting home from work too. I heard the low murmur of his voice with Mum's in the kitchen, the soft whirr of the kettle boiling again. I told myself they were doing better these days. Whether they were ignoring their issues or sorting them out, I didn't care. Mum was back sleeping in the same room as Dad and – bottom line – they weren't arguing any more.

Here were photos of me and Abigail at a play park, here we were on my fifth birthday, my sixth. Here was an earlier picture of Abigail in her new bedroom, a year or so after Uncle Robert came on the scene. She looked so happy, giggling. On Mum's laptop I made a new folder. I called it *Abigail*, and I saved all the best photographs in there. The whole thing would be a beautiful surprise for Abigail. The very best birthday present I could think of.

On Saturday, her birthday, we were the first to arrive: Mum, Dad and me. For some reason my aunt and uncle had picked the posh hotel in the centre of town – definitely not the kind of place we usually ate. Properly fancy: all flock wallpaper, mauve napkins, real silver cutlery. The waitress who came to take our drinks orders wore a little silk necktie. It wasn't the kind of place we usually came to but this was a special occasion. The absolutely most special.

We all had presents and cards for her. It had been so much easier to choose this time, to pick out the obvious messages: *Happy Birthday. Happy 16th.* In just two weeks' time it would be my birthday too: 27th September. I'd be sixteen as well, exactly like her again. I only hoped the trial would be over by then.

I'd wrapped her album in turquoise paper, a colour she'd always liked when we were kids. When I saw her coming into the restaurant with Auntie Anne, Uncle Robert, the twins, I stood up. How long was it, actually, since I'd last seen her? Two weeks, nearly three? Her outfit was lovely: a dark red dress that rose high about her neck. 'You look very grown up,' Mum said to her with a smile. She didn't say anything about how my cousin's collarbones stuck out. Under the make-up she'd put on, Abigail looked like she was coming down with a cold. A bit hot to the touch in my hello hug.

Uncle Robert sat her at the top of the table so she could see us all. I sat on her right-hand side. I'd been right, it didn't matter what Lena had said. Everything was good between us. Everything was fine. As we handed her our cards and presents, Abigail gathered them into a pile at the side of her plate. She didn't seem to know quite what to do with them. 'You can open them,' Auntie Anne said.

'Afterwards,' she said.

I looked at the pile – half a dozen in total maybe – and suddenly I thought of all the presents she had missed out on. Every birthday that had passed by when she was locked up with *him*, away from us. Had he even known when her birthday was? All right, well we'd make up for that now. We'd make this the nicest birthday she'd ever had. I looked around us all at the table, as the waitress lit the candles: Robert, the twins and Auntie Anne. Mum and Dad. And me and Abigail.

When the waitress arrived with our mains, everything smelled amazing. I hadn't realized how ravenous I was, so busy all day with Abigail's album. When my chicken dish arrived I wished I'd ordered a side. It was so tasty but there wasn't much of a portion. Abigail had ordered some kind of risotto, topped with green stuff. She was sort of pushing it round her plate.

'Don't you like it?' I asked.

She wrinkled her nose. 'Not really.'

I looked down at my own plate. 'Here. Wait.' I pulled her plate towards me, made room on it with my fork. With my knife I separated a hunk of chicken for her. 'Have some of mine. I wouldn't manage it all anyway.'

After that, I finished my meal pretty soon and I got impatient waiting for everyone else to finish. When our desserts came, I couldn't wait any longer. I nudged Abigail's elbow. 'Come on. Open your presents.'

All of us had made such an effort. They were beautiful gifts that we had chosen for her: a woven silk scarf from Mum and Dad, a board game from Sam and Laurie, and her own iPhone from my uncle and aunt. I craned across. 'I'll help you set up Instagram and everything. We can Snapchat, it'll be almost like living together again.'

Now she reached for my own present, tied with a bright pink ribbon. I helped her lift the flat, heavy package. She weighed it, shook it, trying to guess. Carefully she picked off the Sellotape, pulling the wrapping paper free. Now at last she could see what

249

it was. I leaned over, unable to hold back. 'Look, I've filled it with all our family photos. There's loads in here you haven't seen; I don't even think anyone else has copies. They're from my mum's collection, photos of you, of me, of all of us.'

'Auntie Lillian's collection?' There was a strange note in Abigail's voice.

'Oh, Jess,' said Mum. 'What a lovely idea.'

Slowly my cousin lifted the stiff cover, turning through the first pages. It *was* a lovely idea, the whole thing was lovely, Abigail and all of us, the pretty restaurant, and the birthday cards, Abigail's pretty outfit, and everyone here, it was *just right*, just how it should be. Abigail turned the pages slowly to begin with, then faster, more urgently. I'd begun with the very earliest pictures, me and Abigail as babies, then as toddlers in those years we'd spent together when Auntie Anne and Abigail lived with us in London. There we were, us with Abigail at two, at three, then all of us arriving and settling in Lincolnshire. Here she was at three and a half, four, Uncle Robert appearing on scene – so many happier shots then. Abigail turned another page and leaned forwards, her neck bent so far it looked painful.

'These are all wonderful,' said Auntie Anne. 'Can I see?'

Instead Abigail gripped the album tighter, the cardboard protesting under her hands. I could glimpse a picture: Abigail smiling, Abigail giggling, Abigail happy. Red dungarees, white and blue-striped wallpaper. I reached out to ease her grip but she pushed my fingers away. The heat was coming off her, like she was burning up.

'What is this?' she said.

My smile made it hard to speak. 'This one is you, in Robert's house. I think it's when you had just moved in.' The words came out almost under my breath. I was frightened of making a scene.

Auntie Anne was saying, 'It's lovely, Jess, so lovely, I'm so glad your mum saved them all,' and Uncle Robert was saying, 'Abigail, won't you say thank you?' We were all leaning in, closing in on her. That flush on her cheeks looked feverish now. She pressed the album covers shut and stood up, pushing back her chair so hard it fell over. For a dumb moment I thought she only wanted to say thank you.

Instead, she stood there and yelled at us all.

Chapter 27

ANNE

'*Stop pretending!*' she yelled. '*Stop pretending, all of you!*'

And then Abigail was bolting from the table.

'Go after her!' said Robert, pushing himself up. For a second I couldn't get my legs to work; Jess had given her a perfect album of perfect family photos, but the table was covered with empty plates, dirty napkins and how could we pretend we were perfect at all?

She had already set off like a hare, twisting through the candlelit tables. I set off after her but I was so slow and clumsy and I couldn't seem to get through. The thick back of someone's chair caught me in the ribs, knocking the breath out of me, and I stumbled out an apology, pushing my way past. Ahead of me Abigail was pulling open the heavy restaurant doors, her thin shape twisting away through the gap.

At the second door, I almost caught her, my hand catching the shoulder seam of her dress, but she twisted away, ripping herself free. 'Abigail!' The outer door swung back on me, clipping my wrist and she was away again, dashing right out into the street. She shoved her way outside, into the dark, where the road in front of us was full of cars, tail-lights, headlights. She went haring up the pavement, pushing through a couple coming towards us, shoving past them. 'Abigail!' I shouted again, running after her, and behind me I could hear Robert shouting too, coming after us, calling Abigail's name. There was a moment when she seemed to hesitate and fall back and I thought, it's all right, she's stopping, you'll catch her up now. I kept running, ready to grasp her and hold her, and she had stopped as though waiting for me, as though all she'd ever wanted was for me to reach her. So I wasn't prepared for what happened next, I wasn't prepared for it at all – was she trying to cross, still compelled to run away, or was it some other instinct that drove her at that point? She jibed right, veering from the pavement. The driver never expected her.

And then all I remember is my shout, a scream of brakes and a sickening thud, the sight of her red dress flying up and the sight of her beautiful, thin body falling.

Minutes later that felt like hours, there were lights, red and blue, and sirens and urgent people doing urgent things; Robert climbing into the back of the ambulance with her, while Fraser got me into our car, telling me Lillian was taking Jess and the twins, telling me to put my seatbelt on and then we were driving in the wake of the sirens.

Fraser was talking as we drove and I wanted to say to him: *I know, I know, I wrote you an email and how I wish now I'd sent it*, but all I could do was close my eyes, unable to speak.

'Will you trust me?' he kept asking. 'Will you trust me?'

Then we were at the hospital, Lincoln A&E, and the light

was greenish. Robert was there, and Lillian, Jess and the twins, but not Abigail, she was with the doctors. We sat in the waiting area, cold, still in shock. She was going to be okay, they had told us. Concussion at most; Abigail had been lucky to miss the car, only falling and knocking her head, a glancing blow, on the kerb. They would run a few more checks and monitor her overnight. They would let us know as soon as we could see her.

Under the harsh lights, the air hung heavy, like the pressure you get when you fly in a plane – it grows and grows until you almost can't bear it, and when it bursts, your whole head rings.

Stop pretending. How could I have thought all this time it didn't matter? How could I ever have thought she'd forgotten what I'd done?

Sam and Laurie lay slumped against Robert, worn out by the ambulance, the panic. Fraser sat with his hands pressed to his knees. 'What is it?' said Robert. 'Please tell me what is going on.'

When Fraser went to speak, Lillian half stood, her voice a warning shot, but he held out a palm. 'We all need to hear this. Yes, even Jess.' Fraser took his daughter's hand in his. Jess was sitting so upright in her plastic chair, ready and not ready, her features a blur of both adult and child.

'Lillian?' said my husband. 'Fraser?'

Fraser looked at me for a long time, then slowly switched his gaze to Lillian. When she sat back down, it felt as though some contract between them had been finally broken.

When Fraser spoke, it was as though he'd been preparing the words for years. 'It was wrong of us, Lillian. It was wrong of us, Robert, and I'm so sorry about it though we all meant well.

Lillian – I think what Anne told you is right. I think Abigail remembers those moments on the train. We should never have kept this buried. I think it's time now to say what happened.'

How many mistakes were you allowed? How many times was too many? What if they were only small mistakes, tiny, hidden stitches that could easily be unpicked? What if they were huge, what if you messed up the stitch that was supposed to hold everything together? Lillian and Fraser had kept my secret for the longest time – too long – Lillian insisting it was for the best.

They had been the first ones to answer my phone call, Fraser lifting the receiver to hear me half hysterical, gasping, *I left her! I left her!* And then Lillian was there, stepping in, correcting, putting everything right, one more stitch in the pattern of our whole lives. She was only doing what we always had done. It was only one more little white lie. *Don't say that, Anne. You lost sight of her, in that crush, in those crowds. That's all that happened, isn't it? That's all.*

We had left it like that ever since. It had caused such conflict between Fraser and Lillian, this decision to hide the truth, and I'd always lived in fear of what it might do to me and Robert if he found out: not only what I had done, but how I had lied afterwards. All these years I'd fought so hard to be the kind of person Robert wanted: good, kind, capable like him. All these years, I'd known I was letting Robert down. Now I knew it meant risking tearing our marriage apart, but for Abigail's sake, I had to tell him. And afterwards, it would be for Robert to choose.

In all the evidence they'd gathered, all the questions they'd asked, nobody had ever probed this one. Why was it that when the train doors closed, Abigail had turned and burrowed away, not screamed or cried or clawed at the glass? Why had she ridden that escalator so quietly? Now I confessed it all to him in the sickly green waiting room, with the twins asleep with their heads in our laps. I was glad that they were there – a precious bond that tied me to Robert, while slowly my words unravelled everything else between us.

Lillian listened to me, stony-faced; beside her sat Fraser with compassion in his eyes. He was a truth-teller, and always had been.

That evening the Underground was heaving. It was rush hour, thousands of rain-drenched commuters scrambling to get home. At the hospital, Robert and I had argued and now I was heading back to the hotel through a downpour: the twins in the double buggy and Abigail big enough to walk by herself. Quite big enough; it was just that she didn't want to. All the tension at the hospital had upset her; I had been so angry. I just wanted to get back to the hotel where I could feed them, run a bath and put them to bed. Robert's mum had made me feel so bad about myself and now I was trying to manage all this on my own: three small children in the chaos of London. All week I'd had messages on Facebook: hope visit goes well, thinking of you, hugs. But Facebook messages didn't help to wheel a double buggy and Facebook messages didn't help keep an eight-year-old in check. Abigail was dragging her feet through the wet – with every step, she was complaining – and the twins were grizzling, hungry; it wouldn't have taken much for one of them to start screaming.

I kept nagging Abigail, telling her to pick her feet up, not thinking of how I was going on and on. Eventually, we got through the ticket gates and down the escalators to board the Northern Line. I was lucky to find a space for the buggy, and Abigail could stand next to it in the vestibule area. There were dozens of people pushing on after us, ramming the carriage full. I hung onto the buggy – I couldn't let go of the twins – and Abigail, with her frowning face, was hanging onto the pole by the door. The bell rang and the doors closed and we were packed in, waiting. But we didn't move. The train was hot, suffocating as we stood stationary. Eventually, an announcement came: this train would go only six more stops.

The train doors grated open again. Now some people wanted to get off. I shoved the buggy in as tight as I could and kept as far in as I was able. The passengers nearest the doors were doing their best to move aside, but Abigail was still just clinging to the pole. She needed to make room, but she was being so stubborn.

I should have realized then what was happening between us, recognized the tightness, the way it would build, where it could take me. But it had been so long. For years things had been so much better, everything else a distant memory and I'd been so sure we'd come past all of that now. All I was thinking was, *everyone's getting so impatient, we are such an inconvenience to them.* So I told Abigail, sharply, to do what other passengers were doing: let go of the pole and step down onto the platform. She would still be right there within arm's reach, and she was only stepping down for a moment.

Now the station was filling up all over again, a disgorge of passengers from yet another train. The doors were still open and the people who'd stepped down were clambering back on, plus other people too, running up the platform. I had to keep hold of the twins in the buggy, but with my free hand I gestured to Abigail: all right then, step back up. I was frustrated and no doubt it showed; but Abigail just stood there on the platform. She just stood there.

Everyone was so busy, only thinking of getting home, mad at the delays; they didn't stop to look at some kid belonging to God knows who, and I was just some woman with a buggy, taking up all the room. But I had been nagging at her for the last twenty minutes, going on and on at her, not minding my tone, not holding onto my frustration, and now Abigail stood there with the hard, furious look of her father on her face, the look that said, *I'm so angry with you.*

Something slipped inside me then. We had come so far, for months, years she had been so good, *we* had been so good. I couldn't bear to see her looking like that. The past was the past, she was supposed to be a happy child now, loving her was supposed to be easy, and *we were supposed to be so much better than this.*

When the bells went a second time, I know what I should have done. I should have grabbed my daughter and hoisted her straight back onto the train, like you do with a toddler screaming in the supermarket, you just scoop them up and carry them off. But in that moment, that tiny sliver of a second, I didn't want to deal with it. I didn't want to deal with a child like that.

So instead I did the other thing you do, when you feel that way, undermined, defeated. Anywhere else, *anywhere else*, it wouldn't have mattered when I turned away, frustrated and exhausted, when for just one split second I said to myself: *Fine.*

But then. But then—

But then the doors closed and the train pulled away and by

the time I got to the emergency cord we were already in the tunnel on the way to the next station, and then it was simply, utterly too late.

All of these words spilled like a river into the harsh light of the waiting room. Robert sat with his hands gripping his knees as though if he let go he might topple right over. 'You knew?' His question was for Lillian, for Fraser.

Fraser answered him, laying a hand over mine. 'Lillian and I – were only trying to do what was best. We made a decision and then it became so complicated to undo. We carried on. We shouldn't have.'

I saw the hurt on Jess's face too, twisting her mouth, tearing up her eyes. It was so hard for me to look at her. What I'd done to Abigail, I had done to all of them. I never meant to, I *never* meant to, but this one moment had brought on everything else, a thousand more wounds that might never heal. A tiny second that turned into seven whole years, and a scar that underlay everything she had suffered.

Robert was about to speak again when a doctor appeared. We could come and sit with Abigail now. At that, Robert told the Bradys to go home. When they protested, he insisted. I watched them go, the jagged secret standing between Robert and me. Now it was just us.

They had moved Abigail to the children's ward. On slippery chairs with the twins in our laps, we tried to sleep. Close to the end of the night-shift they came to say she was being discharged. They let her go with a bandage taped across her forehead. At home let her sleep, they said, but keep a close eye on her. Any blurred vision, any headaches, bring her straight back.

In the five a.m. darkness, Robert carried her out to the car. She was fifteen – no, sixteen now – but he was strong and she weighed almost nothing. I followed behind them, sickened with guilt as I shepherded the twins. At home, just as at the very start, we put her straight to bed. Moving like a sleep-walker, she pulled off her clothes, burrowed her way into her sleeping T-shirt and turned over on her side. I knew and I had known it all the way along: Abigail had taken that moment with her into her abduction and Abigail remembered it when she came back. When I picked up her crumpled red dress from the floor, I saw the smudge of blood on the shoulder.

Dawn was close to breaking outside when I slid into bed next to Robert. I could feel the fury in him. I knew how angry he was.

He covered his face with his hands as we lay there. 'How could you not tell me?'

I could say it now. 'I should have. I was a coward. I know I let you shoulder the guilt by yourself.'

'You did. I always thought I was to blame. I thought it was all my fault. You know I've struggled with that for years.'

'I know.'

'Why then? Why couldn't you have told me?'

I felt the tears come to my eyes, it was so painful for me to voice this other part of it and my throat ached as I brought the words out. 'Because it was such a terrible thing to have done. It was the worst part of me, everything I didn't want to be. I thought if I showed you that, I thought if you knew – ' my words were small as teardrops in the dark – 'Robert, I thought for sure you would leave me.'

In the dissolving darkness, Robert fell silent. For a long, long while we lay there, two bodies in one bed, two paths ahead of us, one choice. There was nothing more I could do. I was no longer hiding from him; he knew my story now, he knew the truth. I knew I might lose him, that I might lose everything, but if I did, at the very least there were no longer lies between us, and knowing that, I felt a strange sense of calm.

At last, in the breaking light, he reached out for me. His hand slipped over my hip, my stomach, feeling for me in a way he hadn't done for many, many months. I felt my skin shiver and tears come to my eyes, too much emotion suddenly to hold in. I hardly let myself breathe and I tried to make barely a sound as I turned myself towards him, ready to accept whatever this meant, whether it was goodbye or whether it was love.

He was rough at first and I couldn't blame him. I felt the deluge of banked up emotion spill out of him as he pushed and pulled. I accepted the jarring embrace, and I let him because I understood all of this was part of our working through, something that didn't have words but had the deepest chords of meaning. Before long he slowed and sank and became gentle; the pain disappeared and his anger lifted away, and in the movement and closeness I understood him as well as if he had spoken out loud: he was saying, *you aren't to be blamed*, or maybe simpler: *I can forgive*.

Afterwards, in the morning light, I showered; the burning water washed all the rest away. With my hair wet, in my dressing gown, I made a mug of tea to take into Abigail. She lay in her bed straight out on her back, as though lying in a coffin. When I set the tea on her bedside table though, her eyelids quivered and I knew she was awake. I gently drew the curtains back, filling the room with bright autumn daylight.

I pulled the chair over from her desk so that I could sit right beside her. The little blue rabbit lay flopped over on the floor. I set it upright on the table, her flopsy who had come through it all.

'Does it hurt a lot?' I lifted my hand towards the white bandage on her forehead.

Her voice was croaky; her throat must have been very dry. 'No. Not much.' She squinted in the glare.

They had given her painkillers when she left the hospital and I was glad she was getting some relief. I took her hand in mine, her skin cool, despite the warmth in the house.

'I wanted to say something the first moment you came home,' I began. 'But I didn't and it's left you with a terrible misunderstanding.'

She listened, lids flickering, while I talked. For the first time, I spoke to her about everything that happened that day while her hand lay unmoving in mine. Having confessed once, the second time was easier, and whenever I asked if she understood, she nodded. I stumbled only a little when I got to the end. I found myself repeating phrases, my words becoming clumsy. I got it out though: what I needed to say.

'Anywhere else, Abigail, it wouldn't have mattered. I'd done that with you before, the same as I did that day. You often dawdled and nine times out of ten I'd walk on the same way. You would only be mad at me for a second and then you'd be right there, catching up. That time wouldn't have been any different, it was only a stupid moment. The problem was just that you were on the platform. Whatever else he's made you think, it was never anything else: just a tiny, stupid mistake. I was tired and not thinking straight and in that split second when I expected you to step up, the doors … Then we were in the tunnel and the driver wouldn't stop and – honestly, Abigail – there was nothing else I could do.'

She squeezed her eyes tight shut. I placed a hand against her cheek. 'Can you see how it was?'

She nodded again and opened her eyes. She had said it didn't hurt, but I could see the pain now in the tightness of her face.

'Yes' she whispered. ' But is there anything else? Anything at all you haven't told me?'

I felt a weight slip away from me then. Finally, I could look at her honestly and say: 'No, Abigail. I promise you. That's all.'

She lay there, unblinking eyes open to the ceiling and I could almost see her fighting with herself: to believe me or not. To accept or push away. At last she let out her breath and nodded, as though she had won – or given up – the fight.

'All right then,' I said. 'I love you.' It couldn't have been, surely, but it felt like the first time I'd said those words to her, directly and aloud, since she came home. Now I would leave her to sleep. She was here, she was safe, and everything was in the open. As I closed her door behind me, I saw her sit up and take a sip of the lukewarm tea.

Chapter 28

JESS

Abigail's voice on the phone was small, flat. But not just that. She sounded – scared?

'Can I come and stay at yours?' Her voice was crackly on the line, like she was calling long distance.

'Now?' I said. Her call had woken me from the dead of sleep. 'I thought you were going to London tomorrow? Isn't it the trial? Isn't it the day after tomorrow it starts?'

'Please, Jess.'

'Where are you?' It was the middle of the night.

'I'm here. Right outside.'

I pulled back my bedroom curtain. A downpour was bashing off our window ledges, pinging off the flagstones of the front drive. Through the sheets of rain, I could make out her huddled figure at the end of the drive.

'Shit, Abigail – wait right there.'

Downstairs, I fumbled open the heavy front door. When I got to her, her face was so thin, her eyes huge hollows under the white strip of plaster across her forehead. 'What are you doing here?'

She didn't answer, just said, 'Is your mum in there?'

'Of course, but she's sleeping.'

Abigail looked up at the dark windows above us. With no lights on, the house looked like a cave. Abigail was shivering. Water had soaked up the ankles of her jeans. 'Jesus,' I said, 'did you walk the whole way?'

Abigail half opened her mouth to answer.

'Never mind,' I said. 'Just come on inside.'

We slipped into the house and I helped Abigail struggle out of her drenched coat. With a finger to my lips, I led her upstairs and switched on the low lamp in my bedroom. Lit up, Abigail looked worse than ever, her hair in wet ropes, her lips bluish. She sat down on my bed, like she'd come to stay for good.

I found her a clean towel from the airing cupboard to rub the worst of the wet from her hair, and plugged in my hairdryer. 'Here. Sit here.'

I pulled out a cushion for her to sit on the floor and I sat cross-legged on the bed behind her. Her hair smelled of raspberry from the shampoo she used – the tall pink bottle I'd seen at their house. She bent up her legs and wrapped her arms around her knees. With the hairdryer on its lowest, quietest setting, I ran the stream of warm air over her, praying that Mum wouldn't wake up. 'Do you remember, when we were little?' I said. 'When we'd plait each other's hair?' I separated the strands, curling them round my fingers. In the low hum, her hair was growing dryer, softer.

I didn't hear her the first time. Her voice was muffled, she still had her forehead resting on her knees. She had to repeat herself. 'I need you to do something for me.'

'Okay … what is it?'

She lifted her head, I felt the tendons of her neck pull under my hands. 'At the trial. When they read out the verdict in court, I want to be there.'

I felt shivery. 'What do you mean?'

She hesitated. I tried to read her expression but sitting behind her, I couldn't make anything out.

'My parents don't want me to go in the courtroom. But I need a chance to see it properly.'

I kept the strands of hair tight in my grasp. 'See what?'

Very carefully, she twisted herself free of me and turned around on her knees to face me. 'Jess. Can you keep a secret?'

I clicked off the hairdryer and stared back at her. My old playmate, my cousin. My mirror image, the other half of me, the person I would do anything for in the world.

'You remember,' she went on, 'about the photo? The one I told you about – the picture John Henry said was sent to him? Well, I have to prove the truth, get through all these lies. I'm going to confront them, there in the courtroom. No one can lie in there, and then I'll *know*. Jess, finally I'll know.'

Something cold and dark rose up in my stomach. Because none of what she was saying made sense. There *was* no photo, not a real one anyway – but maybe that was all she wanted to prove? Finally convince herself she'd been wrong? And I had promised, hadn't I, that I'd never hurt her again. Never betray her, never let her down.

Carefully I set down the hairdryer. 'But what exactly is it you want me to do?'

'Speak to your parents. To your mum. *My* mum always listens to yours. Tell them I have to be there at the verdict.'

I hesitated. 'But they said it's best if you don't go in.'

Her hands were like claws against the floor. 'I need this, Jess, can't you see that? He told me that they didn't want me. He told me that they gave me away! And Mum told me what happened, how on the train she just left me, and now I have to know, Jess, I just have to know!'

It hit me then where this was all coming from. All right, she had reason to still be mad. She had reason to be hurt. But I thought about Dad, what he had murmured to me after Auntie Anne told her story. He'd talked about it with such compassion. I reached out and wrapped my arms around Abigail's cold shoulders. Her hair was almost dry by now, lying across her shoulders like a cloak.

'Listen, Abigail, Auntie Anne told us. What happened between you, before any of the rest.' I let my head rest against her neck. 'It was only a moment,' I went on, 'a mistake, like that stupid night with us at the fairground. Moments like that, they don't mean anything. I promise you, your mum never meant it. She loves you. We all do. You don't need anything to prove that.'

But instead she pulled away, curling into herself. My arms went slipping from her shoulders. In that moment, she looked like some strange animal. When she spoke again, her teeth looked so sharp. 'Somehow, Jess, you think everything's so simple. Even now, you think all of this was some simple mistake. You can't get it, can you? You still don't believe me. You can't see how it's so much worse than that.'

I was a statue, I couldn't move. Her words hung there, dissolving into my silence, breaking completely apart when a door creaked, footsteps on the landing.

'Shit,' I whispered, my lips finally moving. 'Mum's up.'

At that she seemed to cower, like she couldn't bear to get into trouble.

'It's fine,' I said. 'I'll explain to her, she won't mind.'

But Abigail just shook her head, clasping her arms around her knees. 'Don't let her in, Jess. Please, don't let her.' I hardly recognized my cousin at that moment. With the white bandage across her forehead, the bumps of her spine sticking up through her jumper, she looked so bizarre, so not-normal.

Now the footsteps were going past my door, crossing the landing and heading down the stairs. Surely Mum must have seen the light under my door, so why hadn't she knocked? Then I heard it: the growl of an engine out in the street, the click of the front door opening.

'Stay here,' I said to Abigail. I got up from the bed. Now I heard Dad's footsteps following Mum downstairs. Abigail hardly moved as I opened the door. Out on the landing, in the gloom, I took a moment to steady myself. I could hear their voices from downstairs: Mum, Dad, and I already knew who the other person was. I closed the bedroom door tight shut behind me and crept down.

They were in the living room – my parents and my uncle – their voices clearer than ever as I came down. Below me, the hall floor was covered with wet footprints. I pictured Mum's face. Without saying anything, without letting the grown-ups know I was right there, I crept into the kitchen and found the rolls of kitchen towel under the sink. In the hallway I quietly tore off a wad of paper and listened.

There'd been an argument, I made out, a row of some sort. Abigail yelling. Because my aunt and uncle had heard her again in the night. Sleep-talking. Silently I got down on my knees and let the wet soak into the paper. If they found me here, I argued with myself, I would tell them I was cleaning, that I hadn't wanted Mum to find the floor in such a mess.

'Her bed was empty,' my uncle was saying. 'We found her kneeling by the wall.'

On my own knees, my arms locked, I went still. For some reason, the image came to me so strongly. Abigail, the wall – it was like I'd had that image in my head for weeks.

'She was asleep?' I heard the shiver in Mum's voice.

'Yes. But talking.'

I pulled another wad from the roll, tearing down until only the cardboard tube was left. If they heard me, so what? They must know by now that Abigail was here. They must know the two of us were awake.

'Could you make out anything she was saying this time?' said Dad.

Uncle Robert said a word that I didn't catch.

'"Sorry"? She was saying "sorry"?' Mum exclaimed. 'Sorry for what?'

'I don't know,' said Uncle Robert. 'And in the morning, she said she didn't remember any of it.' His words came out faster now, like a rush of ball bearings. 'In the end, we called her therapist. We only wanted to know how to help.'

Above me, a floorboard creaked. Abigail on the move. I got up from the floor, scooped up the sodden paper and bent cardboard tube. My uncle was still talking but I didn't want to hear any more. I stumbled up the stairs to Abigail. I dropped the sodden paper towels in my wastepaper bin and shoved the empty kitchen roll down on top of them. I sat down in the chair by my desk. I wanted her to explain. The story of her

269

sleep-talking was creepy enough, yet all of that I could almost understand except – '*Why do you keep shouting at them?*'

But now, suddenly, there were footsteps on the stairs, a knock at the door. Dad in the bedroom doorway, his face set.

'Abigail? Robert's here.'

Without another word, she unfurled herself from the bed and pushed past me and Dad. I followed her downstairs. Uncle Robert was waiting by the open front door, holding out her still-wet coat. As Mum came out of the living room, I swear I saw Abigail flinch – but then as I stepped forwards, my cousin held her arms out for me to hug her. As I pressed my cheek to the cold of her neck she whispered: 'Ask them, won't you?' In the confusion I had almost forgotten. The verdict. To be there, with him.

I pushed away the part of me that was frightened by what she had said. The secret that I still didn't understand. See, I told myself, no matter what else has happened she *trusts* you. No matter what else, she wants you to help. And you *can* help. Better than her parents, better than anyone. I held her close, breath-for-breath. I didn't hesitate, just said: 'Yes.'

And I did, as soon as they'd gone. I kept my word and spoke to my parents, exhausted in the small hours of morning. I created arguments, elaborated reasons I could safely believe in. I said she wanted the chance to confront him. I said she just needed to see him found guilty. When it came to it, I surprised even myself by how persuasive I sounded.

'Well,' said Mum when I had finished, pulling her dressing gown tight around her. 'Well,' she said, 'you know her best.'

Chapter 29

Saturday 21st September:
Day 118

ANNE

My daughter had done that: walked alone to the Bradys' in the middle of the night. And all because the day before I had called her therapist.

The intention had been with me for weeks, ever since that night when I followed Abigail up into the loft. And the night of her birthday, I'd had to confront her with mistakes of the past, dragging all the pain of that up, and now she was sleep-talking again. It was only days now until we had to face trial and I was so worried that she wouldn't make it through.

Her weekly therapy had been the cornerstone of our routine. In the beginning, I'd driven her there but once she was used to it she wanted to walk by herself. She walked there, she stayed for her hour, she came home.

On Friday, when I rang, the therapist – Jenny Coulson – wasn't available; I did my best to explain myself in my message: who I was, why I was calling, why we were so in need of her advice. It was the next morning, the Saturday, when she called back; Robert was home and Abigail was upstairs. Robert closed the door of the living room. On speakerphone, we took the call together.

From her first words, Ms Coulson sounded confused. I interrupted, trying again to explain myself. I spoke in a rush, my words tripping over each other and my explanation coming out garbled. I took a breath and went back to the beginning. I tried this time to articulate our situation slowly, sanely, point by point. Had Abigail mentioned any of this in Thursday's session? Was there anything Jenny thought that would help?

When I finished there was a silence. Then Ms Coulson replied: 'But Mrs White – I haven't seen your daughter since July.'

I felt myself go very still.

'Since *July*?' said Robert.

'I have your letter here in her file…'

'What letter?' I managed to say. Her words were entering the room like a detonation.

'The letter from you, Mrs White. You wrote she was doing much better and you felt she could stop seeing me.'

'I didn't write anything like that.'

The therapist paused, then said: 'It has your signature – same as on your payment cheques. Abigail said there was no need for me to call you. I'm so sorry, Mrs White, if there's been some mistake—'

I was shaking. I hung up. I opened my laptop, my hands slipping on the keys. I logged into our bank account and scrolled through the weeks, back, back, back and it was true. Since July, there was nothing: no cheques cashed.

'Robert,' I said once I trusted myself to speak, 'can you please call Abigail down?'

When she came down the stairs her face was closed off in a way that was worse than I'd ever seen before. The bandage across her forehead was frayed at the sides as though she'd been trying to tear it off. I thought we had talked and made it okay, but one look at her and I knew I'd been so, so wrong.

'Can you sit down?' I said. 'Here, on the couch.' I thought of that very first night when she came home, when I'd dropped the vase of roses and the carpet got soaked with spilled water, and who was to say there weren't slivers of glass still embedded in the weave?

Abigail lowered herself stiffly onto the cushions. We sat flanking her, one on either side. She looked at her knees – her too-bony knees – and I wished I was close enough to take Robert's hand. I started off as carefully as I could. I started off with: 'We are only trying to understand.'

I tried to keep my shoulders down, my body language open. I asked her: all that time, where had she been going? Where had she spent the hour if not in Ms Coulson's room?

'I walked around,' she said. 'Just walked around.'

'Wandered the streets?' The very thought of it filled my stomach with dread. I imagined her going to the bridge, the railway line.

'Didn't you think you could discuss it with us?' Robert asked. 'If you didn't want to go anymore, that's all right, but we have to know what's going on.'

It felt inconceivable that Abigail had not told us, that she had lied and hidden the lie, that she had forged a letter from us and faked our signatures, and pretended every Thursday to go. And it was inconceivable that *we had not known*.

And now another thought burrowed into my mind. 'What

about all those cheques we gave you? What happened to them, where are they?'

Abigail said: 'I tore them up.'

I saw her scattering them away in the wind as she walked. I saw her again the night of her birthday, the red dress flying out around her, haring up the street away from us. When had she veered onto this trajectory, falling so far from sense and normality? Abigail was pressing herself back into the couch, her neck rigid. My voice grew louder, despite my best efforts. 'But Abigail, *why*?'

And Robert: 'Please, Abigail, you have to communicate with us.'

I hardly knew what Robert or I said next and Abigail just seemed to be mumbling to herself. When I caught the words I could hardly breathe; her lips shaped that awful phrase again: *Stop pretending*.

I could see Robert was on the edge; my husband who was always so careful and controlled now near to losing it in a panic of concern. I held up a hand – wait, stop a moment – but by now we had already gone too far. We had pushed her, we had scolded her, we hadn't been on her side. In a split-second Abigail's mumble became a shout, a confused hubbub, and it can only have been a few seconds – half a minute at most – but it felt like hours that Abigail sat there and screamed at us, with all kinds of accusations tangled up in there.

Then she wrenched herself up from the couch, flew up the stairs and slammed her bedroom door – three, four, five times – so hard that I felt our very house would come apart.

Chapter 30

JESS

But the day after, despite everything that I knew had happened, Abigail seemed so calm. That Sunday morning, I went round to see her, to help her pack for the trial and tell her what my parents had said. But she hardly seemed bothered by any of it any more. Like, why was I even mentioning it? Sleep-talking and a crazy row, but now all that had been like nothing, gone away somewhere or never even existed. Maybe, said Uncle Robert, as he gave me a lift back home, she had just needed to get something out of her system. Maybe all that shouting had done her some good.

The more I thought about it, the more right he seemed. Abigail had done all of that shouting and now, the day before the trial, in her calmness she was almost serene.

Chapter 31

Sunday 22nd September:
Day 119

ANNE

All that remained was to get through the trial.

Abigail had had hours of preparation – with the lawyers, with Caroline from the Witness Service. We had her outfit – the one we had shopped for together; it was ironed, folded and neatly packed. We had made arrangements for the twins to stay with their best friend's family. If the Bradys' were going to join us at trial, we couldn't leave the twins with them. I sent another text to Jack's mum, checking yet again that the plans were okay. A reply came back almost at once. Yes. Of course. And good luck for the trial.

Robert and the children were upstairs packing. I was downstairs, searching for our train tickets. I checked my watch. We needed to hurry: our train was leaving in less than an hour and we still needed to drop the twins off on the way.

I shuffled through another pile of documents on the kitchen surface – the tickets weren't there either, though a bank statement was, a council letter about recycling and a scribbled drawing by Laurie in black and red.

'Have you found them?' Robert called down.

'Not yet,' I shouted back. A sheaf of papers tipped onto the floor and I crouched down to scoop them up. Amongst the scattered pages, I glimpsed a school report of Sam's, half read, but no tickets. Where were they? I remembered booking them, clear as day, three tickets, open return, because who knew how long it would last or when we would be able to come home? I remembered the confirmation email and I remembered—

Wait. I went to the foot of the stairs. 'Robert? Is the printer set up?'

'In the living room. Just plug in the cable.'

I opened my laptop on the arm of the couch, by the little table where the printer now sat. Robert had moved it there from Abigail's room. I opened my email: here they were. Three tickets. I plugged in the cable and set the printer running.

'Mummy!' A wail from upstairs. 'Mumm-e-e-e!'

'Have you got toothpaste?' I shouted up to Robert. 'We always forget toothpaste.'

The tickets came out sharp and glossy, the new ink shining. For a moment I stared at them, my breath catching. We were ready now, we had everything we needed.

Upstairs, in our bedroom, Robert was zipping up our suitcase. 'Everything okay?'

I held out the tickets: three adult bookings. Since her birthday, she no longer qualified as a child. We went through the rest of our checklist together. Nothing forgotten, nothing missed. We had the toothpaste, we had our tickets, no way to put it off and no way to back out now. Robert put his arms out and hugged me.

'All right then,' he said. 'Time to go.'

In her room, Abigail was standing by her bed with her suitcase, like a soldier waiting to go on parade.

'Ready?' I asked.

She nodded.

'Give that here then,' said Robert, beside me. 'I'll take it down to the car.'

Any moment now, we would leave.

She had been so calm since the strangeness of last night, but then Jess had been round and Jess always helped. Abigail had been so calm, in fact, that I'd easily agreed to what Lillian asked for: we would let Abigail come into the courtroom for the verdict. She would remain outside for the rest of the trial; I couldn't bear the idea of her being with *him* for days in the courtroom, the danger of the twisted bond between them. But I could understand how it might help to be there at the end: to see him found guilty, get closure. I didn't want to argue with Lillian now. No distractions, no conflict. Nothing mattered except getting through this process, the final test we had to face.

I took a last look around her room, as Robert lumbered downstairs with our suitcases. Her room was neat and tidy, the way she always kept it. Everything in its place, and the only thing that seemed to be missing was the little blue rabbit, her favourite, her flopsy. What had she done with it? She had packed it perhaps. In the mirror of her vanity, I could see her side-on reflection: nose, eyes, hairline. The angles made me notice something I seemed to have gone blind to. Gently, I tapped a finger to my forehead. 'You don't need that on any more, do you? It's healed now, hasn't it? You can take it off.'

When she reached up to lift the edge, the plaster peeled away easily enough.

'Mum-ee-ee!' Laurie's voice floated again across the hallway.

'What *is* it? Just a minute,' I said to Abigail. 'Just a minute, then we'll go.'

But in the boys' room, Laurie's suitcase lay open on his bunk and his clothes were all over the floor.

'What are you doing? You need to get ready.'

'*I'm* packed,' said Sam.

'Sam says I can't go!' cried Laurie.

'What do you mean?' I began to put his clothes back into the case, half folding them, half shoving them in. It only made him cry harder.

'With Abigail. He says I can't go.'

'Laurie! Come on. We've talked about this. We've been over this for weeks. You and Sam are staying with Jack.' The suitcase was a flimsy, Harry Potter thing and the zip buckled as I tried to fasten it. Abigail slipped into the room like a shadow, leaning her back against the wall by the door.

'But I want to go with Abigail!'

'Shut up,' Sam said. 'I told you, you can't.'

Laurie's face was distorted with grief. 'Why?'

Sam yelled. 'Because babies aren't allowed!'

The zip unsnagged, biting my finger. 'Sam, Laurie, please. We have to leave!'

I was so busy with the suitcase, yanking the zip round, that I didn't see what happened next. It was Abigail who was watching everything from the doorway. One moment, Sam was shouting and Laurie was crying, and the next there was the flash of an arm swinging, a shrieking scream from Laurie, and when I looked up he was holding his hands to his neck and Sam was tumbling to the floor.

'Oh my God, Laurie! What are you doing?'

Sam knelt on the floor with his hands to his face. There were red scratches on Laurie's neck and the collar of his pale blue T-shirt was torn. I didn't even know who to go to first. What was this? The boys – my boys – they almost *never* fought, but a whirl of images came back to me now: Sam raising a fist, Laurie shoving, kicking, crying in the night.

Before I could move, Abigail peeled herself from the wall and crouched down next to them. I'd been wrong. Yet again, I'd been wrong. The mark on her head was red and angry – not healed up at all. She raised Sam to his feet and straightened Laurie's T-shirt. It was the first time I'd seen her touch them like that.

'It's all right,' she was saying to them, 'I promise. You have to stay here and be looked after. You're going to stay away from it, and be safe.'

I let go of the suitcase and found my voice. 'What is it? My sweethearts, what is it?' Laurie wiped his eyes, Sam lowered his hands. His cheek was fine; both of them were fine. The whole thing had looked so much worse than it was. But they still stared at me, wordless; they couldn't tell me. It was as though they had sensed some shadow that none of us had grasped, channelled some current that hung over our whole family. I pulled a wad of tissue from my sleeve, wet it and dabbed the skin under Laurie's chin. I kissed Sam's cheek, soothing the bruise.

I heard Robert beep the horn from outside. I looked at the trio of my children standing there – innocent, bruised – and felt weak with unease. I thought of how Abigail had screamed at us yesterday, bizarre, incomprehensible words we couldn't make sense of, about photographs, betrayals, a terrifying muddle of anger and hurt.

Something is bothering me. The detective's words buzzed through my head, a memory of him staring at us as he played Cassingham's tape. *Something still isn't adding up.*

A thought burst open in me, a tight shoot wrapping its tendrils around me. For the first time I thought: what if DS McCarthy was right all along?

Chapter 32

JESS

The courtroom was cold. That's what I was aware of most, at first. How all of us huddled in the gallery.

The trial had already run for two days, and now finally I had persuaded Mum and Dad to take me down. We have to be there, I'd told them. Abigail would want me there. And I was old enough to be in the courtroom. Fifteen, almost sixteen, the rules said I was allowed, and Dad was able to persuade Mum now. I had been waiting and waiting, and now finally we were here, in the middle of the trial itself.

The public gallery was almost full: I counted fourteen men and twenty-one women. Not long now, Uncle Robert had said; they could move to deliberation any day. I couldn't stop thinking about what Abigail had asked me, what she'd said. *When they read out the verdict, I want to be there. I have to get through all these lies.* I had agreed, thought I'd understood her plan, but what if there was so much more to it than that?

I sat in the gallery, scanning the courtroom. What had I been expecting? For a monster to look monstrous, like some ogre in a fairy tale? Each time, my gaze passed over him, juddering away. I only made the connection with reality when I looked for the cues of the courtroom itself – the features I'd repeatedly Googled before coming. Those were the jurors, and the bench for the judge; there was the witness stand, and there was the dock, and this man was in it. This man. I'd seen his picture all over the news and Uncle Robert had described him when he'd returned from that first hearing – his hair, his height, his shape. But when I finally did set eyes on him it caught me so off-guard. He was so *ordinary*. That pale blond hair hanging over his ears. I thought of the boy I'd seen in the blurred Internet print-out. In the street I would have walked straight past him. I couldn't have singled him out in a crowd. If he had come up to me helpfully in the rain, I don't think I'd have been frightened. The idea sent a shiver down my spine.

I tried to make myself listen to what was going on. I was doing this for Abigail, I had to make myself hear it all. The prosecution called a last witness and a man climbed, light-footed, up to the stand. He settled himself, ready for questions. Ready to tell the truth and nothing but. He was a police officer, there to talk about the evidence they'd found in the house. Abigail had lived there all right, he said. There were the clothes, the DNA on the bed sheets. Packets of sanitary pads under the attic bed. They'd found plates, dishes, knives and forks. Bags of sweets and their empty wrappers. An ashtray. Storybooks and textbooks, paper and crayons. A lack of windows, a lack of light. A heavy lock on the attic trapdoor and a ladder too weighty for a young girl to unfold. Unconsciously, I kept reaching across myself into the space at my side. Reaching for Abigail, but she wasn't there; she was with Uncle Robert, back at the hotel, safely kept away from it all. I felt her absence like a hollow pit, one I was in danger of tumbling right into.

While the police officer spoke, the jury were blank-faced. I couldn't read anything in their expressions. Not the man with the frown lines between his eyes nor the woman with glasses that caught the light, not the elderly man who scratched his stubble, nor the young woman who caught a cough in her fist. And then the defence barrister was standing up. His chin was wide and broad, like a hammer, and his eyes looked like they could see right through anyone. He was so tall, he towered, and his questions were like darts, so sharp you hardly even felt them go in. As I watched and listened, I kept losing my footing. My hand-holds kept slipping out from under me. Again and again he did it – just when I had been so clear, so sure, the very next step I was stumbling, tumbling under his words. This defence barrister presented the very same facts, but he'd wrenched them inside out, turned them upside down. He made us look, then look again, questioning everything we'd just been told. Are you sure, every one of his questions said, are you really *sure*? Locks for imprisonment, the attic a cage. Or could the locks be for safety, for a child's own good? The traces of blood in the kitchen? Take a nosebleed, for example, or perhaps a grazed knee. Who of us hasn't made for the kitchen sink to catch the drips? What child has never hurt themselves?

Next to me, Dad laid a hand on my arm. 'Saying these things,' he murmured, 'it's only his job.' I knew that, but I still felt the muscles in my legs grow weak. We were supposed to come here and see the bad man punished. This was supposed to lay it all to rest, so that Abigail would never be frightened again. All this time I'd thought it so simple. Right and wrong, good and bad. Plain as daylight. That's what I had always believed. Now I was learning, in the very place where it mattered most, maybe it wasn't like that at all.

At the hotel that evening, I went straight to Abigail's room. I knocked, carefully at first, then louder. I wanted to warn her. I needed her to know what I'd heard. It isn't black and white, I had to tell her. There's all these questions, all these doubts. Getting the truth, hearing him found guilty, it's what you need, I know that, but what if the very opposite happens?

It was Auntie Anne who opened the door, dark shadows under her eyes and a finger pressed against her lips. Abigail had gone straight to bed, she said. No, no, she was fine, she just needed her rest. 'Best let her be,' she said as she let the heavy door fall closed.

I crept back along the muffled hotel corridor to Mum and Dad's room. In the single cot the staff had set up for me, all night I drifted in and out of sleep, unable to get comfortable on the stiff mattress. It seemed my back was caught against a cold hard rail and something or someone was pressing me backwards, leaning on me, pushing at me until I was slipping, falling, a terrible fall with something horrifying beneath—

I wrenched myself up from the nightmare, head ringing. Mum's alarm clock was shrilling for morning. Not a sliver of light showed through the heavy black-out curtains. Under me, the mattress was damp with sweat.

Chapter 33

ANNE

Near the end of the week, the defence called an expert witness – a psychiatrist who had examined Cassingham. He had conducted interviews, compiled a report, laid down all his conclusions in there, and yes, he'd concluded that the defendant had no mental illness. On the witness stand he kept referring to his typed report; it was all in there, he kept repeating, everything he wished to state. But the defence barrister kept pushing him – beyond his remit, the lawyers later said, beyond the requirements for the court, but perhaps he was just like the rest of us in that courtroom, wondering, if he wasn't ill, a psychopath or madman, then why?

The psychiatrist had a neat, square face; his grey-dusted hair was clipped short and his voice was soft. To me, he seemed likeable even though he spent his time amongst such unlikeable people. The court was quiet while the psychiatrist spoke and as he talked, Cassingham's eyes skittered. They made the same movement each time, like a tic, a slide, always in the same direction – towards our family – again and again but never quite landing. Yet again I wished Robert could be here with me; I felt so strangely exposed without him. But we'd agreed we would do it this way: he would stay outside, with Abigail. And I would be the one to listen to it all.

The defendant was a complex man, the psychiatrist was saying. He struggled with relationships and with himself. Don't forget, this doctor said, the circumstances in which he grew up. I wanted to close my ears to his voice. I didn't want to know about this man's past. Was I expected to care if he was lonely, childlike, as the psychiatrist said? What did I care that he'd been brought up in foster care, multiple homes, never being loved. It didn't excuse him, not one bit.

Don't forget, the psychiatrist went on, the defendant only wanted a bond, a family. He didn't wish Abigail any harm; he only wanted to keep her. The defendant, he explained, was something of a fantasist. It was his own reality he'd decided to create: that she belonged to him and that he was her guardian.

A surge of nausea rose up in me.

And yet, the prosecution barrister was now saying, cross-examination already underway, he kept Abigail a secret. He kept her hidden. Even in his fantasy world, he knew enough to do that. This man knew wrong from right. And despite his fantasies, he *did* harm her. In some of the worst ways possible. Physically, mentally. Sexually. And when he was done with her, he found himself *another* girl to abuse.

If I could have, there in the courtroom, I would have drilled my fingers into my ears. Instead I imagined a great thick wall around me, layers and layers of perfect lines, like a tight deep weave that would never let anything through.

Yes, the psychiatrist was saying. Because although Abigail

was a child, Cassingham was not. Cassingham was a man with the appetites of a man. And as time went on, Abigail was not so much of a child either. Cassingham, the psychiatrist said, had expressed great remorse about this aspect of his relationship with Abigail. He had never planned for this to happen. But you have to understand this too: Cassingham had nobody else. He was incapable of forming relationships with those his own age. And Abigail had become everything to him.

I kept swallowing, keeping the nausea at bay. The prosecuting barrister pressed on. You say he cared deeply for Abigail. She was everything to him. He made a whole fantasy out of their lives. So I put it to you – why then did Cassingham attempt to obtain himself *another* child, another little girl to keep? Why did he – so to speak – abandon Abigail? If he cared that much for Abigail, how then, sir, do you explain that?

A murmur rose up behind us, people shifting in the gallery. The psychiatrist looked down at his hands, as though trying to find the right words to explain something so unspeakable.

Picture this, he said at last. A china vase, enamelled in exquisite colours. It is perfect – in shape, in form, in design. It's a thing you've always wanted. You love to hold this beautiful vase, to trace its outlines with your fingers. But one day, in your fervour, you grip the vase too tight. A tiny crack appears on its surface.

One crack is not so bad. You can display the vase with the crack turned to the wall. From the front, it looks like the perfect vase you know and love. But soon the same thing happens again – another crack – and again and again, until whatever angle you view the vase from, it shows its defects, its damage. The vase is no longer perfect. In fact, this vase that was once so precious to you, now appears flawed. It is not the same to you now. Now that it is broken.

For a while, you don't know what to do. Things aren't as they were before. Then one day, you are walking past a shop and in the window, you spy a vase. It is perfect, no cracks or flaws ...

Well, said the psychiatrist. I think perhaps you understand.

A fantasist who still knew right from wrong; that was the picture they painted of him. Did it help us, did it explain anything? Not for me. The only person I cared about was my daughter, my beautiful, brave daughter. Only her answers mattered to me and hers was the only voice I wanted to hear.

The video link was designed to let her speak freely, without fear, to prevent any possibility of him intimidating her. She swore to tell the truth, the whole truth, and nothing but the truth and I wondered whether at last this would bring us to the heart of it. I wondered if we would finally hear a story that made sense of the child who had returned to us, or whether it would only be one more story we couldn't understand. The special room she sat in, just for this purpose, was plain; I could only see the pale blue walls. I longed to be in there with her, to comfort her, to help her, but she had to do this part alone. Even Robert would have to wait outside. They asked her a whole catechism of questions, prosecution and defence. Each time there was a pause before she spoke, her voice on the link a fraction delayed, as though she hesitated before each answer.

Yes, she had lived with the defendant for seven years. From the age of eight until the age of fifteen.

Yes, to begin with, there were locks on the trapdoor. Later, he'd decorated the attic, made it her room.

Yes, she'd had food and warmth and water. Was permitted to wash, and use the flush toilet. Yes, he'd guarded and watched her while she did. Later she'd had the freedom of the house.

No, he'd made no attempt to return her home. His house was her home now, he'd said. Yes, it was true, there were times when he'd hit her. But only sometimes. Only when he got tired or angry or sad. No, she had no lasting scars.

As I watched her up on the screen, it was more and more like watching a somnambulist: someone in a dream who hardly knew what they were saying. Was it only the delay in the sound that made it seem like that? She was telling us the truth – the other evidence proved it – so why did I sense this strange falseness in her, as though somewhere there lived another truth entirely?

Yes, he brought her books, she went on. And newspapers with – now she realized – certain pages torn out.

Yes, she had been thoroughly taught. No, she was never taken to school, but sometimes he would take her outside, just to the end of the street and back. No, she had never been recognized. She wasn't very recognizable by then.

Yes, after a while, he'd begun to have sex with her. When she got older. From when she was thirteen. Yes, he always used protection. He was always careful to protect her that way.

No, she'd never really tried to run away. And she told them about the one attempt she had made, when she was still so little, still only eight. One night when she was exhausted, confused and angry with him. She told him that she didn't like him and didn't want him to look after her any more. She didn't want the sweets or the books or the cuddles. She only wanted to go home.

So much of what she said I already knew, but here were so many details that I had never been aware of. All these parts of my daughter I'd never known.

That night, he left the trapdoor unlocked deliberately, the ladder unfolded on purpose for her. She heard him do it. So she packed a bag – used her pillowcase – and put in it the pyjamas he'd given her, one of the little vests and her shoes. She climbed down from the attic, crept downstairs. She found him by the front door, sitting collapsed on the floor with his head all askew. Tongue hanging out. Throttled by the tie he'd looped round the door handle. She was nearly sick. He opened his eyes.

But I would have, he'd told her. And it would have been all your fault.

But the truth was, even despite that, she wouldn't have gone through with it. The truth was, from the beginning she had believed him, the things he had said. When he'd told her that he had always loved her. When he'd said she was always meant to be with him. Because he was right that her family never came, though every day she had waited for them in vain. Because he'd done everything to make her feel special.

And because, in the end, he'd had so much proof.

He'd been so clever. At eight, she had been old enough to think for herself, and that was the worst part of what he'd done to her. Mind games, like Robert had once said. She had formed her own beliefs, reasoning straight from his faulty premises. She had built them up in her own mind from the sliver of doubt any child might have had, and I knew that Abigail's sliver had been wider than most. He'd presented her with layer upon layer of confusion and lies, dressed up as truth and perhaps that was the cruellest abuse of them all.

But from the moment Abigail took the stand and began to speak, I saw that he would be found guilty. Abigail's testimony showed us it all. Whatever he'd told himself and whatever justifications he had given her, none of that would hold up now. I felt it in the ripples through the courtroom as Abigail spoke. I saw it in the shifts on the jurors' faces and in the way the defence barrister lowered his head. They saw exactly what he had done.

Now as the prosecution and defence unfurled their closing speeches, I imagined myself holding Robert's hand and finally being able to hug my daughter. With Lillian and Fraser and Jess beside me, it felt as though nothing could break our family now. Maybe I should have noticed when they showed us the photos, those stark images of how she had lived, kept until the very end of her testimony, projected on a wide, tall screen for anyone who could still be in doubt. The tiny bed, hardly five-foot long, crammed against the wall. The bare floorboards. The lock. The potty by the bed. The sloping attic walls with no windows, papered in a striped design, the single light in the ceiling with a crooked shade. The photographs were crisp and blown up large for display, but it was such a small detail and there was so much else that was awful in them, that I simply didn't notice. Then before I knew it, the judge was summing up and sending out the jury, and we were standing and it was over, no more testimony – we were done.

Now all that remained was to wait for the verdict. Outside the courtroom, we went upstairs to the balcony, trying to stay away from the hubbub of reporters who swarmed the street outside. Caroline brought Abigail and Robert to us, and Abigail let me hug her though she was as stiff as a mannequin.

Caroline crouched down next to her, Witness Service badge shining, her voice a murmur, checking with my daughter once, twice, a dozen times, are you sure you really, really want to go in? 'I need to see,' Abigail kept repeating, like a record stuck in a single groove. 'I need to see it. I need to know.' It was as though her mind was grappling with something that blocked out every single other thought. Eventually, Caroline stood up and stepped back, leaving her to us as though to say, I've done my part, it's your call now.

Robert shook her hand. 'Thank you, Caroline, we appreciate all you've done.'

From the balcony, I could see people milling below: all these people here to see lives broken, changed or put back together. Robert stood beside me and took my hand though we didn't exchange a word. Until the verdict came what was there to say?

Another half an hour crawled by. I saw the detective come in through the entrance, DS McCarthy who had said he would come to check on proceedings. He turned his eyes up at me, his grey gaze falling on me like a shadow. As I followed his movement through the space below, my eyes caught on another figure – impossible but there. In shock, I drew back from the rail.

'What is it?' said Robert.

I couldn't move. I'd recognized, unbelievably, who this was. Ten years etched into his cheeks, his forehead, but the eyes were the same, and the nose and the lopsided mouth.

'It's Abigail's father,' I said. 'It's Preston.'

'Preston? Here?' Robert peered over the balcony.

Somewhere nearby I was distantly aware of my sister and Jess engaged in a whispered argument. 'But didn't you see it?' Jess was saying. 'That wallpaper, the pattern, the *very same one*!'

All those phone calls I had ignored. All those lines I had tried to hold. I glanced behind at my daughter, curled in her chair, blocking out the world, then turned back to the man who was her father.

He was here; it seemed he had only just arrived. Had he flown all this way, just to be here at her trial? As though he had heard my thoughts, Preston looked up and saw me, and I hardly knew whether to laugh or cry. After everything I had done to keep him out of this, after everything he had been to me in the past.

He began to climb the stairs up to us and I pushed myself away from the balcony and hurried to meet him, to stop him. We came face to face, halfway up, halfway down, the father of my child, this man I hadn't seen in a decade.

'Please,' I found myself blurting out. 'Please, Preston, don't make a scene. I'm sorry I never answered your calls, but please don't do anything now, not in the middle of this, please. She won't be able to handle it, she's already dealing with so much.'

He looked at me; even standing on the step below, he still stood that little bit taller than me. I felt as though I was nineteen again, my life all over the place, things spiralling.

'Please, Annie. I only want a chance to see her. I promise I won't even speak to her; everything else can wait until after.'

He took a step to one side and slowly continued climbing, and I hurried after him. As I did, I realized something had changed about him. It wasn't simply that he was older, those lines on his face anyone might have expected, it was that there was a colour to his skin and uprightness in the way he held himself; he had changed and I realized in a rush what it was.

Finally, Preston was sober.

At the top of the stairs he came to a halt. My family were there, scattered on the balcony, Lillian and Jess still whispering together. And Abigail, curled in her seat, knees drawn up, hair half covering her face, thumbs jabbing at her phone, some game she was playing, drowning everything out. She was so thin, so pale; her hair that once had looked so sleek straggling across her shoulders.

I stood there next to Preston, looking at her. It felt like how sometimes in the dead of night we would stand together looking down at our daughter in her cot, those rare times when none of us were fighting. In sleep, she had been the perfect child, but now … I felt almost ashamed. 'Preston, I'm sorry, it's been so difficult, so hard for us all—'

'Annie. Stop. She's beautiful,' he said.

That was the moment she looked up and saw him, dawning recognition on her face. Preston was smiling and raising a hand, *hello,* but then Lillian was moving, crossing the space between her and Abigail, putting her whole body in between like a shield. And it was Abigail who got up and roughly pushed my sister aside.

Before any of us could move a step further, a voice came from the stairs behind me. 'They're ready for us now,' said DS McCarthy, like an order. 'They're calling us back in.'

There wasn't time for anything else; no time for Abigail and Preston to reconcile, no time for me to say a word to Lillian.

I stood there looking at my daughter and I couldn't name it, couldn't say what it was, only the sense again that there was something terrible I had missed, something all of us had missed and I felt the lines – all those lines I had so carefully drawn – start to splinter, only this time I had no idea how to stop it and no idea what was about to be let in.

The gallery was crammed full – a dozen journalists had arrived and DS McCarthy slipped in too – and there now wasn't enough room for us all to sit together. We'd only waited two hours in total – such a short time for a jury to deliberate.

I pushed my way with Abigail and Robert to the front and Abigail insisted that Jess sit with us. Fraser and my sister sat alone, behind, and I saw Preston slip in at the back. Good to his word, he'd let her be. Afterwards, I promised myself, I would put everything right between them, only please, please let us get through this first.

We stood for the judge and when the jury filed in, I saw Cassingham in the dock make one move, just one: running his hands through the lengths of his hair.

Now the head juror was standing up. The court clerk's voice filled the courtroom. 'Foreman of the jury, have you reached a verdict on which you are all agreed?'

I thought of how everything came down to this, how it would put an end to everything Abigail had been through.

'We have.'

I thought how it would draw the ultimate line and allow us to finally be the family I had been trying to make all this time, loving each other and trusting each other and doing everything right. That was all I had ever wanted and because I wanted that so badly I knew they had to find him guilty.

Beside me someone was fidgeting, twisting in their seat. I closed my eyes, every sense and nerve straining for the answer.

'And on the charge of child abduction, do you find the defendant guilty or not guilty?'

Guilty, I whispered to myself. *Guilty, guilty, guilty*. Beside me someone was standing, rising from their seat.

'We find the defendant—'

She was a warrior, she was a broken child, she was an avenging angel, she was my daughter. She was all of these things in that moment.

'*Wait!*'

In the echoing silence that followed, Abigail was the centre of the universe.

She twisted round to face the gallery, her knuckles glaring white on the back of her chair. I reached for her, then pulled my hands back; if I touched her I felt she would burn me right through.

'Sit down!' cried the judge. 'Sit down!'

But she wouldn't. She was staring into the gallery in a blaze of accusation, staring at the one person I never could have imagined: not me, not Cassingham, not even Preston—

Her eyes were locked on the one person I had trusted more than anyone. Huge pieces clashed – those attic walls, Jess's whispers, a picture of a laughing child in an album.

'"Abduction"?' Her voice was fracturing, desperate, terrified of itself, as she hurled these words: '"Abduction"? *You sent him photos of me!*'

Chapter 34

Thursday 26th September:
Day 123

JESS

It was like there was nothing but white space, and no one else in the courtroom but Auntie Anne, Uncle Robert, my parents and me.

I couldn't bear to look at Abigail.

Dad's face was pale as a ghost's, his beard no mask to disappear behind. The horror on his face was a mirror of everything I felt. He stood up, his whole frame shaking.

I dug my nails into my palms, all the safety in my world torn out. 'Please,' I cried, '*please* say that you didn't!' Because if it was true, then the monster wasn't a stranger at all and one of us had delivered Abigail straight into his hands.

My dad stood looking down at her. But she just sat frozen, staring past me at Cassingham. From the look in her eyes alone, I knew.

It was true. She had done it.

My mum.

Chapter 35

Thursday 26th September:
Day 123

LILLIAN

I was looking at him and, in the dock, he was looking at me. His expression said, *Come on now, you remember*. His expression said, no need to pretend. Seconds tumbled past in which I couldn't understand it, until he reached up and dragged his hair back from his face. He scraped it back from his forehead, his fingers stretching the strands so tight that they almost disappeared, his face appearing so much thinner now beneath.

I couldn't pull my gaze away and I finally saw what I had missed this whole time.

Ironic really. After all, I've always prided myself on not making mistakes. I plan, I consider, I am thoughtful. I can see the big picture and the long game. I know what's best. This is who I am.

My sister Annie made mistakes. Big ones. Ones I always ended up trying to put right. Take the night of the fight, the biggest fight they'd ever had. It was me who'd had to extricate her from there. God knows when – if – she'd ever have left otherwise.

It wasn't the first time I'd had to sort things out – between them, or with Abigail – but that night was the worst. When Preston's brother called me, it made me so angry. I could tell on the phone he was still just a kid, still in his teens, an immature voice saying, *please come now, you have to do something.* He didn't even know me, but he'd found my number and he'd been that desperate. This seventeen-year-old kid trying to look out for a two-year-old because her own parents had run completely off the rails.

One a.m. and they weren't even in the house when I arrived. The front door was half open and the inside reeked of smoke. Cigarettes and more. The place was a mess, clutter everywhere; it was clear Preston was hooked on something again. I could see places where Annie had tried to keep order, but she'd never been good at taking control.

I found them out in the back garden. The neighbours up and down the street must have heard everything. Preston was drunk, or high, who knows, yelling, swearing, I'd no idea about what. Annie was standing there in flip-flops – flip-flops, for God's sake, in the middle of December – and pyjama bottoms and a jacket she'd shoved on. She was in tears trying to calm him down, unable to see she was only making things worse.

I marched out there – I actually marched – and grabbed my sister without saying a word to him. You can't reason with someone in that state. He started doing something with the garden bench then, dragging it off the patio, trying to tip it over. I managed to get Annie back into the house and I didn't stop to pack her clothes. Her handbag was slung over the back of a kitchen chair so I just grabbed that. *Where is Abigail?* I kept saying. Every time she replied, *What are you doing here?* I'd expected to hear my niece wailing away, but no, not a sound.

It wasn't till I got back out into the front hallway that I found her. Preston's teenage brother was bringing her down from upstairs. He was as young as I'd pictured: this skinny kid in a tracksuit, all shaved head and big eyes. She was clinging to him, completely silent. That disturbed me more than anything, far more than if she'd been bawling her head off. Back through in the kitchen, Annie was in a hopeless state, hardly able to pull her shoes on. I didn't say a word to the kid, barely looked at him, as I stepped up the stairs and grabbed Abigail, stuck a coat on her and hauled her and my sister out of there.

I got us a taxi straight to our flat in West London where Fraser was up waiting for us. Anne was exhausted; we made up the sofa for her – we didn't have a spare room back then, not with London prices. Abigail we put down in the cot with Jess. We found them both in the morning with their arms wrapped round each other, sleeping like angels. I told myself then, thank God she's too young to remember any of this. But my God, I thought now. Perhaps she always did.

It was two more years of arguments and mess before Annie finally cut contact with Preston. When she met Robert, when she at last had the chance to make a new life with him, I finally, finally put my foot down. Preston contested, but the courts decided otherwise. He was an addict, after all.

Afterwards, though, his young brother kept texting. So many texts saying, why wasn't Abigail visiting any more? I felt for him, I really did. I'd never forgotten the way Abigail clung to him that night, huddled in his thin arms. That was how

I'd remembered him. But clear lines, clean breaks; they're so important, especially for someone like Annie. Leave a gap and she would tumble through it; leave a loophole and she would tangle herself in it.

For the longest time I ignored those texts; I never mentioned them to Annie. I suppose I'd assumed he'd eventually lose interest, but he never did. Finally, I remembered what Annie had once told me: *You think you're setting an example to people. Instead you shame them into giving up.*

I mentioned courts and legal proceedings, but I sent the picture to make it clear: she had a good life now, with us. I sent him the picture to show him the evidence: Abigail aged five in red dungarees, smiling, happy in her brand-new house with a backdrop of white wallpaper with diagonal blue stripes. I never told Annie what I'd done. I sent him the photograph, and it worked. I didn't hear from him again after that, the young man I'd always believed was Preston's brother.

Now I looked at the figure in the dock, thirteen years on from when I'd last seen him, pulling back his hair so tight it appeared his head was bald – or shaved.

Such an innocent. Such a monster. I could have slapped myself for what a fool I had been.

Chapter 36

ANNE

The judge was shouting, 'Take her out of the court!' and they were pulling Abigail away from me. I tried to hold onto her, but my arms and fingers were weak as straw, as though in a dream when you can barely move. She was breathing hard, full of fire. She was frightened and she was furious. The judge was calling for a recess in the trial. From somewhere, out of nowhere, other officers were leading Lillian, Robert, Fraser and Jess away. My sister's face was hard as a statue's. If they tried to put her in handcuffs, I imagined she would hold out wrists of white marble.

DS McCarthy rose up beside me, a hand on my arm, his voice low. 'You need to come with me.' He was pushing me out of the courtroom and at the back, through the crowds, I caught sight of Preston, his face stiff with shock. As we passed, words came tumbling out of him – *'Fuck, Annie, I've realized who he is!'*

I tried to call out to him, but the detective was pushing me relentlessly ahead. He led me to an interview room, an empty space among the tumult of the courthouse. 'In here,' he said. 'Don't speak to anyone until I come back.'

I fought to catch my breath. 'Get Preston as well,' I told him as he turned to leave. 'Abigail's real father, he's out there.' I thought, Preston, we need you, I'm sorry I never answered you before, we need you because maybe you know what this is.

The detective went out without a sign that he'd heard.

I sat there and waited for three long hours.

When he returned, he had no one else with him.

'Where is my daughter?' I said. 'My husband?'

'In separate rooms. We had to interview you all separately.'

'And Lillian?'

'We've taken her statement too.'

'What has she done? Please, David. Tell me what she's done.' But I needed to tread slowly, for the sake of my own sanity. I started where it felt easiest. 'Preston knew him, didn't he?'

'Yes.'

'Tell me how.'

'In foster care. They overlapped a few months. Preston didn't recognize him until now.'

In foster care. How could anyone have known? I pressed my hands to my jaw. 'Did you check? Is it true?'

He nodded. 'We've tallied the records.'

I lifted my head. 'He told Abigail he was her uncle.'

'Now you see why. They both lived in the same foster home, when Preston was fourteen and Cassingham seven. Preston knew him as "little Johnny" – a sad kid with bruises he tried to help. I imagine it was the closest thing to a family that Cassingham ever knew.'

He was known to us, a bizarre extension of our complicated family. This time, when my eyes met the detective's, a new thing passed between us, all the previous antagonism gone. My look to him said, *It's true, you were right*, and his look to me said, *Yes, and I'm sorry*.

Now the detective was talking about the night Lillian came, the worst fight with Preston, the final straw. 'Do you remember someone there?' he was saying.

'Lillian...'

'And who else? Try to think.'

But I couldn't think or I didn't want to or even if I wanted to remember, there were only flashes – 'Someone holding Abigail. Fraser? A neighbour?'

'Lillian believes that he was there. That he was the one who rang your sister, pretending to be Preston's brother.'

I felt sick and terrified of what this meant. I wanted Robert here with me but it was just me with the whole world cracking under my feet.

'If he was there that night,' the detective went on, 'if he had Lillian's number, we suspect that he was stalking you. We imagine he tracked down Preston at first, became obsessed with him. Then later, you and baby Abigail.'

I dropped my head into my hands, my scalp crawling, and I told DS McCarthy about all those times I'd felt someone had been invading that flat. 'Preston never believed me and I thought it was just me, my mind going crazy. But you're saying it was him. In our home? In our lives?' It was so hard to breathe; my chest was so tight. 'I still don't understand. I don't understand! Did she give her to him? Did she give her...?'

DS McCarthy shook his head; a slow, graceful movement.

'I don't believe it was like that. No conspiracy. Lillian claims her intentions were good. That she only sent the picture to get him to stop contact.'

This awful thing, this terrible act. How could I be sure she hadn't done this on purpose – my sister who never, ever made mistakes? But to believe otherwise would be to tear everything apart and I had to trust in the goodness of my family.

'But why didn't he tell all this to the police? Why did he never say that he knew us? He could have put the whole blame on us.'

'Because you heard it, didn't you, in the trial? A fantasist maybe but he knew right from wrong. He had stolen from you, he had trespassed. Prior knowledge of you would suggest premeditation. None of that would have worked in his favour.' DS McCarthy smoothed a hand across his cheek. 'We suspect his stalking continued even after Lillian's message, and after you moved away to Lincolnshire as well. You can do it – the Internet, Facebook.'

My stomach dropped to the floor again. 'That's how he would have known we'd be down in London,' I whispered. 'At the hospital. I put it on Facebook. David, I put everything on Facebook back then and I didn't even know how to make my account private.' Because back then I was happy and naïve and stupid, and because I always, *always* made mistakes.

'We can check for him on CCTV there.'

'How long had he been planning this thing then?'

But the detective was shaking his head. 'I don't think he planned it at all. I think he only meant to see her. He didn't follow you into the Tube station, did he, and he couldn't have known that she'd come back out. The rest was a coincidence. The rest was opportunity.'

I gripped the edges of the table in front of me and fought with myself to push away the guilt. If I hadn't left her, their paths would never have crossed, it was because of me that moment happened, a million to one moment that sealed all our fates.

The words I'd heard on the police tape came back to me: … *at the station steps, I'd thought that was it. I was simply wandering, outside in the rain.* Suddenly I could see the whole scene so vividly, as though I'd stepped right into his mind. He is there with us, quite deliberately, at the hospital, seizing his chance to see her even for the briefest time. Afterwards he tails us to the Tube station, extending the precious minutes before he has to say goodbye, hearing me nagging at her the whole way. Outside the station entrance, from under his umbrella, he watches Abigail disappear inside. He has seen her, filled his eyes with her, all that he wanted, but he's too overcome with emotion to return home yet. Half in a daze, he circles the station. Then just as he's about to head home, the impossible happens, telling him this was always meant to be: he turns around and like a miracle *my daughter reappears.*

And he takes her.

I wiped my eyes and looked up at the detective. 'So what happens now?'

'Now I present these facts to the judge. And he will decide if this trial can continue.'

He led me back to where the rest of my family was waiting: Fraser and Lillian, Jess, Robert, Abigail, in a room with chairs round a conference table. I sat down, straight across from my sister, feeling Abigail's dark eyes on me. We sat there and went through everything, bringing each piece of the jigsaw to light.

'You did it,' I said to Lillian. 'You sent him photographs.'

'Yes.' My sister lifted her eyes to me. 'Though for the record, there was only one.' It was the first time in our lives I'd ever heard her confess to a mistake.

Now, for the first time since her outburst, Abigail spoke. Her voice was slow and thick, the way she sounded when she talked in her sleep. 'He said he used to watch over me. He said he knew me since I was born. He did, didn't he? He was there the whole time, and you never knew.'

'But why didn't you tell the police about the photo?' It was Lillian speaking and it took me a moment to realize it was my daughter that she was asking.

My daughter curled herself back in her seat. My sister was right though: why hadn't Abigail told them? Instead she'd waited to shout it in a courtroom, instead of telling the police so that we all could have known. Her voice came out barely above a whisper. 'Because for so long I was so scared of making it true.'

I felt my eyes fill with tears. I imagined the horrors that Abigail had lived with these last four months. No wonder she had lashed out at us. No wonder she had feared she was going mad. Now, more than ever, I had to convince her. I had to wipe that whole slate clean. I leaned towards her across the wide table though she was too far away for me to take her hand.

'Cassingham twisted everything,' I said. 'He's guilty of more than we ever thought. He lied to you and he made victims of us all. He used it all against you, Abigail, but none of it was true. *We* are your family. None of us did this.'

In the wake of my words came Lillian's quiet, commanding voice.

'You do believe us, Abigail. Don't you?'

Chapter 37

Friday 27th September:
Day 124

JESS

She did believe us, she told us so, and so did the prosecutor and so did the judge, and the next day the trial restarted and they read out the verdict and Cassingham was found guilty.

He was guilty!

They came to get him and take him away. He didn't even struggle, he knew it was over. In the hubbub that erupted in the courtroom, I grabbed Abigail's arm, saying, 'Aren't you glad?' She had to be – as glad as me.

'He hurt me,' she whispered as I put my arms around her. 'He hurt me so much.' She was all stiff and rigid in my arms, but that only made me hug her harder.

Now her lawyer came wrestling his way through the crowd, dabbing at his brow with the heel of his hand, leaving damp patches on the cuff of his shirt. His eyes were shining and his mouth wore a smile. 'I rarely do this,' he said, 'the police usually speak. But come with me – the reporters will be waiting at the western exit. If you'd let me, I'd like to make a statement for you all.'

We followed him out along a tall, wide corridor, with windows high up on the walls and sunlight that sparkled on rain-spattered glass. Outside there was a whole crowd to welcome us, joy at the verdict, and everyone so happy. Puddles on the ground, but bright sun shining – the kind of weather that rainbows came from. I kept hold of my cousin, my arm around her, so close her bony elbow dug into my waist. I wanted to shout to the waiting crowd, *Look at us! Look at the two of us together!* I wanted everyone to see us like this, with nothing in the world to separate us now.

Tomorrow the papers would be full of our story. The happy ending at last, *at last*. To the clatter and flash of cameras, sun catching the wet, the lawyer was making his statement, praising our family for our courage, our love. He would have known about everything that had gone wrong, everything we had missed, everything our family had mistakenly done, but his words showed that none of that mattered. It could be forgotten, wiped away like raindrops, because Cassingham had been found guilty and everything, *everything* else was over.

I was so happy it was like walking on air.

Chapter 38

Friday 27th September:
Day 124

ANNE

On the long train journey home, Abigail curled herself into her seat. Across from her, Jess stretched out her legs so that their feet were touching. They fell asleep together like that, the way they used to as tiny children.

None of us needed to speak any more: Lillian, Fraser, Robert and me. We had come through it. Everything had been laid bare in that courthouse, layers of the story we had never dreamed of, but now it was over. Cassingham was guilty – guilty of everything – and now we were free, finally, to be Abigail's loving family. As we rode through the soft dusk, I had never felt closer to them. Even Preston – left to make his own way back to Heathrow – was one of us now.

Outside the courthouse, I'd gently introduced him to her. She'd huddled next to me, not quite ready yet to fit him back into her life. But he hadn't got upset or angry, just told her he loved her and how much he cared, and I was so proud of him for that. I could see it then in his clear, healthy face: he had always cared so much for Abigail, he just could never before find the right way to show it.

Beside me, Abigail's eyes rolled beneath their lids; her head flopped sideways and rattled against the window. She had barely spoken since the verdict. If I was honest, she seemed to have shrunk into herself again. The thought made a heavy hollow in my stomach but I pushed it away. All right, so the trial had overwhelmed and exhausted her. So many huge facts and questions to deal with and no doubt that would be hard for her right now. But all that mattered was that Cassingham was guilty.

From here on, I told myself, she would only need time.

When we reached our station close to dusk, my sister stood to pull down our bags. It was only when I stretched up to help her that I realized she was no longer taller than me. Somewhere in the span of years, I had caught her up and as we lifted down my suitcase together, I glimpsed how changed she looked.

'Lillian?' I said. 'Why don't you all stay with us tonight?' It had never been like this: she'd never been the one in need of rescue. Without looking at me, she nodded.

Back at home, with the twins collected from Jack's house, all of us headed, exhausted, to bed. I tucked the twins in and brushed my teeth next to Robert. It was only once I was lying in our old familiar bed, the room lit by a bright flat moon and Lillian sleeping at the end of the hallway, no longer all-knowing, no longer perfect, that the thought struck me: who am I to turn to now?

Chapter 39

Friday 27th September:
Day 124

JESS

You could always hear trains from Abigail's house – the soft clatter, the echoing horns. You could imagine the passengers going here and there, freight carriages running through the night. When she was little, Abigail used to say they kept her awake. Later she got used to the sounds.

When I woke – to the sound of a train or a voice, I couldn't really tell – the room was dark, the lamp was off, but the curtains were drawn back from the window. A bright white moon was shining outside, an almost-full moon, and Abigail was awake, sitting cross-legged up in bed. Her hair was loose over her shoulders and growing long now, bright blonde. In the moonlit dark, it was like she was glowing.

'Happy Birthday, Jess,' she whispered.

In the middle of all the chaos, I'd forgotten. Today was my birthday. I was sixteen. Abigail and I were the same age again.

I reached out to turn on the little Mickey Mouse lamp she still had in her room. 'Will you come with me?' she said, blinking in the brightness. 'I've something to show you.'

'You mean – ' I rubbed my eyes – 'like, a present?'

'Sort of, yes,' she said. She pushed herself off the bed. Only now did I notice – she was fully dressed. I had a moment of strange-dream logic, when behind the surprise everything easily makes sense. Abigail, there in front of me, was so clear.

Without questioning her, I pulled on my jeans and jumper. Silently she opened the bedroom door. The landing outside was dark. Behind their own doors, all the bedrooms were dark, but the moonlight shone through the landing window. It was like it was following us, lighting the stairs up in silvery-grey.

Softly Abigail opened the door opposite – the door to the twins' room. I heard a snuffling murmur – Laurie or Sam turning over in his sleep. 'Look.' She pulled me forwards into the doorway beside her. The twins were tucked-in humps in the gloom. They looked so young, so peaceful. 'Do you see?' said Abigail.

See what? It was Sam, it was Laurie, her brothers. They were fast asleep, they were fine. As if hearing my thoughts, she let the door close again. Her voice was thick, her words almost slurred, like she was talking to me without being properly awake. 'Come on then. Let's go.'

I thought about saying to her, no, come on Abigail, let's go back to bed. Whatever it is, we can do it in the morning. It was dark and the house was cold, but in the morning everything would be warm and bright. Instead I followed her down the stairs, holding onto the banister like I was afraid I'd tumble the descent head-first. The bare floorboards downstairs were chilly. I shivered in my thin jumper, my bare feet. But Abigail was already at the back door, lifting our coats down from their hooks.

'Where are we going?' But she just pressed a finger to her lips. She looked so beautiful to me then, my old familiar play-mate. Here she was, my friend, my family, the single person who mattered to me most. I took my coat from her and tugged it on, took my scarf as well to wind about my neck. Together we sat on the kitchen floor to pull on our shoes.

Silently, she unlocked the back door. Outside, the night was beautiful. A sharp bright cold after the cloudiness of London, and the sky was crystal clear. No sign of rain and the moon so close to full. In its light and under the glow of the streetlights, we headed across the decking and to the little fence at the bottom of the garden. As she opened the gate and I followed her through, our breaths made white clouds in the pure air.

I had no idea of the time. It could have been midnight, it could have been almost dawn. It was like time had stopped entirely and in these moments only Abigail and I existed. As if only the two of us had ever existed and somehow everything had been leading to this.

We made our way up the silent street, like shadows. No birds, no cars, no barking dogs. The whole world was still. We wove our way up the street to the lopsided railings at the end, to the path that led all the way to the embankment. Of course. Where else would we have gone? In the moonlight, like a spell, I could see the outlines of old footprints on the muddied ground ahead, marking the way, as if this was the way we were always meant to come. The path through the scrubby bushes was like a tunnel, mired in shadows as the streetlights fell away behind us. Brambles caught at my elbows and shins. I twisted and turned against them in the dark, yet Abigail slipped through ahead of me so easily, like she was a fairy-spirit or a ghost. A branch whipped my cheek and then my scarf caught and tangled, dragging away from my neck. 'Wait.' I tried to pull it free, but it wouldn't come. Instead Abigail pulled at my elbow. 'Leave it,' she said. 'You won't need it.' The air on my bare neck sent electric tingles through me. I was suddenly so aware of being alive.

At the end of the path, we came out onto the sweep of grass where once we'd sat in the sun, picking daisies. Was this where she wanted to bring me, to this place where months ago I'd given her my own simple presents – the bracelet of daisies, the childhood photo? What did she have for me here now? The tangled ground was bare, the grass muddied. The moonlight was bright, but the air, the night, was so cold.

'What is it? What do you want to show me?'

But Abigail only pointed, and I saw it now – the fencing below us that blocked off the tracks and the hole in the mesh that would so easily let two girls slip through. 'From here you can get to the bridge,' she said. 'And from the bridge you can see everything.'

Still at that point I could have turned back. But I didn't. On the other side of the fencing, the ground fell away steeply. We slip-slithered down, our fingernails catching on clumps of damp grass, roots, mud. It should have hurt, but the pain didn't seem to reach me. At the bottom, we skidded to a stop, breathless. Down here the moonlight struggled to get through and there were no more streetlamps, just shapes in the dark and the smell of iron. She pointed. 'Look.'

Along the track, sixty, seventy yards away, the bridge spanned over the railway, its signal light shining red like a beacon. Red for no trains coming, no trains allowed through, but still a dangerous place, we both knew that. A thick iron structure of struts and railings, the two heavy girders that ran along the sides. A workman's bridge, closed to the public.

'We can climb up onto it,' said Abigail. 'I know a way.'

'But why? What's up there?' My voice came out faint, little more than a puff in the dark. I felt the words fade and disappear. She only said, 'You'll see.'

And so I followed her. I would have followed her anywhere. After all, what had I ever been without her? We padded along the gravelled edge of the railway line, our feet slipping on the shifting stones. At the foot of the bridge, under its shadow where the night fell deeper than ever, I made out the spiralled iron staircase, tight and narrow, that led up to the flat crossing span at the top. This far away, the hoot of a train carried like music. Abigail grasped the thin handrail and we climbed, the iron ringing with each step. We passed the tiny workman's walkway, suspended from the girder that ran parallel to the bridge. And then we were at the top, on the wide safe flat. We were high up now, above the tracks, higher than the grassy embankment. From up here, the sky was vast, a deep pit. In the crystal-clear night, the black was forested with stars, brilliant clusters of them, so many that one blurred into another. I took hold of the smooth safety railings that ran the length of the bridge and tipped my head back.

'The Milky Way,' said Abigail, pointing.

'It's beautiful.' I gazed up into the starry cavern, the cold night air pinching my throat. I could have yelled straight into that beauty.

Beside me, Abigail was leaning over the rounded railings. Her hair swung like a curtain as she looked down. 'I had to bring you here to show you. To make you see.'

She didn't mean the stars, I knew that. What then? 'Be careful!' I giggled. But she shook her head, like my warning made no sense.

'You can't see from here.' She put a foot on the lower bar of the railing, like it was a rung, a ladder she was climbing. Before I could stop her, she swung herself up.

She was like an eel, the way she slithered right over. One minute there, and the next only her fists, and her body dangling. Then she dropped, landing with a clang on the tiny walkway below, little more than a thin shelf, suspended from the girder by a line of iron ropes. 'You have to climb down here,' she said. 'From the girder, you'll be able to see.'

Even then, I didn't question her. I hardly remember following her over the railings. My body seemed to move by itself. It was like the movements of childhood, scaling a climbing frame, swinging from a tree branch, everything in balance, everything easy. For a moment, I hung, full stretch from the railing, fishing with my feet and then I was down, dropping to the iron-mesh walkway beside her, the girder at my elbow and the real bridge just above.

The distant train hooted again, louder this time and I thought I could feel its vibrations now too – the faintest hum in the wires above our heads.

Abigail pulled herself right up to sit on the girder that paralleled the length of the bridge. Its surface was punctuated with thick iron rivets, handholds for our small cold hands. She was sitting now with her back to the tracks, her feet in her laced-up trainers hooked into the thin iron ropes below.

'Come sit beside me.'

In the moonlight I could see her so clearly, the perfect

reflection of myself. The iron girder was freezing, but when I pulled myself up beside her, the structure was wider, safer than I'd thought, a flat seat like a bench for the two of us. She tipped her head back and I did the same.

She was right. It was better than ever up here. The silhouette of the bridge's railings, two feet, three feet in front of us, but beyond and above them, nothing at all. Sitting here, on the wings of the bridge, it was like floating in mid-air. Here, perched on the girder, we were flying. Abigail's blonde hair glowed ruby, lit up by the signal light. 'I believe everything they've told me,' she was saying. 'All the explanations they've given.'

In the excitement of climbing over, and the beauty of it all, it was a moment before I could catch up with her. She was talking about the trial. The adults, the whole history that had come rolling out in the courtroom. 'Me too,' I said, holding tighter and letting out my breath. I tried to find Orion or the Plough in the stars. There were so many pricks of light, I could hardly separate them. 'In the end, we got to the truth.'

'You saw the twins sleeping, didn't you? Peaceful and safe.'

The twins? Abigail wasn't making much sense, her voice had become slurred again, but sitting up here beneath the Milky Way I hardly cared. Better to breathe in the bright air, to fly and float in the exhilaration of it all.

'That safety is all I've wanted. But it isn't like that for me, it isn't.'

'How do you mean?' I kept searching the sky.

'Jess – ' her voice cracked in the cold – 'do you remember our game – *Do-you-trust-me*?'

I almost laughed. It was like she'd read my mind. 'Of course!'

With every breath I felt the air rush to the bottom of my lungs, setting my blood fizzing. I let my eyes close. I could still see the stars behind my eyelids.

I heard Abigail let out a huge breath, and I imagined it billowing up white into the sky. 'Jess, will you play that with me now?'

It was like a dream. 'Of course,' I said, my eyes still closed, lost amidst the stars.

I was aware of her slipping down from the girder, her feet clanging on the thin iron below. I opened my eyes – and found her standing right in front of me, pressed up against me on that tiny walkway. Standing between my legs, the way a boy might stand with a girl. For the strangest, brightest moment, I thought she was about to kiss me.

Instead: 'I thought it would be better,' she said, 'when he was found guilty. I thought I'd feel safe then, Jess, but I don't. It became worse because it made me see everything I'd been through. I feel more frightened than ever now, do you get that? So I need you to play it with me. Do you trust me?'

She circled her hands about my wrists and I glimpsed now a film of blankness in her eyes. She was like a dreamer, a sleep-walker, or maybe it was only the glare of light, the far-off headlight of the train as it rounded the corner in the distance behind me.

'Do you think you can understand, Jess, how that feels? When it's supposed to be someone you trust?'

She smiled at me and I let myself lean backwards, the way it always was in our game. One of us leaning and one of us holding. I thought I understood what she was doing. She only wanted that feeling again; that sensation of perfect trust, perfect safety. After everything she had been through. I let myself sink backwards, laying myself down on the bed of black air.

'*Do-you-trust-me?*' she said, the magic mantra.

'Yes,' I whispered. *Yes, yes yes*.

I was leaning back now further than ever, further than we'd ever played before. It filled me with a burning thrill. I closed my eyes, safe in her grasp, counting the seconds – *seven, eight* – until she would pull me up. The sound of the distant train came clearer. The hum of the engine seemed all around us.

'When you're terrified because you thought you could trust them...'

Thirteen, fourteen ... Still I hung there. 'Abigail?' Her hands began to burn against my wrists. She was still tipping me, tilting me. Blood rushed to my head, spots of light dancing in my eyes.

Eighteen, nineteen ... I clutched at her arms. It had never been like this, she had never held me so far, so long. Was this honestly still a game? I was tipping backwards, like in my nightmare, there was nothing to hold onto, and she wasn't pulling me back, she wouldn't lift me! I was sliding backward, my weight pulling her over the girder too. 'Abigail!'

'This feeling deep down, ever since I came home. This is what it is!'

I was hanging nearly upside down. It wasn't red in her hair any more, but green.

'I need you to feel it, Jess,' she cried above the train's warning siren. 'I need just one person who can understand! Please, I need you to know how it feels.'

I clutched at her as the world upended. But I didn't know, I didn't understand, all that I knew was that I was slipping and a train was coming and she didn't realize, or she *did* realize it and – 'Please, Abigail! Stop, stop, *STOP!*'

Chapter 40

Friday 27th September:
Day 124

ANNE

I was trapped in a dream in which all I could see was the long slow arc of a judge's gavel coming down, dropping onto me from above like a hammer or a guillotine blade, down, down until it smashed on the crown of my head with a bang and I sat up, slick with sweat, trussed in the covers.

I had woken so many times before like this, heart scrambling, listening to some noise in the house, or outside, some untoward feeling: Abigail's sleep-talking, the creak of the loft ladder, all those other moments of drama.

As though moving along such familiar grooves, just like every other time, I pushed back the tangle of covers and slid my legs from the bed, leaving Robert to sleep his deep sleep. Like an automaton, well programmed, I unhooked my dressing gown from the back of the door and slipped it over my goose-bumped shoulders. I knew the drill by heart: out onto the landing, stop and listen. No movement, no sound, nothing yet out of place. The sound that had woken me seemed to have come from below, but I trod quietly, not startling anyone. It might still be nothing but a dream.

I listened at the twins' door but there was no sound or movement from there. Now softly, gently, I pushed open Abigail's. Her little Mickey Mouse lamp was on, casting a warm glow of light across the rose-pink walls. Everything in her room was in its place, except Abigail's bed was empty and Jess's sleeping bag sagged from the camp bed. Their mobiles both lay, abandoned, on the desk.

I turned off the lamp and pulled the door to. I was still perfectly calm; no need, I kept telling myself, to panic yet.

I went quietly downstairs. In the kitchen the fridge hummed. I checked the downstairs bathroom: maybe Abigail had taken ill and I would find her huddled, green-skinned, over the toilet with Jess crouched beside her holding back her hair. But the moonlit bathroom was cold and silent. Out of habit, I twisted the tap that had a tendency to drip. In the living room the red light glowed on the Skybox, a programme recording, some series link that Robert must have set. On the couch, the cushions were plumped and neat and the moon peeped in at the window, reflecting in the mirror that hung above the hearth. The hearth where red rose petals had once scattered.

I stopped. Through the French windows, I saw the garden gate – shut but not latched. The bang that had woken me – that was what it had been.

They weren't in the house, I realized. They'd gone out.

Without waking anyone, I got myself into my boots and coat, armed myself against the dark with a torch. I told myself they wouldn't have gone far, only into the street maybe to look at the stars. After the trial, after everything had come right, I couldn't believe that they weren't anything but fine. I would find them, lying somewhere on their backs on a patch of grass, two silly teenagers, immune to the cold. I would find them, bring them in, make them hot chocolate and put them safely back to bed.

I pulled open the back door – unlocked, more proof – and went outside. Standing in the empty back garden, I fought the fear that rose up in me: stomach, chest, throat. Stop it, I told myself. You need to work out where they are. Stop it, think and be sure.

I remembered how many times I had warned her, how many times I'd caught her trying to slip off that way. Now in my marrow I sensed that she had gone to the one place she had always been drawn to, a place that had always held such a fascination for her. The railway line.

I didn't wake anyone else; I didn't let them know. It was as though I knew I had to do this on my own. And yet as I set off up the street to the path, I thought I saw in the house behind me a single upstairs light come on.

Twigs and thorns caught at me as I pushed my way through the tangle of bushes. Something was caught, wrapped on a branch and when I pulled it free and shone my torch upon it, I immediately recognized Jess's scarf. So they'd come this way after all. I pushed the scarf into my pocket and prayed that they had gone no further than the embankment.

In the dark, the stretch of grass was muddy. I stood on the embankment panning my torch across the thick black. In its thin beam something appeared, disappeared. I steadied my hand, trained the light on the bridge and then the figures on it, wavering, dancing, but I could hardly make sense of the shapes they made; the placement of those figures was all wrong. Behind me, up the track, I could hear a distant rumble and then I thought, oh my God, the signal light is green.

I pushed my way back along the embankment, to the hole in the fence that I knew the girls had slipped through, the only way up to the bridge. Somehow Abigail had discovered this place for herself and all its secret ways, its danger games and teenage dares, a place I'd tried so hard to keep her away from.

I slithered after them down the bank, the air dense with the scent of torn grass and mud. I heard the distant train hooting as I reached the steps and above a voice was shouting, *Stop, stop, stop!* – and whether it was Abigail or Jess I couldn't tell, but either way I was coming for them. Whatever wild game they were playing, it would end.

I hauled myself up the twisting staircase, my hands raw in the cold and when I finally clambered up to the top, I realized immediately what was so horribly wrong. They weren't on the bridge. My God, *they weren't on the bridge*, they had climbed right over the safety railings, to the walkway beyond and the girder that hung across the tracks, like nothing but a tiny shelf with no safety, nothing at all to prevent them from falling. I pulled myself along the railing towards them, choked for breath.

'Abigail?'

'Auntie Anne!' Jess's voice.

My God, my God, what were they doing? My daughter, my beautiful daughter. This was no game, no make-believe. I could see the weakness of my daughter's arms; Abigail was unable to pull Jess up.

Four yards away from them, three, I tried to shine my torch

without scaring them. When Abigail craned at me over her shoulder, her eyes had the glaze of a dream, like those times before when I had seen her sleep-talk, unknown to herself. 'Abigail!' They hung frozen; Jess wasn't struggling now. She hung from the girder, almost upside down, her thin legs clutching at Abigail's waist, fingers hooked at Abigail's wrists, but not struggling. If she struggled, I realized, she would fall.

I edged closer, another foot, another inch, and the train was still coming. I was almost right next to them now, but the railings were a barrier between us. 'Abigail, please, what are you doing? You love Jess, she loves you!'

Abigail's breath was thick and laboured. She was still holding Jess, but for how much longer? 'But nobody feels it! I only want her to know how it feels!'

'What do you mean? Abigail, feel what?' I couldn't stop my own voice rising. From the corner of my eye I thought I could see a ball of torchlight wavering on the embankment. 'Abigail, this is crazy, this is madness, there's a train!'

'It hurts and it scares me!' Abigail cried over the rumbling of the train. 'It doesn't matter if they were only stupid moments, just mistakes! It's worse, that makes everything *worse*. Robert should have been there and on the train you shouldn't have left me and Auntie Lillian met him and Preston should have *known*.'

'Abigail, stop. You have to stop!' I couldn't climb over, I didn't dare when the railings were so thin and the walkway below so narrow. There wasn't time, there wasn't room when the train was coming. Jess was slipping, slipping and any wrong move I made could trigger her fall, but if I stretched, if I leaned over and reached—

'Please,' cried Jess. '*Please*!'

'It's worse to say you never meant to. You were my parents, I should be able to trust you—'

I couldn't hold the torch, I needed both hands. I let go and it fell, whirling away somewhere and now we were lit by the train's headlight only. I leaned over the railing, my jacket catching on some jagged, twisted metal prong, holding on with one hand, grasping for Abigail with the other.

'You were my *parents*, the grown-ups, and I was your *child*!'

Every word of Abigail's was like a hammer blow. I was so close, but I still couldn't reach them and each time I leaned further I felt the jagged spike bite my flesh. 'Auntie Anne, please!' Jess screamed above the shriek of train brakes, her hands clutching at nothing, her body slipping, her weight dragging both of them down.

'It makes it worse if you didn't mean any of it,' Abigail shouted, her body slipping further still, 'it makes it worse because the truth is, *the truth of it is* that I was your child and your one job was to protect me. The one single thing you were meant to do if you loved me! But you didn't! If you loved me, then you were meant to protect me and you failed, and that's what I'm most scared of and *this* is how it feels!'

I went deaf in the roar of the train crashing up to us and the train was the horror of her words, a great rushing mass that I couldn't escape. Time slowed right down, the night became silent, the train moving only a centimetre at a time and it was as though I had stepped right out of myself and had all the space in the world to think. In that slow arc of time, it was as though I saw myself from far above, a mother who had so

327

horrendously failed and I thought, how could I have pretended anything else all this time?

With Abigail's words, the guilt poured through me, guilt I'd blocked and hidden from and lied for, guilt that I'd always assumed would break me. Instead, its scorching pain was like purification, releasing me, filling me with a strength I had never known before. I was no longer blind and no longer frozen and for once in my life I was going to act as I should have from the very start, not holding back and not caring if she pushed me away or was angry or stubborn or pretended not to care, trusting myself because this was the truth, she was my daughter, my child, my responsibility through the entire of space and time, and if I couldn't protect her now, how would I ever live with myself and how could I ever be forgiven?

And so I hooked my legs round the railings' posts and leaned right out, feeling that spike of metal tear a deep gash through my flesh, stretching myself so far that if I slipped I knew it would be my end. I reached both my arms, my whole self out to my daughter and my niece, leaning into the abyss, risking my whole life to stop Abigail committing a mistake we could never recover from. I clasped my hands under my daughter's arms and I pulled, a cantilever, somehow finding the strength to do the impossible and lever them both up. I felt the deep weight of my daughter in my arms; I heard Jess's cry of relief from below.

I heaved Abigail back from the edge of the girder, until Jess was close enough for me to grasp too. I pulled them back together, my daughter and niece, levering them to safety, a hand on each of them, ignoring the pain from the wound in my side From the corner of my eye, I glimpsed torchlight on the embankment – glimpsed Lillian watching it all. I felt the world righting itself as I pulled them up, warm blood spreading at my hip, the train rushing through beneath us.

My daughter flung an arm around me, crushing herself to me, unbalancing me with the sheer force of her embrace. I had her safe in my arms, cradled against me and for the lightest moment Jess hung there with us—

Then my fingers slipped—

And I lost my hold.

Chapter 41

Friday 27th September:
Day 124

JESS

In those moments the stars were bright, brighter than I had ever seen. I saw my cousin, my twin, my soul mate, the person I'd have followed to the ends of the earth. Abigail hung above me against the black pit of the sky, and for a moment it seemed to me we were both falling – her up into the black stars and me down into the deeps. Then she was lifted away and I was alone and there was nothing but the cold, the black and the empty air.

I saw it then like never before. How different we were, how far apart we'd fallen. How blindly, how naïvely I had clung to her. Following her, refusing to see danger, blindly walking straight into this. Because I'd refused to accept the traumas she'd been through, too needy, too frightened to let her be changed.

Well, now I was feeling everything she had gone through. There was no escape from the danger now.

I opened my eyes to the blackness as I fell.

Chapter 42

Friday 22nd November:
Day 180

ANNE

Who could have thought it would end that way? How could any of us have imagined we would reach such a point? We thought what we had been through when Abigail was missing was the worst. I had thought that once Abigail came home there couldn't ever be any more pain. How wrong I had been. How wrong about it all.

The rest of that night had been a blur of shouts and dark, mud and torches. There were sirens, paramedics crashing down the banks. They took her away in an ambulance with its blue lights flashing, Lillian riding with her.

On the embankment, Lillian had been there and witnessed it all.

Sometimes in my mind, I confused that terror on the bridge with another night, when Abigail had turned away from us and there had been such terrible, awful danger. Sometimes it was as though everything had stopped up there on the girder and time was stuck and hadn't restarted since.

Two weeks after, we came abroad, here, to Morbihan in
Brittany. Robert was recruited for a renovation project, and
we all had come out with him. When Robert presented the
opportunity to leave Lincolnshire, it had taken no time at all to
decide. Now we were renting a cottage – a gîte – by the week
and we had been here for over a month: me, Robert, Abigail
and the twins.

There was a stretch of water that flowed not far from the
cottage: a slow-moving, graceful curve of the Nantes-Brest
canal. Since discovering it a few days after our arrival, I often
came for walks along its peaceful towpaths. It reminded me of
the canal back home, familiar and yet so different. We were in
a whole other country now. I was here, I had my daughter, but
after everything that had happened, I still had no idea what
would become of us. There had been so much upheaval in the
weeks since that night, so many things had come to an end,
and Abigail was still struggling, I could see that. All I could
do now was try to keep loving her; keep that at the centre and
pray it would hold.

Today, for the first time, she had agreed to come on this walk
with me. We had left Robert and the twins at the gîte, settled
down in front of a gentle French cartoon. It was a late, mild
autumn here, and even towards the end of November there was
bright sun, blue sky. Abigail and I traced our way beneath the
tall trees that lined the banks, our boots making a clumping
sound on the tramped earth, hers like the second pulse of a
heartbeat to mine. As I walked, I felt the skin across my hip
pinch and twist. I had needed a multitude of stitches. When I

looked in the mirror, the raw line that ran from my waist to inner thigh was like some strange Caesarean scar. Abigail had been reborn to me that night, but there on the bridge a whole edifice had collapsed. We were revealed as a family broken like that vase – a family that had failed in its singular duty, a family that had allowed their child to come to harm. All of us, and me especially. Not deliberately, never intentionally, but we had.

Abigail had needed us to see that and did she know now that I finally understood?

As we walked, she tilted her face up to meet the sun and pushed a few strands of hair from her eyes. The exercise had brought a flush to her cheeks, cheeks that were rounder now; she had been eating better since we'd come out here. She was picking up the rudiments of the language too; learning had always come easily to her. We'd talked about her going to school here, if we chose to stay long enough for that. Robert and I had talked about not going back and I knew for myself I didn't want to return.

Abigail and I were approaching a lock now, one of the few manual ones on the canal. I wondered if the lock renovations back in Lincolnshire had ever been completed; I wondered what volunteers Martin and Cory were doing now.

Cassingham was sentenced to fifteen years in the end. That was his punishment to live with. I hadn't seen or spoken to DS McCarthy since the trial. I knew he was still working for the Lincolnshire police and I hoped he was doing well, that quiet detective with the cool grey eyes. For so long, he had been an enemy to me, but perhaps in the end he had seen our little family, with all its sorry histories, more clearly than anyone.

Faintly, we could hear the rushing of water, the steady

waterfalls from the overspill weir. As we climbed the gentle incline, I pointed out to Abigail a boat coming up from downstream, low in the water, only the top of its flat roof visible until we reached the top. The lock was set for them; they would only need to close the downstream gates and crank open the panels above. We stopped to watch. As they came closer I could make out two children, a boy and a girl, tucked in the prow. One nine, perhaps, the other ten. The little girl waved at us. Of the two of us, it was Abigail who waved back.

This morning, I'd received an email from Lillian, one of the infrequent communications we had now. I remembered a time when I'd called her every day. She wrote with snippets of news and it wasn't hard for me to read between the lines: she and Fraser weren't doing well. I knew their marriage had been under strain a long time, with problems that went far beyond what happened with Abigail, or with Jess, and perhaps the realities of that were finally coming to the surface. With this new distance between us, perhaps we were both seeing things more clearly.

I cupped my hands around my mouth. '*Voulez-vous l'aide?*' I called out in clumsy French. Do you want any help? My voice just about made it across the water. The little boy turned to call to someone inside and a moment later, as the prow of their narrow boat nosed into the lock, a man – their father – came out, carrying the windlasses. '*Ah oui, Madam, s'il vous plaît,*' he called back, then switched to English. 'Thank you.' Everyone spoke good English here.

The man jumped lightly from the boat, landing with a little grunt on the neat grass beside us. Now I could see the woman – his wife – in the stern, her face tanned, her hair caught up in a red bandana, pulsing the motor in reverse, skilfully slowing the boat as it eased into the lock's tight hug. The little girl ducked through the low doors in the front and a moment or two later she appeared at the other end, next to her mother, the boat rocking from her movements running through. I heard the babble of their voices, the stream of French too fast for me to translate.

The father, the husband, held out a windlass to us and Abigail took it, her arm dipping from the unexpected weight.

'Got it?' I said, and she nodded.

'You will take this side?' the man said and we agreed and he headed across the thin metal bridge.

In the narrow space of the lock, the engine churned.

Jess had survived that night: two broken arms and a wrenched ankle but the train had missed her and she had survived. When I went to visit her in hospital, she didn't seem to bear me or Abigail any ill will. In fact she said something that seemed strange at the time, but maybe not so much now. 'Maybe it had to happen,' she'd said.

Lillian's email said Jess had changed a lot since that night: she went out all the time now, came home late, hung around with a whole new set of teens. The way Lillian wrote it, I could tell she was worried; in how I read it, Jess had simply grown up. She and Abigail still kept in contact: Snapchat messages and the odd phone call here and there. I knew how sorry Abigail was for what had happened that night; I knew that Jess had forgiven her, a hundred times over. But Jess was discharged from hospital it was as though that night on the bridge had seperated them from each other, somehow. There was a space between them now, their lives reaching in different directions, these two cousins who had once been so entwined. I could only hope the two of them would always remain friends, always love each other. But now I could see too that perhaps they had always needed this space. Perhaps only like this could they become their own selves, true to all the differences between them.

As for me, sometimes I missed Lillian with a wrenching pain. Other times I couldn't imagine how I'd lived under her influence so long. Sometimes it felt as though after that terrible accident on the bridge, our family had been broken into pieces. And then I'd wonder if we hadn't had to break up to survive, find new ways of reconfiguring ourselves.

'All right,' I said to Abigail. 'First, help me close the lower gates.'

I gave the man on the opposite bank a wave and together we three tugged the heavy downstream gates closed. Now the boat was secured in the staircase of the lock. It sat centre and snug, ready to ascend.

At the other end, I showed Abigail how to fit the windlass to the crank that would open the release panels upstream. Her first efforts were stiff, awkward, but I could see she was determined to do it. Opposite us, the smiling husband kept pace. Slowly, stately, the boat began to rise, the water climbing the dark, glistening walls. The little boy reached out a hand to touch the slick sides and his mother called out sharply to warn him back. Water rushed in through the panels we'd opened above and I signalled across to the father. 'You can go back on board. We can do the rest from here.' The boat was high enough now for him to step straight onto.

'Here,' I said to Abigail. 'You stand ready to push on this

one while I do the other.' I crossed the ringing metal bridge and took up my position on the other side. I leaned my weight against the lever, testing it for give. Not yet. If you pushed too early, nothing would move, but once the waters balanced and equalized on either side, the upstream gates would open as easily as yawning. On the barge, the woman turned the engine up, fighting the currents. 'Thank you!' she shouted up in English. 'So helpful that you know what to do.'

Abigail straightened. 'Yes,' she shouted back. 'She does. She's my mum.'

I couldn't move then. I could hardly keep breathing. She must have known all she was saying with that one simple statement. I felt shaky from the knowledge of what was there between us, the wide sluice of hope her words had let in. She was answering a question I'd been lost in for weeks. *I am your mother, but will you have me? After everything I've done and everything I haven't?*

I pushed again against the opening lever and felt it give a nudge beneath me. I braced myself. When we were done with this – if she could do it – I would cross the bridge back to her. I would put my arms round her, no holds barred.

'Abigail?'

But now she was unmoving; she stood there staring into the water, lost in her own thoughts. Above the revving of the engine, the woman shouted up, '*Vous êtes capable?*'

Can you do it?

For one awful second I thought she might turn and run, abandoning the boat and the family and everything. Then she lifted her chin and pushed up her sleeves. 'I'm ready, Mum.'

Copying me, she set herself against the weight. From either

side we pushed in tandem, the gates giving, easing through the water. We went on pushing together, like that, until the lock stood open, and the little family sailed through.

ONE PLACE. MANY STORIES

Bold, innovative and
empowering publishing.

FOLLOW US ON:

@HQStories